THEY WALK IN DARKNESS

Horrifying events in the village of Fendyke St. Mary left lambs with their throats cut. This was followed by the disappearance and murder of six young children — all with their throats cut. Then the bodies of two men and two women were found in Witch's House, a derelict cottage — all poisoned. Yet strangely, the murder had occurred whilst the cottage was surrounded by snow; and after locking the door, the murderer had escaped leaving no tracks . . . !

GERALD VERNER

THEY WALK IN DARKNESS

Complete and Unabridged

LINFORD
Leicester

First published in Great Britain

First Linford Edition
published 2011

British Library CIP Data

Verner, Gerald.
    They walk in darkness.- -
    (Linford mystery library)
    1. Serial murders- -Fiction
    2. Detective and mystery stories.
    3. Large type books.
    I. Title II. Series
    823.9'12–dc22

    ISBN 978–1–4448–0803–2

Published by
F. A. Thorpe (Publishing)
Anstey, Leicestershire

Set by Words & Graphics Ltd.
Anstey, Leicestershire
Printed and bound in Great Britain by
T. J. International Ltd., Padstow, Cornwall

This book is printed on acid-free paper

FOR
MY WIFE
WITH LOVE

PART ONE

THE EVE OF ALL-HALLOWS

'Is it a party in a parlour?
Crammed just as they on earth were
   crammed —
Some sipping punch, some sipping tea,
But, as you by their faces see,
All silent and all damned.'

             —WILLIAM WORDSWORTH.
                 Peter Bell, Part I.

1

The engine emitted a queer sound, like a rather pompous old gentleman clearing his throat, stalled, and the big car came to a sudden and jerky halt. Peter Chard uttered a mild expletive below his breath, fiddled with throttle and ignition, and pressed on the self-starter. It whirred noisily, but the engine was disconcertingly unresponsive. He tried again without any better result and gave a sidelong glance at the tip of his wife's nose which protruded pinkly from a nest of furs and was the only portion of her that was visible.

'What's happened, Peter?' she asked, drowsily. 'Why have we stopped?'

'I don't know,' he confessed, reluctantly. 'It can't be lack of petrol. I had the tank filled up at Norwich . . . ' He made another attempt but it was quite useless. The engine remained silent and lifeless. 'It won't go,' he declared, rather unnecessarily.

'That,' remarked Ann, rousing herself, and emerging from the enveloping furs like Aphrodite rising out of the sea, 'is quite obvious. But why won't it go?'

Peter shook his head. He had not the faintest idea why it wouldn't go. It had brought them smoothly, and without any trouble at all, from Bishop's Thatcham to Norwich and, from thence, to this desolate part of East Anglia, and the stoppage had been unexpected and, to him, unaccountable.

'I can't understand it at all,' he said in perplexity, after a further and equally futile assault on the starter. 'I'd better get out and see if I can find what's wrong.' He opened the door nearest to him and slid out from behind the wheel. An icy blast swept into the comparatively warm interior of the car, and, with a shiver, Ann retired once more into the depths of her furs.

Peter crunched through the snow and, without feeling very optimistic, lifted the radiator cover. He was a very good driver, but he knew practically nothing about the construction of the internal combustion engine. The hot mass of metal with its tubes and wires and springs was almost a complete enigma to him, and after peering and probing for some time, with only the vaguest idea of what he was doing, he came back, readjusted the throttle and ignition, pulled out the choke, and tried again, hoping for the best. But the engine stubbornly refused to give even an encouraging splutter. Peter gave it up eventually with a grunt of disgust and stared helplessly at the wheel.

'I don't know what's the matter with the thing,' he growled. 'It won't go and that's all I can say about it. It's as dead as a pole-axed bull . . . '

'Surely, Peter,' said his wife in dismay, 'you don't mean that we're stuck here indefinitely . . . ?'

'I'm afraid it looks very much like it,' he admitted, ruefully. 'I can't do any more . . . '

She sat up and peered through the windows at the uninviting landscape spread around them. It was rapidly growing dark, and before, behind, and on either side stretched a flat, dreary expanse of white, unbroken except by a few clumps of trees and patches of reeds, a solitary windmill in the distance, and, nearer at hand, the slender spire of a church. The snow-covered country merged with the greyish-yellow of the sombre sky and combined to produce a queer, unreal twilight that added to the general effect of deadness and desolation.

'Not a very salubrious prospect, is it?' said Peter, fumbling in the pocket of his heavy overcoat and pulling out a packet of Players. 'Have a cigarette?' He gave her one, took one himself, and lighted them both.

'How far are we from Fendyke St. Mary?' asked Ann.

'The last signpost we passed said three and a half miles,' replied Peter. 'That was about a mile and a half back . . . '

'Peter, what *are* we going to do . . . ?'

He frowned and blew out a thin stream of smoke from pursed lips.

'Well, there seems to be only two things we *can* do,' he said, slowly. 'We can stay here until somebody comes along and rescues us, or we can get out and walk to Fendyke St. Mary . . . '

'Darling — two miles in this snow!' said Ann with a shiver. 'I'm wearing the flimsiest of high-heeled shoes and my sheerest and most expensive Aristoc stockings to impress your Aunt Helen ... Do you think anybody *will* come along if we waited?'

Peter shook his head.

'Candidly, I don't,' he said. 'We haven't seen a sign of anything human since we left the main road, and it will be quite dark in another half an hour ... '

'Which means if we wait for help we might go on waiting all night,' broke in Ann. 'That doesn't sound a pleasant prospect to me. I'm cold, ravenously hungry, and dying for a cup of tea ... '

'I think we'd better walk,' said Peter, firmly. 'You can have both tea and food when we get to Aunt Helen's ... '

'*When* we get there,' said his wife with a grimace. 'Have you ever heard something about counting chickens ... ?'

'Come along,' said Peter, opening the door and getting out. 'If we've got to walk, we may as well take advantage of what little light there is left.'

Ann sighed resignedly, gathered her furs around her and followed him, stepping gingerly down into the snow. Her foot sank up to the ankle and she gave a little squeal, balancing herself on one leg and clutching wildly at Peter's shoulder for support. He laughed.

'It's all very well for you,' she declared, indignantly. 'But my shoe's full of snow, and it's wet and cold . . . '

'I know,' he said, soothingly, 'but I'm afraid it's going to be worse before it's better, darling. The only thing to do is to get it over as soon as possible.'

With extreme reluctance she set her other foot beside the first and removed her hand from his shoulder. Peter leaned inside the car, switched on the lights, and closing the door, locked it.

'Come along,' he said, taking her arm. 'With a little luck we ought to reach Aunt Helen's before it gets quite dark.'

'I hope you know the way,' said Ann. 'It's difficult to see which is the road and which isn't with all this snow.'

'We can't go far wrong if we make for that church spire,' said Peter, nodding towards it. 'That's the church of Fendyke St. Mary.'

It was difficult going. The powdery snow was four inches deep and in places even deeper. They came upon these unexpectedly for there was no warning of their existence until they found themselves floundering in the middle of them. To add to their discomfort the wind, blowing in fitful gusts across the flat broadlands, was icy and penetrating, finding its way under Ann's furs, and beneath Peter's thick overcoat, with remarkable persistence. It stung their faces and brought tears to their eyes and made their ears ache.

'How much farther have we got to go?' asked Ann, after they had been walking for nearly twenty minutes. 'That spire doesn't look to have got any nearer, to me.'

'It's deceptive in this light,' answered Peter, encouragingly. 'I should say we'd come, roughly, about halfway.'

'Roughly is a very good description,' said Ann, fervently. 'Both my legs are completely numb and I don't think I've got any feet left at all . . . '

'Isn't that a house?' interrupted Peter, peering ahead through the gathering gloom.

'Where?' she demanded.

'There — on the right — by that clump of willows.' Peter pointed. 'It's not very distinct, but . . . '

'Yes, I think it is,' said Ann. 'Oh, Peter, do you think they'd give us some tea if we asked them?'

'I don't know whether we ought to stop,' said Peter, doubtfully. 'If we want to reach Fendyke St. Mary before dark . . . '

'I don't care whether we reach it before dark or not, darling,' said Ann with determination. 'If there's a chance of getting a cup of tea and a moment's rest, I'm going to take it. I'm frozen to the marrow, Peter.'

As they drew nearer, the shadowy smudge of the house became clearer and they presently saw that it was a low-built cottage of stone with a steeply sloping roof. A broken wall, also of stone, separated it from the road, and four pollard willows grew close up to one end, their thin branches fanning up from the stunted, club-shaped trunks like the quills of a porcupine. There was no sign of life about the place. The windows were dark and dirty and no feather of smoke rose invitingly from the squat chimney.

'It looks to be empty,' remarked Peter, halting by the gap in the stone wall which faced the broken porch.

'Perhaps they live in the back,' suggested Ann, hopefully. 'Let's knock anyway, Peter, and see.'

She entered the gap and began to walk towards the front door and, after a moment's hesitation, Peter followed her. He noticed that the snow within the enclosing wall was smooth and unmarked. No one had, apparently, passed that way before them since it had ceased falling that morning. Ann raised her gloved hand and knocked.

2

The rusty iron knocker, shaped like a goat's head, sent hollow echoes through the house, but there was no other sound of any sort.

'You can't wake Duncan with thy knocking,' said Peter. 'It's no good, Ann, the place is empty.'

He stepped back from the porch and moved over to one of the small lattice windows at the side of the front door, trying to peer in through the lozenge-shaped panes. But they were so encrusted with dirt and grime that he could see nothing at all of the interior. Ann knocked again, but without any better result than the first time.

'We're only wasting time,' said Peter, coming back to her side. 'Let's get on.'

Rather reluctantly she turned away and they retraced their steps to the road. As they came out of the gap in the low, broken stone wall, she paused and looked back.

'What's the matter?' asked Peter, quickly, as he caught sight of the expression on her face.

'I don't know,' she answered, slowly. 'I got a sudden queer feeling — as though someone were *watching* . . . .' She gave a little shudder, still staring apprehensively at the deserted building.

'Imagination,' declared Peter, taking her arm. 'The place is obviously empty and, from the look of it, has been empty for years. Come along, darling.'

She allowed herself to be led away, but the impression had been very vivid.

It was almost quite dark when they eventually reached the outskirts of Fendyke St. Mary, and the first glow of light from a cottage window was a welcome and comforting sight, for they were both wet and cold and weary.

'Last lap,' said Peter, cheerfully. 'We turn round here by the church, and Aunt Helen's house is about a hundred yards farther on.'

'Thank heaven for that!' breathed Ann, fervently. 'I think I can just about manage to last that far.'

They rounded the massive bulk of St. Mary's church, which towered up into the cold gloom, and came into a broad, hedge-lined road, and, presently, to a wide gate which Peter held open for Ann to pass through.

'Here we are,' he said. 'This is Wymondham Lodge.'

Ann stumbled through the gate with a gasp of relief. She could see very little. The hint of a shrubbery and a faint glimmer of light somewhere ahead that suggested warmth, food, a hot bath, and rest for her aching and frozen limbs. That was what was uppermost in her mind. Rest. She felt at that moment that she could not have moved another yard if her life had depended on it . . . A house rose up suddenly out of the darkness and she saw that the glimmer of welcoming light came from a chink between drawn curtains. And then she was standing under a pillared porch, and Peter was beating a loud and impatient tattoo on the doorknocker . . .

There were footsteps and the door opened, flooding them in a bath of warm light that gushed out over the steps and snow-covered drive, and in the light stood a grey-haired man in the black garb of a servant, peering forward questioningly.

'Hello, Hewson,' said Peter, and the questioning look changed to a smile of recognition and delight.

'Mr. Peter, sir!' exclaimed the old man. 'Come in, sir. Come in. The mistress has been wondering what had happened to you.'

A door on the right of the wide, square hall was flung open and a short, fat, rosy-cheeked woman with snow-white hair bounced out.

'Who is it, Hewson?' she demanded, and then before he could reply: 'Peter! So you've got here at last! And this, of course, is Ann. My dears, you must be frozen . . . Hewson, tell Roberts to make some tea and bring it into the drawing room . . . I'm sure you'd like some tea, wouldn't you? You poor things, you look frozen to the bone. Come straight along in and get warm by the fire. Take off those furs, dear, and leave them on that settle. Roberts will look after them when she's

15

brought the tea. It's lovely to see you both and I think Ann is even prettier than I expected, Peter. Now come along in by the fire, for I'm sure you must both be very cold after travelling such a long way in this wretched weather. It's quite the worst we've had for some time and looks like continuing for several days . . . ' Still talking rapidly, Miss Wymondham led the way into a long, cosily-furnished room with a great log fire blazing in a wide, open hearth. A little overwhelmed by the spate of words which gushed unceasingly, like a freshly tapped oil well, from this cherubic old lady, Ann followed, thankful for the warmth which enfolded her comfortingly, and began to drive away the chill of the icy wind and snow.

' . . . You come and sit over here, dear,' went on Miss Wymondham, after a slight pause for breath, and shaking up the cushions on a deep settee by the fire, 'I'm sure you'll find it very soft and restful. And you, Peter, can sit in that chair. Roberts won't be long with the tea and when you've had that, I'll take you up to your room and you can have a hot bath

16

and change. Hewson can take your luggage up. You'll find the room beautifully warm, there's been a fire there all day . . . '

'The trouble is, Aunt Helen,' interrupted Peter, shedding his heavy overcoat and dropping it over a chair, 'we haven't got any luggage . . . '

'Not got any luggage?' echoed Miss Wymondham in evident surprise. 'My dear boy, what *do* you mean? Surely you . . . '

'All our luggage is in the car and that's about two miles away,' explained Peter. 'You see, we had a breakdown or something — anyway, the car wouldn't budge an inch farther, and so we had to walk the rest of the way.'

'Good gracious!' exclaimed Aunt Helen, with wide blue eyes. 'Two miles in this dreadful snow! You poor darlings! No wonder you both look so tired and cold. How terrible for you. Never mind, you've got here at last, thank goodness. I'll get Hewson to telephone to the garage — Acheson, such an obliging man — and I'm sure they'll send someone to fetch the car or,

17

at any rate, bring the luggage . . . ' She rang the bell insistently. 'My dear, you ought to take your shoes and stockings off *at once* in case you catch a chill. There's nothing so dangerous as wet feet, you know. I could lend you a pair of bedroom slippers, though I'm afraid they'll be a little large . . . '

'Please don't trouble,' said Ann, stretching her soaking shoes towards the blazing fire. 'They'll soon dry and . . . '

'It's no trouble at all,' interrupted Miss Wymondham, firmly. 'I . . . oh, there you are, Hewson. I want you to telephone to Acheson's garage and ask them to send a car and pick up some luggage. Mr. Peter had a breakdown about two miles away and had to leave all the luggage in the car and hasn't got a thing to change into. Neither has Mrs. Chard, so they must do something about it *at once*. Tell him whereabouts you have left the car, Peter . . . '

Hewson listened attentively while Peter gave him a detailed description.

'I don't know whether you'll be able to persuade them to turn out on a night like this,' he concluded, doubtfully. 'But . . . '

'Persuade them?' said Miss Wymondham, indignantly. 'I should just like to see Tom Acheson refuse, that's all! Go along and ring up at once, Hewson, and tell Roberts to bring me my blue slippers — the satin ones. They're in the bottom of the little cupboard beside my bed . . . '

'They'll have to call here for the key,' said Peter, as Hewson was departing on his errand. 'I locked the car before I left it.'

'I'll tell them, sir,' said the old man, and went out.

'You really shouldn't bother about the slippers . . . ' began Ann, but Miss Wymondham refused to listen.

'Nonsense, my dear,' she said, firmly. 'I'm not going to have you catching cold if I can prevent it, and spending your stay with me in bed. Just you be a good girl and take off your shoes and stockings at once . . . '

'It's no good arguing with Aunt Helen,' said Peter. 'I found that out years ago, didn't I, Aunt Helen?'

'It took a long time for you to realize

it,' said the old lady. 'As a little boy you were a most argumentative and stubborn creature.'

'He hasn't changed,' remarked Ann, taking off her shoes and beginning to remove one of her stockings, showing a great display of very shapely leg in the process. 'He can be like a mule at times . . .'

'Don't I know it,' declared Miss Wymondham, with an affectionate smile at her nephew. 'Oh, well, it runs in the family, I suppose. Peter's father was the most obstinate man that ever lived. Even a mule can be persuaded, I believe, not that I've ever had much to do with mules, but the Angel Gabriel would have had his work cut out persuading Robert Chard to do anything that he'd decided not to . . .'

'That is strength of will,' broke in Peter, loftily.

'Rubbish!' exclaimed his aunt. 'Don't you let him stuff you up with *that*, my dear. That's what his father always called it. Strength of will has nothing whatever to do with it. Sheer, stubborn obstinacy, that's what it is.'

'It seems to run in the Wymondham

family as well,' said Peter with a grin, 'so I must have inherited it from both sides . . . '

'I always thought you had double your fair share,' said Ann, sticking out her naked feet to the fire and luxuriously wiggling her numbed toes. 'Never mind, darling, you're very sweet. I always had a soft spot in my heart for mules . . . '

'You'll have a soft spot in your feet for chilblains if you do that,' broke in Peter, reprovingly.

There came a tap on the door and it opened to admit an elderly woman with a pleasant face and a laden tray.

'Oh, here you are, Roberts,' said Miss Wymondham, as though her arrival was a great surprise to her. 'Put the tray down on this table. Did you bring the slippers . . . ? Oh, yes, I see you did. Here you are, my dear. Now put them on and you'll feel more comfortable. Roberts, take Mrs. Chard's stockings and shoes and clean them — the shoes, I mean, of course. You can wash the stockings. Is the fire all right in Mr. and Mrs. Chard's bedroom?'

'Yes'm,' said Roberts, smiling cheerfully

at everybody. 'Will that be all, 'm?'

'Yes, I think so,' said Miss Wymondham, busy with the tea things. 'Did Hewson get through to Acheson . . . ? Oh, here is Hewson. Well?'

'Acheson's are sending to tow Mr. Peter's car back, madam,' said the butler. 'It will take about an hour, they think.'

'That will do splendidly,' said Miss Wymondham. 'Thank you, Hewson. There you are,' she added, triumphantly, when Hewson and Roberts had gone. 'I told you, didn't I? I *knew* Tom Acheson would never dare to refuse. Here you are, my dear, here's a nice hot cup of tea, which I'm sure you're dying for. You'll be able to have hot baths and change in time for dinner — a really hot bath is always so comforting and refreshing when you're cold and tired, I always think. I've asked one or two people to dinner. Doctor Culpepper — a charming man, and such a clever doctor, I'm sure you'll like him — and the Sherwoods — such a nice young couple — and Laura Courtland. She's the daughter of Felix Courtland, the man who bought Priors Keep three years ago. He was a stockbroker, or something, but he's retired. He was coming, too, but he's in bed with a chill, poor man, so he can't. They're all looking forward to meeting you, Peter. They've read all your books . . . '

Peter groaned and held out his cup for more tea.

'Am I being 'shown off', Aunt Helen?' he demanded.

'No, dear, not exactly,' said Miss Wymondham, complacently, 'but I thought it would be more cheerful for both of you if I asked some people along. There's not much fun in spending an evening alone with an old woman like me, and since you're staying for a month you may as well get to know some of the neighbours. It will be more amusing for you. Now do either of you want any more tea? Because I must go and talk to cook about dinner. She's very good, but she *does* want supervision. Just make yourselves quite at home, both of you, won't you?'

Miss Wymondham bounced across the room with great energy, beamed at them from the doorway, and went out.

3

Peter came into the cosy bedroom clad in his dressing-gown, warm and fresh from a boiling hot bath. His wife, partially dressed, was sitting at the dressing-table brushing her dark, chestnut hair. Tom Acheson had been better than his word and brought the stranded car, and the luggage, back in under the time he had stipulated.

'I feel much better,' said Peter, stooping and kissing one of Ann's bare, soft shoulders. 'There's a lot to be said for civilization and good plumbing. How do you like Aunt Helen?'

'I think she's a darling,' said Ann.

'Some people find her a little over-whelming at first,' said Peter, lighting a cigarette and drifting happily about the room, 'but they get used to it. Her energy is amazing.'

'She's altogether sweet,' said Ann, laying down her hairbrush and getting up.

'I hope she approves of me.'

'Nobody could help approving of you, darling,' said Peter, struggling into a shirt. 'I wonder what these people are like she has invited tonight?'

'I'm sure they're quite nice, or your aunt would not have asked them,' said his wife.

'H'm. Aunt Helen seems to have made a definite conquest,' said Peter. 'I should have preferred a quiet evening on our own, but I wouldn't say so for the world.'

'So would I,' agreed Ann, slipping a black frock over her head and pulling it down round her slim figure. 'But I think it was very thoughtful of her to try and guard against the possibility of our being bored. I do hope, though, that it's not going to be a late party, darling. I feel terribly tired . . . '

'I don't suppose it will be,' said Peter. 'I shouldn't think people kept late hours round here. Where the devil has my tie got to . . . ? Have you seen it anywhere . . . ? Oh, here it is. How did it get there?' He retrieved it from the mantelpiece.

'You put it there yourself, darling,' said

his wife, calmly. 'Will you fasten this dress for me?'

He came over and dealt with it, kissing the top of her head before resuming his own interrupted toilet. Ann was ready first. She gave a final touch to her hair, and turned away from the mirror.

'How do I look?' she asked, half mockingly and half seriously, pirouetting in front of him.

'Lovely!' said Peter, enthusiastically. 'But then I've never seen you looking anything else but lovely.'

'You're the most satisfactory husband, darling,' she said, smiling at him. 'You always say the right thing at the right moment. How long are you going to be?'

'I'm ready now,' said Peter, putting on his dinner-jacket. He pulled down his waist-coat, gave a pat to his tie, and slipped his hand under his wife's arm, giving it a little squeeze. 'Come along,' he said.

When they reached the drawing room they found that two of the expected guests had already arrived. Miss Wymondham, looking more rosy-faced and cherubic than ever in a black lace dress, was chattering volubly to a fair, rather nice-looking man, and a pretty, dark girl, while Hewson gravely dispensed sherry.

'Oh, here you are,' she exclaimed, breaking off in the midst of what she was saying. 'My dear, how very nice you look. What a lovely frock . . . This is my nephew, Peter Chard, and his wife, Ann. Peter and Ann, this is Anthony Sherwood and April. Two more sherries, Hewson, please.'

Peter's outstretched hand was gripped firmly.

'I've been looking forward to meeting you,' said Anthony Sherwood in a deep, pleasant voice, 'and so has April. Haven't you, dear? She's a great fan of yours, Mr. Chard . . . '

'I've read all your books,' said the dark girl, smiling, 'and thoroughly enjoyed them.'

Now this was a remark that Peter always found embarrassing. There was such a limited way in which it could be answered without appearing a fatuous idiot. He was saved the difficulty of finding anything reasonably suitable by the opportune arrival of Doctor Culpepper and Laura Courtland, who were ushered into the drawing room by Roberts. Miss Wymondham introduced them, and Hewson brought more sherry on a silver tray. Peter gave an inward sigh of relief when neither of the newcomers said anything about his books, or even hinted that they were aware that he wrote at all. Doctor Culpepper was a stoutish man of medium height with one of the largest noses that Peter had ever seen, and a mass of unruly grey hair. He wore shell-rimmed spectacles, behind which a pair of shrewd and very dark eyes twinkled humorously.

Laura Courtland was a cat of a very different colour, and Peter thought 'cat' was quite an apt description, for there was something definitely feline about her. She was tall and sleek, with smooth dark hair which she wore dressed close to a well-shaped head. Her voice was deep and rather husky and she looked at you through her thick lashes without fully raising her heavy eyelids, which gave her a sleepy, langorous expression that some people might have found attractive but which Peter most definitely disliked. She was wearing a scarlet dress which fitted so closely, what there was of it, that it left very little to the imagination, and very high-heeled shoes of the same shade. A rather unexpected and surprising person to find in a small village in East Anglia, thought Peter. Much more suited to the sophistication of a nightclub, or restaurant, in the West End of London. He wondered what on earth there could be in common between this exotic girl — she couldn't be much more than twenty-five — and his aunt. Ann was evidently thinking much the same for he saw her turn an appraising gaze from Laura Courtland to Miss Wymondham, and there was a slightly puzzled, questioning look in her eyes.

'We met on the doorstep. It was quite coincidental. There was nothing prearranged about it.' Miss Courtland was explaining, although nobody had asked her, the reason why she had arrived with Doctor Culpepper.

'Not quite on the doorstep — at the gate,' said the doctor, jovially, sipping his sherry with evident approval.

'Why make me a liar for the sake of a few yards?' said Laura, languidly. 'Has anybody got a cigarette? I left mine at home . . .'

Both Peter and Anthony Sherwood pulled out cases and extended them. After the fraction of a second's hesitation she took a cigarette from Peter's case.

'Thanks,' she murmured, as he snapped a lighter into flame and lit it for her.

'How is your father, Laura?' asked Miss Wymondham. 'I do hope he is not any worse. Colds are so treacherous, particularly in this weather, unless you take the utmost care of them . . .'

'He's not any worse — except in temper,' answered Laura. She trickled smoke lazily from her nostrils. 'That's pretty foul at the moment.'

'There's nothing like a cold for bringing out the worst in people,' said Doctor Culpepper, with a little throaty chuckle. 'Always makes 'em irritable and depressed. Part of the symptoms. Even the vicar's like a bear with a sore head.'

'Oh, dear, has poor Mr. Benskill caught

a cold, too?' chimed in Miss Wymondham with great concern. 'I *am* sorry to hear that . . . '

'Half the village have got colds,' said Doctor Culpepper. He finished his sherry and stared gloomily into the empty glass. 'I wish that was the only trouble,' he added, seriously.

The rosy, smiling face of Miss Wymondham changed. She became grave and concerned, and Peter could have sworn that there was fear in her eyes as she looked at the doctor.

'Oh,' she said, in quite a different voice to her usual one. 'There hasn't been . . . anything more . . . ?'

Doctor Culpepper nodded.

'I'm afraid there has,' he began, and stopped as Hewson appeared at the door.

'Dinner is served, madam,' he announced.

4

The memory of that dinner in the pleasant, panelled dining room at Wymondham Lodge lingered long after in Peter Chard's mind. When the whole horrible and ghastly business, that brought something akin to panic to the village of Fendyke St. Mary, was over and done with, he was able to recall that scene so clearly and vividly, and with such a wealth of detail, that it might have been actually taking place all over again. For it was during that dinner, in so far, at least, as Peter himself was concerned, that the dreadful and beastly sequence of events had their beginning.

Doctor Culpepper's interrupted reply to Miss Wymondham's question had introduced an entirely new atmosphere into the little gathering. Whereas before it had been gay and light-hearted; the normal reaction of a group of people who had met to eat and drink and spend a pleasurable evening in each other's company, there had now descended a curious kind of gloom that had settled over five of the septette like a blight. Neither Peter nor Ann had, at that period, any knowledge of the cause for this sudden blanketing depression, but it was so obvious that it was quite impossible to ignore it. They took their places at the long refectory table in almost complete silence, even Miss Wymondham's usual verbosity having become quenched. While Hewson served the soup, Peter stole furtive glances at the faces of the others.

Laura Courtland, the remains of her cigarette still smouldering between her fingers, looked suddenly tired and rather bored. Anthony Sherwood was frowning gravely at his plate, and his wife, who was sitting next to Peter, was crumbling her bread with nervous fingers and staring straight before her at a large vase of yellow and rust-coloured chrysanthemums in the middle of the table. Doctor Culpepper fidgeted with his napkin and made repeated, and apparently ineffective, attempts to clear his throat. Peter's eyes met Ann's, who was immediately opposite him, and she raised her eyebrows slightly, and almost imperceptibly shook her head, a tacit signal that she was as much puzzled as he. He was on the point of asking his aunt to explain the cause of this sudden change which had come over them, when she saved him the trouble.

'What has happened now?' she asked in a subdued voice, looking down the table at Doctor Culpepper. 'You were going to tell us, weren't you, when Hewson announced dinner?'

Doctor Culpepper picked up his soup spoon, looked at it attentively, put it down again, and once more cleared his throat.

'It's Mrs. Coxen's little girl,' he answered slowly, at last. 'She disappeared this afternoon . . . '

'That makes the fifth,' muttered Anthony Sherwood. 'Thank God we haven't any children, April.'

'Somebody ought to do something about it,' broke in April, passionately. 'Instead of letting it go on and on . . . it's horrible . . . '

'The police are doing all they can, my

34

dear . . . ' began Doctor Culpepper.

'All they can?' cried April, scornfully. '*All they can?* What have they done? Nothing. And now there's another . . . ' Her voice, which had risen shrilly, cracked and broke. 'All they can,' she repeated, contemptuously.

Laura stubbed out her cigarette on the side of her bread plate.

'It *must* be a lunatic,' she said, huskily. 'It *must* be.'

'May I ask,' said Peter, looking from one to the other curiously, 'what you are all talking about?'

'Oh, my dear, why of course I forgot,' said Miss Wymondham, turning quickly towards him. 'You don't know anything about it, do you, Peter? No, of course you don't. How could you? It's really dreadful and shocking, and it's been going on now for over eighteen months. It started with the Robsons' baby . . . '

'It started with the lambs,' corrected Doctor Culpepper, quietly. 'That was the *real* beginning.'

'Well, yes, I suppose it was,' agreed Miss Wymondham, who was recovering a little of her normal volubility. 'But nobody took it really seriously, did they? until after the Robsons' baby . . . '

'What happened to the Robsons' baby?' asked Peter, as she paused. It was Doctor Culpepper who answered him.

'Somebody stole it while it was lying in its pram in the garden,' he said, very slowly and clearly. 'Three days afterwards the poor little mite was found in a clump of reeds on the edge of Hinton Broad with its throat cut . . . '

'Such a lovely baby she was too,' murmured Miss Wymondham, shaking her white head sorrowfully. 'A sweet, chubby little thing, only ten months old . . . '

'How dreadful,' said Ann. 'What a horrible, beastly thing . . . '

'That was only the beginning,' said Doctor Culpepper, grimly. 'There were three more after that and each case was practically identical . . . ' He broke off and began to drink his soup with almost savage intensity.

'Do you mean . . . they were all found dead in the same way?' said Peter, and the doctor nodded curtly.

'Ghastly, isn't it?' said Anthony Sherwood, and the lines of his young face were set and stern. 'The eldest was only two and a bit . . . '

'And the police haven't done a thing about it,' put in April, angrily. 'Not a thing . . . '

'That's hardly fair, my dear,' remonstrated Doctor Culpepper. 'They've done everything they possibly could do . . . '

'Well, it hasn't done very much good, has it?' said Anthony. 'They haven't caught the brute, whoever it is, who's responsible?'

'It's not such an easy matter,' said Doctor Culpepper. 'I'm not holding any brief for the police, but I have had several chats with Superintendent Odds about it, and it's quite easy to realize his difficulty. There's very little doubt that these horrible atrocities are the work of a homicidal maniac, which means that the normal motive is lacking. This monster kills for the sheer lust of killing . . . '

'Colonel Shoredust should have called in Scotland Yard,' remarked Laura Courtland, languidly. 'Father said that a long time ago.'

'Could Scotland Yard have done anything better?' replied Doctor Culpepper, doubtfully.

'It couldn't have done anything worse,' snapped April. 'And you must admit that, at least, it probably has more experience . . . '

'In ordinary crime, perhaps,' agreed Doctor Culpepper. 'But I very much doubt whether it would have been more successful in this case. However, I should imagine that Shoredust will be forced to call in help sooner or later.'

'When all the children in the village have been butchered, I suppose?' said April, sarcastically. 'It'll be a little late then, won't it?'

'Isn't there any suspicion against anybody?' asked Peter, cutting in to prevent the heated argument which looked likely to develop. Doctor Culpepper hesitated and then shook his head.

'No,' he said. 'At one time the police did, I believe, have some idea that a fellow called Twist might be responsible, but . . . '

'Oh, I'm quite sure they're wrong,'

broke in Miss Wymondham with conviction. 'Poor Twist wouldn't hurt a fly. He's never been — well, 'all there' as people call it, but he's quite harmless. I can't think of anyone in the village who *would* be capable of such a dreadful thing . . . '

'That, of course,' said Doctor Culpepper, 'is the whole trouble. Except for this abnormal and terrible kink the person concerned is, no doubt, quite normal and ordinary in every respect. Just like anybody else. He may not even be aware of what he has done. That is sometimes part of the symptoms in these cases . . . '

April Sherwood gave a little shiver as though a cold draught had struck her.

'It's rather horrible that, isn't it?' she muttered. 'To think that it might be somebody we all know and . . . and are friendly with . . . '

She stopped as Hewson removed the soup plates and served them with fish.

'If it wouldn't harrow anybody too much,' said Peter, 'I'd like a more detailed account of these outrages. I'm not asking out of morbid curiosity. The psychological aspect interests me.' He caught his wife's eye as he finished speaking and, from the momentary expression he surprised, came to the conclusion that she, at least, was not completely satisfied with this explanation for his curiosity. 'Didn't you mention something about lambs, Doctor Culpepper?'

The doctor nodded and swallowed the portion of turbot he had been masticating.

'Yes,' he replied. 'In my opinion that is how it all began. Several lambs were stolen, not all at the same time, but with various intervals in between, and were later found dead with their throats cut.'

'And you believe that this was the prelude to the baby murders?'

'Yes. I believe it was a sort of rehearsal, if you can put it like that.'

'It seems rather extraordinary to me,' Peter went on, frowning slightly, 'that if this maniac was out to kill, he didn't kill at once. Why do you imagine he took his victims away and killed them later?'

Doctor Culpepper shrugged his shoulders.

'There's no accounting for a deranged

mind,' he answered. 'It's no good expecting anything logical, you know. At the same time there may be an explanation in the fact that it was too risky to carry out his intention on the spot.'

'Perhaps that might apply in the case of the children,' said Peter, thoughtfully. 'But surely not in the case of the lambs? However, I suppose as you say it's useless looking for reason in a maniac. You said another child disappeared today?'

'Little Joan Coxen,' said Doctor Culpepper. 'She was playing in the snow in the garden of her mother's cottage. When her mother went to call her in for tea she wasn't there . . . She hasn't been seen since . . . '

There was a sudden hush round the table. Peter's eyes caught Ann's and saw in them a look of horrified incredulity. Miss Wymondham was slowly shaking her head and making clicking noises with her tongue. Anthony Sherwood was silently engaged in dissecting a portion of fish, or appeared to be. His wife was staring at his bent head with her pretty face set and rigid. Laura Courtland gave a fluttering sigh, as if she had been holding her breath, and leaned back in her chair. Only Doctor Culpepper went on eating his fish. And then the telephone in the hall began to ring . . .

5

The telephone bell went on ringing and then ceased abruptly as somebody lifted the receiver. There was the sound of a muffled voice and, presently, heralded by a discreet tap on the door, Hewson entered.

'Doctor Culpepper is required on the telephone, madam,' he said.

The doctor wiped his lips hastily with his napkin, dropped it beside his plate, and with a muttered apology, got up and hurried out.

'I wonder who that can be?' murmured Miss Wymondham, speculatively, turning her head towards the door.

'The call was from the doctor's residence, madam,' said Hewson from the sideboard.

'Well, it must have been very urgent for them to have disturbed him here,' remarked Miss Wymondham, obviously consumed with curiosity. 'Did they say why he was wanted, Hewson?'

'No, madam,' replied the old man. 'Are you ready for the entrée?'

'Not quite,' said his mistress. 'Do you think?' she addressed the table in general, 'it could be any news of . . . little Joan Coxen?'

'I should say it was more probably a patient,' answered Peter. 'However, if you possess your soul in patience, Aunt Helen, perhaps Doctor Culpepper will tell you himself.'

Doctor Culpepper did a few seconds later. He came back with a grave and serious face.

'I'm afraid I shall have to go,' he informed them. 'It's unfortunate, but one of the many drawbacks to my profession. Mrs. Coxen has been taken seriously ill . . . '

'Oh, I'm so sorry,' said Miss Wymondham, looking really distressed. 'Poor soul, I suppose it's the strain and worry . . . '

'Yes, I think it is,' agreed the doctor. 'They tell me that she has developed a high temperature and is delirious . . . '

'Has any news been received of the

child?' asked Peter.

Doctor Culpepper shook his head.

'No,' he said. 'The search is still going on, of course, but I doubt if there will be any further news until they find her — as they found the others.'

He took a brief farewell of everybody, apologized once more to Miss Wymondham, and departed to give what succour he could to the unfortunate woman who had broken down under the tragedy of her loss.

The rest of the evening was not very cheerful for any of them, in spite of Miss Wymondham's valiant attempts to make it so. Such gaiety as she tried to infuse was only on the surface, and its thin crust kept breaking, letting through the cracks writhing tentacles from the ugly monster that lurked at the root of all their minds. And it *was* ugly, thought Peter, as he tried to keep up a desultory conversation with the others: ugly and beastly and utterly horrible, this spiriting away and slaughtering of lambs and little children. The terrible and perverted amusement of a mad brain that yet went to work so cleverly and cunningly that eighteen months of searching had failed to discover to whom it belonged. Somewhere among this community of Jekyll's was an unknown Hyde, outwardly indistinguishable from his fellows, but inwardly suffering, either knowingly or unknowingly, from an unquenchable blood-lust that he strove at intervals to slake. The knowledge was horrifying to Peter, who had only become aware of it in the last few hours. How much more horrifying must it be to the people of Fendyke St. Mary, who had lived in its shadow for all these months? The dread must be with them day and night, particularly those who had children. Anthony Sherwood's remark at dinner was understandable. There must be many who felt the same. Surely the police could have done something in all that time to bring the person responsible to book? It was all very well for Doctor Culpepper to make repeated assurances that they had done all they could, and to point out the difficulties which beset them, but Peter rather sympathized with April's attitude. Without minimizing any of the difficulties, the result had, from what he had heard, not redounded to their credit. He made a resolve to go more thoroughly into the whole thing. It was gripping his interest and he wanted to know all the details. After all, he and Ann were due to stay with Aunt Helen for a month, and for that period, at least, he would be part and parcel of this little community. Perhaps he might be able to do something to lift the pall of horror which lay over it. It would be well worth trying, anyhow, and he *had* succeeded in finding out the truth about that other affair at Bishop's Thatcham in the summer of the previous year. It would add a fillip and a zest to his holiday, at any rate, and supply the necessary mental stimulant that he needed. It was over a month since he had completed his latest novel and his mind was barren of any ideas for the next. Working on this problem might give his stagnant brain just the tonic it required. It appealed to him strongly for, apart from any other consideration, this wholesale murder of helpless children had roused him to a cold anger against the person responsible, homicidal maniac notwithstanding, and it would give him the greatest satisfaction to put a stop to his dreadful activities.

So Peter's thoughts ran in an undercurrent to the polite surface conversation which he forced himself to make.

The party broke up comparatively early. Laura Courtland was the first to go, pleading that she ought to return to her father in case he needed her. They all realized that it was the flimsiest of excuses, but nobody made any real effort to persuade her to stay. Anthony Sherwood and April left very shortly after, and, when they were alone, Miss Wymondham broke into a flood of apologies.

'I'm so sorry, my dears,' she said. 'I did *so* want your first evening here to be cheerful and happy, but I'm dreadfully afraid it was nothing of the sort. Such a dismal atmosphere, I'm really quite relieved that the evening is over. But, of course, you couldn't expect anything else with this terrible thing hanging over all of us, and poor little Joan Coxen being spirited away. I *do* wish, though, that it hadn't happened today of all days. It would have been *so* nice if we could have had a really jolly evening . . . ' and so on *ad infinitum*.

Poor Miss Wymondham was so genuinely distressed that her well-meant efforts to entertain them had not been successful that both Ann and Peter did their utmost to reassure her. But the old lady was too disappointed to be pacified by anything they said, and she was still apologizing volubly when they parted for the night and went to bed.

6

'Peter,' said Ann, sitting up in bed and thoughtfully watching her husband as he pottered restlessly about the bedroom and got slowly undressed by easy stages, 'I believe the detective fever has bitten you again.'

'What makes you think that?' he demanded.

'Oh, various signs and portents,' she replied. 'I thought so earlier this evening when we first heard about this horrible business.'

'Well,' said Peter, undoing the studs in the front of his shirt and then pausing uncertainly as though rather vague about what he would do next. 'Well . . . it did occur to me that since we are here for a month I might . . . well, look into the matter . . . '

'I guessed as much,' said Ann, her eyes twinkling. 'So this is where I resume my well-known role of Watson, is it?'

'You've been promoted since then,'

retorted Peter. 'Besides, I didn't actually *say* that I was going to . . . '

'You don't have to actually say anything, darling,' broke in his wife. 'Not to me, at any rate. The symptoms are very obvious.' Her face clouded and she suddenly became serious. 'It's rather beastly, isn't it, Peter?' she said in an altered voice. He nodded, fiddling with his braces.

'Yes,' he said. 'A very nasty, unpleasant business. Anything that has to do with an unbalanced brain is always peculiarly horrible, I think.'

'There's no doubt, I suppose, that that *is* what's at the bottom of it?' said Ann.

'I shouldn't think there was any,' answered Peter, reaching for his dressing-gown and pyjamas. 'What makes you say that?'

She gave a slight twitch to her bare shoulders.

'Nothing in particular,' she said. 'It just occurred to me, that's all . . . '

'I don't see how there could be anything like that — any planned motive, I mean,' said Peter, thoughtfully. 'It's not that type of crime at all. If it were it would be far easier. Find the motive and you've found the murderer. No, I think it must be a maniac . . . '

He disappeared into the bathroom, and Ann was almost asleep when he came back in pyjamas and dressing-gown and carrying the remainder of his clothes over his arm. She moved drowsily as he slid into bed beside her and lay staring up at the ceiling.

'Aren't you going to put the light out, darling?' she murmured. 'I'm so tired . . . '

He reached out an arm and turned the switch of the bedside lamp, but although he, too, was tired, it was a long time before he fell asleep. The glow of the dying fire filled the room with a rosy gloom, and on this background his imagination painted vivid pictures which, as he drifted into sleep, became broken and nightmarish dreams, dominated by a great shapeless figure that loomed menacingly through a swirling, smoky fog: a figure that was dreadful and obscene and utterly and incredibly evil . . .

7

Colonel Shoredust was tired and a little irritable. Superintendent Odds was tired and more than a little irritable. Sergeant Quilt was tired and more irritable than either of his superiors, though his position prevented him from showing it as much as they did. He came to the irate conclusion, not by any means for the first time, that Colonel Shoredust was a pompous, incompetent old nincompoop. Colonel Shoredust was convinced beyond all shadow of doubt that both Superintendent Odds and Sergeant Quilt were incompetent, woodenheaded, blundering jackasses. They sat in Fendyke St. Mary's small, rural police station, with the chill November dawn turning the windows to a ghostly grey, and the setting, even under the most salubrious conditions, was not conducive to cheerfulness. The converted cottage was small and cramped, large enough for Police Constable Cropps, who lived there and was usually its sole occupant, but quite inadequate for the conference which was at present being held there. In the white light from the broken gas mantle, Colonel Shoredust looked yellow, with bulging, jaundiced eyes under which folds of skin hung loosely. His moustache, usually trim and jaunty, drooped wearily and there was a white stubble on his chin and heavy jowls.

Superintendent Odds, dishevelled, dirty, and dejected, slumped in a horsehair chair and moodily tugged at his lower lip, pulling it down and letting it flip up against its fellow with monotonous regularity. His short, greying hair was untidy, and his boots and trousers were wet and muddy. Sergeant Quilt, since there was no chair for him to sit on, leaned against the mantelpiece, the picture of physical and mental weariness, his round, fullish face an unhealthy grey and, although it was cold, faintly dewed with sweat. All three had been up all night and looked it.

'For God's sake stop that!' grunted the Chief Constable, crossly. 'Blasted silly habit.'

Superintendent Odds stopped plucking

at his lip. He thrust his hand into the pocket of his overcoat but made no reply. Sergeant Quilt yawned widely and long. Colonel Shoredust shifted restlessly in his chair behind the battered desk.

'There's going to be a damned lot of trouble about this, you know,' he said.

'Yes, sir, I know,' said Odds, tonelessly.

'We've got to find this child before anything happens to her,' went on the Chief Constable. 'We've *got* to. There's going to be a hell of a row if we don't.'

The superintendent shrugged his shoulders. Why did the old fool keep harping on *that*, he thought, irritably. As if he didn't *know*. Aloud he said:

'What more *can* we do, sir? Every available man we can muster is out searching for her. And we've roped in a lot of volunteers as well. They've been searching ever since we got the news. Sergeant Quilt and I have been searching half the night, too. If you can suggest anything else, sir . . . ' He stopped and looked at Colonel Shoredust expectantly.

The Colonel met the look for a second or two, and then his eyes shifted.

'Blast it,' he said, 'what *is* there to suggest?'

'I don't know, sir,' said Odds, wearily. 'But if you're dissatisfied . . . '

'Don't be stupid, man,' broke in the Chief Constable, impatiently. 'Aren't we all damned-well dissatisfied? Look here, this is the fifth of the blasted disappearances in eighteen months and we're no nearer finding the feller who's responsible than we were when we started. If the sequel to this one is like the others, that poor bloody kid's going to be found stuck somewhere with her throat cut, *and* we shan't be any nearer finding who did it . . . '

'The trouble is there's nothing to go on,' said Superintendent Odds. 'You can't search for a motive because we already know the only one there *can* be, and it doesn't help us. We *know* we've got a lunatic to deal with . . . '

'That blasted feller, Twist,' interrupted Colonel Shoredust.

'No, sir.' Odds shook his head. 'I'm satisfied that Twist has nothing to do with it. He's just a bit soft . . . '

'You never can tell with these fellers,' said the Colonel, stubbornly. Tom Twist had been his favourite, and only, suspect, and he was reluctant that he should be so completely dismissed. 'Damned cunning.'

'Yes, sir,' said the superintendent with a patience he was far from feeling. 'But Twist has a constitutional aversion to the sight of blood.' They were not his own words. He was quoting Doctor Culpepper. 'It makes him sick, an' there's no fake about it. We had him tested by two doctors . . .'

'Doctors!' grunted Colonel Shoredust, disparagingly.

'They both asserted,' Odds went on, without taking any notice of the interruption, 'that if Twist had wanted to kill, he wouldn't have killed *that* way. They were absolutely convinced of that.'

The Chief Constable uttered a sound that was suspiciously like a snort. It was quite evident that he placed no reliance at all on the verdict of the two doctors and would have been equally unimpressed if the doctors had numbered two hundred.

'Well,' he remarked, 'there's not much

point in proving who couldn't have done it. What we've got to do is to blasted-well prove who *did* do it. If you could hit on some bright ideas about that . . . ' The bell of the wall telephone broke out loudly and insistently, and so unexpectedly, that Sergeant Quilt gave a violent start and his elbow slipped off the mantelpiece. To save himself from falling, he grabbed wildly at the shelf, dislodging a tea cannister which fell with a clatter into the fireplace.

'Clumsy fool!' muttered Colonel Shoredust under his breath, but not so softly that Quilt didn't hear the comment and glared at his superior 'Odds! For God's sake answer the blasted thing . . . ' The order was superfluous for Superintendent Odds was already at the instrument.

'Hello?' he called, with the receiver to his ear. 'Oh, yes, sir . . . No, I'm afraid not . . . Yes, sir. I will, certainly . . . I'm very sorry . . . We're doing everything we possibly can . . . Yes, sir, I'll let you know at once.' He hung up the receiver and looked at Colonel Shoredust. 'It was Doctor Culpepper, sir. Wanted to know if we'd heard anything. It seems that Mrs. Coxen is very ill with shock, an' in a dangerous condition. The doctor's been with her most of the night . . . '

'Damned sorry,' said Colonel Shoredust. He passed a stubby hand over his thinning hair, and frowned. 'Look here, you know,' he burst out suddenly, striking the desk in front of him with his fist, 'this can't blasted-well go on. We've got to damned-well pull ourselves together and go into action.'

'What do you suggest, sir?' asked the superintendent.

'This business has got to be put a stop to,' replied the Chief Constable 'This blasted butcher has got to be found . . . '

'Yes, sir,' said Odds. 'We're all agreed on that, but how?'

'If we can't do it off our own bat,' said Colonel Shoredust, 'we'll blasted-well get help . . . '

'You mean Scotland Yard?' said Odds, and the Chief Constable nodded.

'I don't like having to ask for help,' he grunted. 'Admission of defeat an' all that. Goes against the grain. But damn it all this can't go on . . . '

'Do you think, sir,' said Odds, 'that Scotland Yard could do any more than we have . . . '

'I don't know. They couldn't blasted-well do any less,' said the Colonel, candidly. 'Oh, I'm not blaming you fellers,' he added, as he saw the expression that came into the tired face of the superintendent, 'any more than I'm blaming myself. We've done our damned-est, all of us. But we haven't been successful, and that's all that counts.'

'Well, sir,' said Odds. 'It's up to you, of course.'

'There's nothing else we can do,' declared Colonel Shoredust. 'We've tried and we've failed. If we don't call in the Yard there's going to be a damned unholy row, and we shall bear the whole blasted brunt of it. I'll get in touch with 'em today.'

He postponed carrying out this decision until the evening of that eventful day and was glad that he had, for by then the horror of Fendyke St. Mary had taken a new turn, and in addition to the slaughter of lambs, and the murder of children, he was presented with a problem so weird and extraordinary, so completely inexplicable, that it was more like the wild imaginings of a nightmare than anything real.

8

Mrs. Sowerby came out of her small cottage in the High Street into the cold grey gloom of the morning just as the clock in the tower of Fendyke St. Mary's church chimed half-past seven. It was not a novel experience, for she left her cottage at that time every morning except Sundays. It allowed her to reach Robin Mallory's little house on the Green by a quarter to eight, get his breakfast ready, and take it up to him at half-past. Mrs. Sowerby did not altogether approve of Robin Mallory, but he paid well and regularly, and the work was comparatively light. Her disapproval was based principally on the fact that he was an artist and that he invariably stayed in bed until midday. Mrs. Sowerby had strict and rather narrow views about art, and Mr. Mallory's pictures decidedly shocked her. The naked and unadorned female form should, properly, be confined to the privacy of the bathroom and not allowed to blatantly disport itself, in every conceivable pose, from the walls of dining room, studio, and bedroom, even if it was only in pictures. And some of the pictures . . . well, really, it made her blush every time she saw them. Apart from this, Mr. Mallory seemed to be a fairly respectable young man. He spent a great deal of his time painting in the big room which he used for a studio and, although Mrs. Sowerby had found traces, in the way of bottles, dirty glasses, and laden ash-trays, of innumerable parties, there was no evidence that he indulged in any of the more erotic vices.

Mrs. Sowerby hurried along with a rather waddling gait, her breath issuing in steamy clouds from her parted lips, and thankful that the night had not brought with it any more snow. There were lights in some of the cottages she passed on her way, but she saw no one during the short distance from her house to the Green. Robin Mallory's house was one of the few modern ones in the village, which is to say that it was not more than two hundred years old. The exterior was not very beautiful to look at, and had been rendered less so by the door and window-frames which Mallory had painted a vivid orange, and which thoroughly offended the critical taste of Mrs. Sowerby. She let herself in with her key and looked for any signs of a convivial evening. But this morning there were no empty bottles, used glasses, or laden trays of cigarette-ends. The place was fairly neat and tidy — as tidy anyway, as it ever was. She went through to the kitchen and filled a kettle at the sink. Lighting a ring of the gas stove she set the kettle on to boil while she prepared toast and bacon.

When it was ready, she made the tea, laid a dainty tray — Robin Mallory was rather finicky about the way things were served up to him — and carried it up the stairs to the bedroom. With the edge of the tray she tapped gently on the door. There was no reply, which was unusual, for he invariably answered at once, and after a moment she knocked again. Still receiving no reply, Mrs. Sowerby shifted the tray so that it rested on one arm, and turning the handle of the door, gently went in.

'Well, I do declare!' she exclaimed in surprised annoyance, for the room was empty. Instead of Mr. Mallory, in flamboyant pyjamas, reclining at ease in the old French bed, it was unoccupied and, apparently, had not been occupied that night at all, for it was as smooth and undisturbed as when she made it on the previous day.

'Well, I do *declare*,' said Mrs. Sowerby again, staring about her in resentful astonishment. 'What can have become of the man.'

She stood uncertainly, with the large breakfast tray held out in front of her, moving her head from side to side as though she expected Robin Mallory to make a sudden and miraculous appearance. But he did nothing of the sort. Mrs. Sowerby put the tray down on a table near the bed head and waddled out to the bathroom. After knocking loudly on the door, with no better result than her previous knocking on the door of the bedroom had achieved, she opened the door and peered gingerly in. The bathroom was empty. Mr. Mallory's rather startling dressing-gown of jade green silk hung on a hook behind the door, but of Mr. Mallory himself there was no sign. Disconcerted and slightly alarmed, for such a thing had never happened before during the entire period she had worked for him, Mrs. Sowerby began a hasty but thorough inspection of the house. The big, untidy studio, with its litter of paints, brushes, and canvases, was empty. The dining room was empty. The small lounge was empty. In another five minutes, during which time she had been all over the house, Mrs. Sowerby was forced to the incredible conclusion that Mr. Mallory was not there and had not been there since the previous day.

'Well, I never did,' declared Mrs. Sowerby to the world in general. 'What can have happened to the man?' Since there was nobody to answer this question, she had to try and find an explanation for herself. And this she did while she ate Mr. Mallory's breakfast and drank his tea in the kitchen. He must have gone to visit some friends and stayed the night. Certainly he had never done such a thing before, but that was the only thing it could be. Very definitely he hadn't slept in his own house.

'Oh, well,' thought Mrs. Sowerby, philosophically, as she set about her work, 'I suppose 'e's his own master an' can do as 'e likes.'

She began to wash up the breakfast dishes energetically.

9

Mr. Felix Courtland woke from an uneasy and troubled sleep and blinked into semi-darkness. His head felt as though it had been stuffed very thoroughly and completely with cotton wool, and his throat was dry and rough. He had tossed and turned through most of the night, and now, at last, when he *had* succeeded in dropping off to sleep, some infernal racket had woken him.

The 'infernal racket' was, he discovered, only a soft tapping on his bedroom door and he growled a hoarse 'come in.' The door opened and a housemaid loomed through the gloom. She carried a tray which she set down on the table beside his bed and then went swiftly and quietly over to the windows and drew back the curtains. Mr. Courtland sat up in bed as light flooded into the room; the weird, artificial light that is produced by the reflection from snow.

'What time is it?' he grunted, ungraciously and thickly.

'Ten o'clock, sir,' said the housemaid. 'I was told to wake you, sir, and ask if you knew where Miss Laura was, sir?'

She was a very young girl and she was a little nervous and apprehensive of Mr. Courtland, even when he hadn't a severe cold in the head.

'Where Miss Laura is?' repeated her master, rubbing his bald head vigorously and looking like a depilated ape. 'Isn't she in bed?'

'No, sir,' said the maid, backing slowly towards the door.

'Well, I suppose she's somewhere about the house,' growled Mr. Courtland, turning to the tray of tea and preparing to pour milk into his cup. 'Why come to me?'

'But she ain't in the 'ouse, sir,' said the maid. 'She hasn't been in the 'ouse all night, sir . . . '

Mr. Courtland paused with the jug poised over the cup.

'Nonsense,' he declared, curtly.

'Miss Laura's bed hasn't been slept in,

sir,' persisted the housemaid. 'When I took in 'er tea it was just like it was yesterday, sir. Miss Laura 'adn't been to bed . . .'

Mr. Courtland put down the milk-jug and glared at her with slightly bloodshot eyes.

'What's that?' he rasped, and coughed. He continued to cough violently until the tears were running down his fat cheeks. After a minute or so the paroxysm stopped, leaving him red in the face and breathless. 'Ugh,' he gasped, wiping his lips with his handkerchief. 'Now what's all this? Miss Laura hasn't been to bed? Why the devil didn't she go to bed?'

The maid, having no answer to this question, contented herself with opening her eyes very wide and shaking her head.

Mr. Courtland blew his nose noisily and with great energy.

'Where did she go last night?' he said, when this operation was over. 'Oh, I know. She went to dinner with Miss Wymondham. Probably stayed there. Tell Pitt to ring up Wymondham Lodge . . .'

The maid was glad of an excuse to

escape; Mr. Courtland was equally glad to be rid of her. He poured himself out a cup of tea and gulped it with enjoyment. It eased his dry throat. Confoundedly unpleasant things colds. Why couldn't the doctors find a quick and reasonable cure? They were pretty good with more elaborate complaints, but the common cold had always beaten 'em . . . Silly to make such a fuss over Laura. She was old enough to take care of herself, and if she didn't want to, that was her affair. It wouldn't be the first time she'd stayed out all night . . . usually there was some man or other at the bottom of it. Laura collected them like some people collected stamps or old china. None of 'em lasted very long. Variety, that's what Laura liked . . . There wasn't much choice, though, in Fendyke St. Mary . . . She'd have to be careful. You couldn't carry on in a village like you could in the West End of London . . . It would be just as well if he had a word with her about it. Not that it would do much good. It was impossible to argue with Laura. She just flared up, and that was that . . . Who could be the attraction this time? Must be somebody local, but who? He'd thought for a long while that there was something going on. There'd been a sort of undercurrent of excitement about her for the last year . . . Oh, well, he supposed it must be pretty dull for a girl of Laura's temperament in a place like Fendyke St. Mary, so if she'd found something to amuse her it would, at least, keep her in a good temper, which was something to be thankful for . . . Oh, damn! here was somebody else to disturb him . . .

A knock heralded the entrance of Pitt, stout, dark, correctly dressed as a butler should be dressed.

'What is it now?' demanded Mr. Courtland, irritably.

'I have telephoned Wymondham Lodge, sir,' said Pitt, respectful without any trace of being servile. 'Miss Wymondham informs me that Miss Laura left shortly after half-past ten, expressing her intention of returning home because you were ill. She did not do so, sir, and the small car which she took out last night is not in the garage.'

Mr. Courtland frowned.

'Where the deuce can she be?' he muttered. 'If she'd had an accident we should have heard. She must have gone on to some friends of hers . . . '

'Very possibly, sir,' said Pitt, without emotion. 'I thought it only right that you should know.'

'Yes, yes, quite.' Mr. Courtland nodded. 'You did quite right, Pitt . . . ' He rubbed his chin, continuing to frown.

'Is there anything you would wish me to do, sir?' inquired the butler, and Mr. Courtland considered for a moment before he answered.

'No,' he said, at last. 'No, I don't think so, Pitt. Miss Laura will probably come back during the morning. When she does, ask her to come and see me at once.'

'Yes, sir.' Pitt gave a slight bow and went out, closing the door softly behind him. But the morning wore away, and lunchtime came and went, and still Laura Courtland had not come home.

10

Old Ted Hoskins, the postman, trudged stolidly through the snow, a bundle of letters in his hand and more in the satchel slung round his neck. The weather made no difference to him. Snow, rain, hail or sunshine, it was all the same. Many years at his job had hardened him. Sometimes there were few letters; sometimes many. That was all the same to him, too. This morning there were quite a number. One for Miss Flitterwyk; three for the Sherwoods; half a dozen for the vicarage, four for the Reverend Amos Benskill and two for the curate, the Reverend Gilbert Ray; a very ornate, perfumed one for Miss Fay Bennett, and one for Miss Helen Wymondham. There was a registered parcel for Monsieur André Severac and a bundle of magazines for Miss Tittleton. Ted Hoskins gradually shed his load, passing from house to house with his shuffling hobble which was the result, partly of old age, and partly of bunions. He came at last to the isolated house of Monsieur André Severac which stood in a narrow lane running off the Green. The exterior of the house was neither imposing nor prepossessing, but Hoskins had seen the interior and knew that it was furnished both tastefully and luxuriously, for Monsieur André Severac was a rich bachelor who liked to surround himself with every comfort. Hoskins took the parcel out of his satchel, with the receipt slip neatly tucked under the string, as he hobbled up the short path to the front door. He beat the usual double tat-tat on the bronze knocker, which was in the shape of a coiled snake, and waited. He expected Monsieur André Severac would appear in the heavy flowered silk dressing-gown which seemed to be his habitual apparel indoors. But Monsieur André Severac did not appear, either in the dressing-gown or out of it. Hoskins knocked again, and then a third time, but there was no reply. The door remained closed and no sound came from within.

The postman frowned. This meant that

he would have to take the parcel away and come back with it later. It was very inconsiderate of Monsieur André Severac to be out, and very unusual. Old Ted Hoskins turned reluctantly away and departed, grumbling under his breath, to deliver the rest of the mail.

11

'Nice to be some people, that it is,' grumbled Mrs. Bossom, 'lyin' in bed 'alf the day an' no consideration for people as wants to get on with their work.'

'Do you think I'd best take up 'er tea?' suggested Rose, the maid.

'No, I don't,' answered Mrs. Bossom, pouring herself out a second cup of strong black tea and splashing in a generous quantity of milk. 'You know what 'appened when we did that once. She flew into such a rage that the roof nearly came off. We've got orders not to disturb 'er Royal 'Ighness until she rings.' She put three spoonsful of sugar into her tea, stirred it vigorously, and swallowed half of the horrible decoction at a gulp.

'What time did she come in last night?' asked the maid.

'I neither know, nor care,' snapped the cook, irritably. '*I* was in bed an' asleep by ten, an' I slep' sound an' never 'eard nuthink until the alarm woke me at seven.'

'So did I,' said Rose. 'I was that tired.'

'We 'ave ter work for our livin',' remarked Mrs. Bossom. 'We can't get up at noon and paint our faces to make ourselves look younger'n what we are an' then lay about all day in silk pyjamas, smokin' cigarettes an' readin' books that didn't oughter be allowed . . . '

''Ow old do you think Miss Bennett is?' asked Rose, curiously.

'Nearer forty than thirty,' said Mrs. Bossom, unkindly. 'An old 'en tryin' ter make itself look like a chicken, if you ask me.'

'She's very smart, though, ain't she?' said the maid. 'An' 'er hair's lovely . . . '

Mrs. Bossom sniffed. It was an expressive sniff. It destroyed the loveliness of Miss Bennett's hair more effectively than a hundred words could have done.

'You'd best be gettin' about your work, my gel,' she said, 'or you'll be all behind, an' then there'll be ructions.'

Rose sighed, collected her brushes, brooms, and dusters, and departed, leaving Mrs. Bossom in possession of the kitchen and her tea.

At half-past twelve when there was still no summons from her mistress's bed-room, Mrs. Bossom called Rose.

'You'd better take this tea up to 'er now,' she said, crossly. 'I can't wait about all day. If she's cross, you'd best say you thought she rang.'

Rose took the tray rather reluctantly. In a few minutes she was back again with it, her small face puckered up in an expression that was both worried and astonished.

'She ain't in 'er room,' she announced, breathlessly.

'Oh, well, I expect she's in the lavatory,' said Mrs. Bossom, unconcernedly. 'Why didn't you leave the tea . . . '

'But . . . but she 'asn't been to bed at all,' cried Rose, excitedly. 'It ain't been touched. It's just as I made it yester-day . . . '

'Ho!' said Mrs. Bossom, tossing her head. 'Been 'avin' a night out, I s'pose. Well, if she thinks she's goin' ter walk in 'ere an' find lunch all ready for 'er, she's

goin' to be unlucky, that's all . . . ' But
Fay Bennett did not 'walk in' at lunchtime, or any other time, and late in the
evening of that day Mrs. Bossom learned
why . . .

12

Peter Chard woke feeling depressed and out of sorts. The horrid fantasies which had disturbed his sleep had left him very tired, almost as though he had had no sleep at all. He felt better after his morning tea, a bath, and breakfast, but the vague memory of those distorted visions stayed with him, though he couldn't have described one single incident in detail. There *was* no detail. Only a tremendous sense of something terrible and evil — an atmosphere that came from hell. He said nothing about it to Ann or Aunt Helen. Miss Wymondham had recovered something of her normal spirits and volubility. She chattered inconsequently about anything and everything; anecdotes and descriptions of the people living in Fendyke St. Mary that made Ann laugh. From thence she drifted to places of interest in the vicinity. The church of Fendyke St. Mary, they learned, was exceptionally fine. It had an open timber roof with carved corbels, and on the ends of the hammer-beams small figures of angels. It was generally acknowledged to be one of the finest churches in the county. The screen contained panels with paintings of the twelve Apostles and an elaborate cornice.

' . . . And then of course, my dear,' went on Miss Wymondham, 'there's Lucifer's stone about half a mile outside the village. This place was a hot-bed of witchcraft in the Middle Ages, you know, and the witches used to hold their sabbaths, and all kind of horrible orgies, at which the Devil was supposed to appear. The stone was used for his throne — at least that's the story, and it looks very like one. You'd be surprised how many of the villagers still believe in witchcraft. Oh, and then there's Mrs. Knap's cottage. She was a poor old woman who was accused of being a witch by Matthew Hopkins and burned to death in 1644. Her place is still known as Witch's House. It's empty now, of course, and has been empty for a good many years because nobody can stay there very long. They say that *something* still lives there, though of course that's all superstitious nonsense. You must have passed the cottage last night, on your way here . . . '

'Oh, is that the place?' said Ann with interest. 'We thought it might be inhabited and knocked to see if we could get some tea, didn't we, Peter?'

Peter, who had only been partly listening, nodded.

'You did,' he said.

'I had a horribly queer feeling, too,' said Ann, remembering. 'As though somebody were watching me from behind the windows. It was a most unpleasant sensation . . . '

'None of the villagers would dream of going near it,' declared Miss Wymondham. 'You chose a particularly bad time to visit it, didn't you?'

'Why?' asked Ann.

'Don't you know? Last night was the Eve of All-Hallows,' said Miss Wymondham with a smile. 'Though, I believe, that the spells and things don't become potent until midnight. Such a stupid lot of nonsense, my dear . . . Oh, there's the telephone.

I'd better go and answer it myself because this is Hewson's day for cleaning the silver and he always starts very early so that he can get it done . . . Do excuse me, both of you.' She bustled away.

'What are you going to do today, Peter?' asked Ann.

'I don't know.' He looked out of the window. 'It's fairly fine. We might have a look round the village — only you don't like walking in the snow, do you?'

'I don't mind if I'm suitably dressed,' she answered. 'Sheer silk stockings and high-heeled shoes are not my idea of suitability. I'd rather like it, Peter.'

'All right, then we'll go,' he said. 'You pop along and get suitably dressed.'

Ann looked at him with her chestnut head slightly on one side. Her eyes were quizzical and mischievous.

'Is this excursion the beginning of the great detective's investigation?' she asked. Before Peter could reply, Miss Wymondham bounced back into the room bubbling over with excitement.

'What *do* you think?' she cried. 'Laura Courtland hasn't been home all night . . .'

'Hasn't been home?' said Peter, sharply. 'But she left here about half-past ten . . . '

'I know, my dear, that's what I told them,' said Miss Wymondham, nodding several times. 'But she didn't go home. Her bed hasn't been slept in and she's nowhere in the house. Isn't it strange? Where *could* the girl have gone to?'

'She *said* she was going home,' remarked Ann. 'She said she thought she ought to go in case her father wanted her . . . '

'I knew *that* was just an excuse, my dear,' said Miss Wymondham. 'Laura isn't as dutiful as all that, by any means. But I thought she was bored. I suppose she went along to some friends, or something, where the party was more gay and hectic. Laura likes excitement and not always of the best kind, I'm afraid . . . '

'H'm,' said Peter. 'I suppose that's what she must have done . . . ' Something in his tone attracted Ann's attention. She looked round. He was frowning thought-fully.

'But you don't believe that's what she *did* do?' she accused.

He shrugged his shoulders.

'Well,' he said, hesitantly, as though he were rather unwilling to put his thoughts into anything so concrete as words. 'I wouldn't definitely say that. I was only wondering if this might not be an extension . . . '

'An extension?' said Ann, a little puzzled.

'Lambs first, then children, and now . . . ' He stopped, abruptly, leaving the sentence unfinished as Miss Wymondham uttered a cry of horror.

'Oh, Peter . . . You can't mean *that* . . . ' she exclaimed. 'You don't *really* think . . . '

'What a horrid idea, darling,' said Ann, with a shiver.

'Somebody else round here has got some pretty horrid ideas, too,' said Peter, gravely. 'We know that. Why shouldn't he have had another?' He pulled out a packet of Players, took a cigarette and lit it. 'Has anything further been heard of Joan Coxen?'

'No, poor little thing,' said Miss Wymondham, shaking her head. 'At least not that *I* have heard, and I'm sure that if anything had, I *should* have heard. Peter, you don't really think that the same thing can have happened to Laura Courtland . . . ?'

'I only suggested it as a possibility,' said Peter.

'Oh, I don't think you can be right,' said Miss Wymondham. 'Laura Courtland's rather . . . well, flighty and . . . and impulsive, you know. It would be just like her to go off somewhere on the spur of the moment . . . '

'Has she ever done so before?' asked Peter.

'Well, no. Not in quite the same way,' admitted Aunt Helen. 'She's always going off for weekends and things. But they've always *known* that she was going . . . '

'Exactly,' said Peter. 'So does it seem likely to you that she would leave this house at half-past ten and, dressed as she was, suddenly decide not to go home but to drive somewhere else and stay the night . . . '

'Perhaps she didn't suddenly make up her mind,' said Ann. 'Perhaps she'd arranged to go on somewhere before she came here . . . '

'In that case,' said Peter, 'surely she would have told them at her home not to expect her back?'

'She may not have had any intention of staying the night,' argued his wife. 'Something may have happened, after, to make her decide to do that . . . '

'And then she would have telephoned,' said Peter.

'Oh, no, my dear,' chimed in Miss Wymondham, shaking her head. 'I don't think she would. If you knew Laura as well as I do, you wouldn't expect her to do anything as sensible as that. It would never occur to her that anyone might be worried or anxious. I think Ann is most likely right and that she had it all arranged before she came here to dinner. It was probably the reason she left early. I *can't* believe that anything can have happened to her . . . '

'Peter *always* prefers the dramatic explanation to the simple one,' said Ann. 'Don't you, darling?' She got up with a swift, graceful movement. 'I'll go and put my things on, if we're going out,' she said.

Miss Wymondham demanded to know where they were going and when she was told, beamed.

'I think it's a splendid idea,' she declared. 'Do wrap up well, though, both of you, because it's very cold. And don't be late for lunch. Cook gets so very irritable and bad-tempered if she's kept waiting and the whole household suffers for it. So try and get back by half-past one. I'm sure you'll both be very hungry by then, anyway . . . '

It was quite a nice morning, they found, when they got out; still freezing hard, but bracing and invigorating. The cutting wind of the previous evening had gone completely and with it the heavy, lowering clouds. A pale sun, without being warm enough to melt the snow, provided a touch of brightness and cheerfulness. The church of Fendyke St. Mary was open and they went in. Miss Wymondham had not exaggerated its beauty. The screen and the roof were really lovely, and so was a canopied font. The cover was richly carved and rested on six pillars, delicately representing twisted foliage. The font itself was six-sided and panelled with tracery. A lovely piece of workmanship, made in the days when men were craftsmen and took pride in superb craftsmanship for its own sake and not for the amount they were going to make out of it. As they left the church they met a short, stoutish man whose clerical collar proclaimed his profession. He was accompanied by a younger clergyman, a dark, handsome, olive-skinned man who had a slightly foreign appearance. The elder man was blowing his nose violently, but he removed the handkerchief to eye them speculatively and, after a moment, stopped.

'It's Mr. and Mrs. Chard, isn't it?' he said in a voice that was rendered nasal and husky from a severe cold in the head. 'I thought it must be. Your Aunt, Miss Wymondham, said you were coming to stay with her and strangers are not — ah — very prolific in Fendyke St. Mary. My name is Benskill. I am the vicar of this parish. This is the Reverend Gilbert Ray, my curate.' Peter and Ann acknowledged the introduction suitably, and the Reverend Amos Benskill went on: 'You have been admiring the church? It is truly beautiful, don't you think? One of the finest in Norfolk . . . ' He expatiated at considerable length on the beauties of his church, while the xanthomelanous curate stood by in silence. 'But I mustn't keep you,' ended the vicar, suddenly recollecting that they were standing in the snow and that it was cold. 'I apologize for being so inconsiderate. You are staying here for a month, I understand. Good, good! I trust that you and your wife will call and see us at the vicarage? It is only a step from here — just along the road — you can see the gate. A bachelor establishment, I'm afraid, but we shall be happy to offer what hospitality we can at any time . . . '

'What a dear old gentleman,' said Ann, when the vicar and his assistant had said goodbye and disappeared inside the church.

Peter nodded.

'Very charming,' he answered. 'I don't much like the curate though, do you?'

'He didn't strike me as being entirely English,' said Ann. 'He's very good-looking in a Latin way . . . '

'More French, I thought,' said Peter. 'There's certainly a touch of something foreign, anyway. Let's go and see if we can find the village pub.'

'Darling,' said his wife, reproachfully, 'surely you don't want a drink yet . . . ?'

'According to Sherlock Holmes,' replied Peter, 'the public-house is the centre of country gossip. Hence my desire to find our own particular centre.'

'Oh, I see,' said Ann. 'Well, I suppose that *is* as good an excuse as any . . . '

The 'village pub', which was disappointingly called by the hackneyed name of the *Red Lion*, was discovered at the end of Fendyke St. Mary's short High Street. It stood in a kind of shallow bay and was a low-built, whitewashed building of considerable age. There were very few people in the bar, which was made warm and cheerful by an enormous fire that burned in an old red-brick fireplace at one end, but the few that were ceased their conversation and stared curiously at

92

Ann and Peter when they entered.

'What would you like?' asked Peter, following his wife over to the fireplace.

'If they've got any Gordon's I'd like a gin and 'it',' she answered, holding out her hands to the blaze. 'If they haven't any Gordon's I'll have a sherry.'

Peter walked over to the bar and gave his order to the pleasant-faced woman behind it. The low hum of conversation broke out again, but it was more subdued, and Peter guessed that the subject was themselves. The *Red Lion* *had* got Gordon's and he carried the gin and Italian for Ann, and a pint tankard of beer for himself, back to the fire.

'Here's to us, darling,' he said. 'H'm, whatever else may be wrong with this place, the beer is excellent.'

'That means that the *Red Lion* is going to see quite a lot of us, I suppose,' remarked Ann, sipping her drink slowly. 'We seem to be causing a great deal of interest.'

'We're strangers,' said Peter, in brief explanation. 'We have aroused a certain amount of curiosity and quite a lot of resentment. It's the normal reaction of the villager. By tomorrow everybody will have found out who we are and accepted us as part of the community. In the meanwhile we are regarded with suspicion.'

'I think you're right about the suspicion part of it,' murmured Ann, looking at the eight or nine people in the bar. They were eyeing them both covertly, and with a vague suggestion of hostility. Even the buxom woman with the pleasant, florid face was watching them while she pretended to busy herself among her glasses and bottles.

'We'll have another and then we'll get back to Aunt Helen's,' said Peter, as they finished their drinks. They had another. As they left the bar, Ann glanced back and saw that all the customers, and the buxom woman, were staring after them . . .

'Well,' she said, as they walked up the High Street past the small collection of shops which served Fendyke St. Mary as a shopping centre, 'if that is your idea of 'the centre of country gossip' I don't think very much of it.'

'You've got to break the ice in a village

like this . . . ' began Peter.

'I doubt if we've even cracked it,' said Ann, 'or made the tiniest dent . . . '

'The morning is not the best time,' he broke in. 'There were very few people there. The place is probably packed in the evening, with a much warmer and more human atmosphere . . . '

'Is that,' said Ann, with a quick, sidelong glance that Peter thought was very fascinating, 'the preliminary to suggesting a visit this evening . . . ?'

'No, no,' said her husband, hastily. 'Not at all. I might, of course, pop along . . . '

'I thought so,' she said, dryly.

'It all depends on the circumstances,' he went on, taking no apparent notice of her interruption.

'What circumstances?' she demanded.

'I want to get the village reaction to these baby killings,' he answered, suddenly serious. 'I want to know if the village suspect anybody, and, if so, whom. If there is any news of Joan Coxen it will be discussed at length and I want to hear what is said.'

'I see,' said Ann. A sudden silence fell

between them, and they were nearly at the gate of Wymondham Lodge before either spoke again, and then it was Ann.

'Peter,' she said, earnestly, taking his arm impulsively. 'I do hope you're going to be successful, darling. It's such a horrid, beastly thing . . . '

He pressed her arm tightly against his side.

'I'm going to do my damnedest,' he answered.

'I think you will be,' said Ann. 'I've a feeling, somehow, that you will be . . . '

'I hope you're right,' said Peter.

13

'Peter,' said Ann, after lunch. 'I wish the car was in working order . . . '

'Oh, it is, my dear,' exclaimed Miss Wymondham. 'I meant to tell you but I forgot all about it. Tom Acheson came up, himself, this morning while you were out and put it right.'

'What *was* the matter with the thing?' asked Peter.

'I really couldn't tell you that,' said Miss Wymondham. 'Tom Acheson did try to explain, but it conveyed nothing to me — a short something-or-other I *think* he said . . . '

'Circuit?' suggested Peter.

'I believe that's what he said, but I wouldn't be sure,' agreed his aunt. 'Anyhow it doesn't matter, does it? The main thing is that it's all right again.'

'What do you want to do, darling?' Peter turned to his wife.

'Well,' she said, 'I thought it might be

nice if we went for a drive round the district this afternoon. Perhaps Aunt Helen would like to come, and . . . '

'No, my dears, not me,' interrupted the old lady, shaking her head. 'You go on your own. I always have a nap after lunch. It puts me right for the evening — I think it's so good for one when one gets to my age, and Doctor Culpepper agrees. He says it helps to keep the arteries from hardening, or something like that . . . '

Peter laughed.

'What you really mean is that you like it and you'd do it whether it was good for you or not,' he said, and Aunt Helen gave him a beaming smile.

'Well, dear, perhaps you're right,' she remarked, complacently.

It was three o'clock when they set out from Wymondham Lodge, and they planned to be back at half-past four for tea. But for a whim of Ann's they would, in all probability, have carried out this intention and would never have made the ghastly, and almost incredible, discovery which was to delay their return to Wymondham Lodge for so long. Peter often wondered, during the ensuing weeks, whether some queer, subconscious prevision, unknown to her conscious mind, had not prompted Ann to make that request. Whatever it was, pure chance, or something more difficult of explanation, she made it.

'Which way shall we go?' he asked, as they came to the turning by the church.

'Let's go the way we came,' answered Ann. 'I mean, last night when we had to walk. I'd rather like to look at that old cottage again . . .'

'Witch's House?' said Peter, and she nodded.

'Yes,' she said. 'Now that we know something of its history, it's interesting.'

'Are you hoping to see 'the something that still lives there'?' said Peter, as he swung the car round into the road along which they had walked.

'No,' she said, seriously. 'But I got a very strange impression before. I'm wondering if I'll get it again . . .'

'You probably will, if you *think* you will,' said Peter. 'It'll be interesting to see what sort of impression *I* get.'

They passed a few scattered cottages, and then the road ran straight with nothing on either side but the flat, snow-covered marshland. In the pale sunlight it looked less bleak and forbidding than it had done under the lowering, grey-yellow sky and gathering dusk of the previous evening — less bleak, but still desolate. They could see traces of the great dykes that drained the fens, and the rushes that marked the edge of the broads. Presently they came in sight of the pollard willows that grew beside the old stone cottage, and Peter slowed down.

'Surely, darling,' said Ann, in surprise, 'we haven't got there already? It seemed much farther than this from the village . . . '

'You were walking then,' said Peter. He brought the car to a halt. 'That's the place. There's the old broken stone wall and . . . ' He stopped abruptly, staring through the window.

'What's the matter? What is it?' asked Ann, quickly.

'Somebody's been here since we left last night,' said Peter, in surprise. 'Several people, apparently. Look at the snow . . . '

She twisted round in her seat and peered past him. The snow which had been smooth and white in front of the porch when they had last seen it, was now marked with innumerable footprints.

'We made some, but we didn't make all those,' muttered Peter. 'Who could have been here, do you think?'

Ann shook her head.

'I don't know,' she answered. 'It's — queer, isn't it?'

He looked round sharply, attracted by a change in her voice. Her face had gone pale and her eyes were unusually large.

'Last night was the Eve of All-Hallows,' she said, almost in a whisper.

'Nonsense!' said Peter. 'Those footprints were made by real people . . . ' He twisted the handle, opened the door, and got out. For a moment he stood looking at the cottage, and then he walked across to the broken gap in the stone wall. The footprints were a confused jumble. They came from the direction of Fendyke St. Mary, turned in through the gap, and proceeded towards the porch. There were many different ones; the large size of men's and the smaller size of women's, each partly obliterating the other, so that none was very clear. Peter was able, after a moment or two, to pick out the footprints made by Ann and himself on the previous evening, and it was while he was doing this that he saw a very extraordinary thing. With the exception of Ann's and his own, *none of the footprints returned!* They went in the direction of the cottage but there was none coming back in the opposite direction. It was curious, and the discovery sent a queer little quickening of the blood through his veins. These people, who had come to Witch's House since the previous evening, had either left by the back way or *they had not left at all!* Stepping cautiously over the tracks in the snow, Peter entered the gap in the wall.

'Where are you going?' Ann had left the car and joined him.

'Up to the cottage,' answered Peter. 'There's something very strange been going on here. I'd like to find out what. Be careful how you walk, darling. Don't tread on those prints if you can help it.'

Avoiding them himself, he moved slowly up to the porch, with Ann close behind him. The door was closed but, to his surprise, when he pushed it, it opened with a rasping of rusty hinges. Peter peered into the gloom of the musty-smelling passage beyond. The place was thick with dust, and the cobwebs of a dynasty of spiders hung in grey shrouds everywhere. The confusion of footprints were clearly visible in the dust that covered the rotting floor, but there was no sound anywhere. Complete silence that was almost oppressive. There was a closed door in the left-hand wall, just below the narrow staircase that led upwards, and the prints all merged and concentrated in front of it. Delicately, on tiptoe, Peter went to the door and tried it. It refused to move. It was either jammed or locked. He experienced a sudden and intense desire to see what was behind that closed door. He frowned at it for a second, and then, making up his mind, he flung himself against it. It flew open with unexpected ease — so unexpected that he only saved himself from falling by clutching frantically at the frame . . . Ann uttered a startled exclamation at the noise.

'Peter, what's happened?' she called from the porch. 'What was . . . ?'

'Stay where you are!' snapped Peter, sharply. 'Don't come any farther, Ann . . . ' But she was already at his side and peering through the open door into the room beyond, although he tried to prevent her.

'Peter . . . look!' she whispered, huskily. 'Look . . . '

The room, which was small and low-ceilinged, was lit with a dim grey light that filtered in through the small, dirt-encrusted panes of the lattice window. A very old worm-eaten table occupied the centre of the floor and this was laid for a meal. There were lace table-mats, an array of shining glass, expensive-looking china, and a six-branched candelabra in which six candles had guttered out. Places were laid for five people, two on either side of the table and one at the head, and four of the guests at this ghastly meal were *still present*. They sat in strangely contorted attitudes, their set, rigid faces and staring eyes turned towards the empty chair at the head of the table with such appalling expressions of horror that they looked like a company of the damned. Peter recognized Laura Courtland, still wearing her dress of scarlet, but the two men and the other woman were strangers to him. Mrs. Sowerby could have told him that the dark man next to Laura was Robin Mallory. Old Ted Hoskins could have identified the man with the greying hair, seated opposite, as Monsieur André Severac. Mrs. Bossom would have known that the rather *passée*, fair-haired woman on his right was Fay Bennett . . .

'Peter,' Ann's voice was husky and almost inaudible. 'Peter . . . they're *dead* . . . . They're *all* dead . . . It's horrible . . . they look as if . . . as if they've been *blasted* . . . '

Peter nodded. They *were* all dead. There was no doubt about that. A line from Wordsworth's *Peter Bell* came flashing, unbidden, into his mind. ' . . . All silent and all damned.'

Without removing his eyes from that incredible and dreadful tableau, he spoke:

'Take the car and go back to Fendyke St. Mary,' he said. 'Get hold of the police and tell them what's happened. I'll wait here . . .'

PART TWO

THE BLACK MAN

' . . . black it stood as night,
Fierce as ten furies, terrible as hell . . . '
— JOHN MILTON. *Paradise Lost*.

1

Peter Chard heard the sound of the car dwindle away to silence, and fumbled mechanically in the pocket of his overcoat for his cigarettes. He had taken one from the packet and raised it halfway to his lips when he concluded that perhaps, in the circumstances, he had better not smoke, and put it reluctantly back again. There would be a certain amount of time before Ann could find the police and bring them back, and the interval offered him a chance, that might not occur again, of putting in a little investigation on his own account. Now that he had, more or less, recovered from the first shock of his incredible discovery, his mind was able to take in and record more details of that horrible room. The table, he saw now, was not only laid for a meal, but a meal had been partly eaten. The plate in front of each of those dreadful figures still contained the remains of food, and the glasses were half full of wine. Death had come, suddenly and unexpectedly, in the middle of that uncanny supper, leaving them in an awful and grotesque semblance of life, like a waxwork tableau, only more hideous than any waxwork tableau could have been. Peter noted that they were all in evening dress. The fair-haired woman wore a very low-cut, backless gown of some flimsy black material, and was elaborately made up; the two men were in dinner suits and black ties. Laura Courtland's fur cape, which she had worn at Miss Wymondham's on the previous evening, hung over the back of her chair, and a heavy cloak of deep blue, fur-trimmed velvet was draped over the back of the other woman's. The men's overcoats hung on a rusty nail in the wall by the fireplace. Amid the dirty dilapidation of that low-ceilinged, grimy room, the effect was, somehow, queerly tawdry. Why had these people dressed with such care to come and eat an uncomfortable meal in this damp, draughty, and neglected old cottage? Why had they come there at all, and in what manner of way had they died? What was it that had stamped that look of stark, naked horror on their dead, distorted faces? Something, or somebody, that had occupied that empty chair at the head of the table and towards which those sightless eyes were all staring with hideous and horrified intentness? The plate in front of that chair was clean; the polished glass empty. Had the person for whom that place had been laid failed to come, or ... Fantastic and impossible ideas began to creep insidiously into Peter's mind. Last night had been the Eve of All-Hallows ... He pulled himself up sharply. It was absurd to what lengths one could go if one let their imagination run riot. The thing was gruesome and unusual, but it must have a practical explanation. There was no such thing as an effect without a cause. Here were four dead people, and somebody had killed them. That was quite obvious and indisputable. Or was it? Perhaps they had met here together, in this strange way, to carry into effect some extraordinary suicide pact? It was possible, but Peter found himself rejecting the explanation almost before it occurred to him. The expressions on their faces were not the expressions of people who had been *prepared* for death. Death had come without warning, or with so little warning that they had only realized its approach when it was too late . . .

He entered the room cautiously and made a closer inspection of the table. The remains of the food on the plates looked like kidneys and liver. There was a big dish in the centre, close beside the silver candelabra, standing on a spirit-heated hot-plate, which also contained traces of liver and kidneys. Somebody had gone to an enormous lot of trouble to provide this meal in the empty cottage to which death had come as an unbidden guest. Was it the person who had occupied, or should have occupied, the vacant place? There were several bottles of wine on the floor beside the empty chair, but only two had been opened. The corks of the other bottles were intact, with the wax seals unbroken. Reluctantly, and with every nerve in his body shrinking from the contact, Peter laid his hand on one of Laura Courtland's bare arms. It was icy cold and stiff, as though it had been made of stone. Rigor mortis was apparently in an advanced state, which accounted for the distorted and unnatural attitudes of the bodies. The freezing cold had contributed to that, of course, though there were signs that a fire had recently been lighted in the rusty, broken grate. It couldn't have been a very large one, however, and must have long since burnt out . . .

If Laura Courtland had come straight from Wymondham Lodge to this gathering, whatever it was, she would have reached the cottage at about eleven, and it was only reasonable to suppose that the others had arrived at about the same time. Yes, thought Peter, and *how* had they come? They wouldn't have walked through the snow . . . He stooped and looked at their shoes. No, they definitely hadn't walked. The shoes were stained, but not as much as they would have been if they had walked very far. But if they had come by car, where was the car? The footprints in the snow outside came from the direction of Fendyke St. Mary, but there had been no sign of any car tracks, or of a car. If it had been left farther along the road, he and Ann would have passed it on their way to the cottage. Laura Courtland might have picked the others up somewhere in her car, but what had she done with it? Even if they had all got out before reaching Witch's House, which it seemed they must have, what had happened to the car?

Peter looked at the vacant place at the head of the table and his eyes narrowed thoughtfully. Had the fifth member of the party taken the car? It was a plausible explanation, always supposing there had ever been a fifth person present. It might be possible to prove that from the footprints, if they were not too confused and jumbled. That would be a job for the police. If there *had* been a fifth person, and this was murder, then he, or she, must be the murderer. Peter thought there was very little doubt that it *was* murder — some kind of quick-acting poison either in the food or the wine. More probably the wine. That, also, was for the police to find out. He was more interested in the psychological aspect of the crime than in its mechanics. Was this an extension of the lamb and baby killings, or something entirely apart? The result of a careful and logical plan with a more practical motive behind it than the blood-lust of a homicidal maniac? Until he knew more about the people concerned it was difficult to conjecture. Something had brought them all to that empty cottage on the previous night to eat that last weird meal together, which seemed to point to a plan of some kind, but whether the plan had been originated by the murderer, or whether he had merely taken advantage of the opportunity presented, was impossible to say.

Peter decided to have a look at the rest of the cottage. Beyond the staircase, at the back, he found a kitchen littered with the accumulated rubbish of years; a small, dark, gloomy room that smelt of decay and rats. There was a door here which evidently led to the garden, but it was bolted and barred and hung with festoons of cobwebs. The place was filthy. Great holes gaped in the rotten floor, and the walls had huge cracks running from floor to ceiling due, he concluded, to a subsidence of the foundations. There was nothing of any interest to be seen, and since this, with the passage and the room in the front, constituted the entire ground floor, he decided to explore above.

Very gingerly he went up the narrow staircase. The treads creaked under his weight and he fully expected the whole structure to collapse at any second, but it held and he arrived on a small landing. There were two rooms up here with low, sloping ceilings and narrow casement windows. Like the kitchen they were full of rubble, and in one the ceiling had partly fallen, leaving a great irregular black gap with broken laths sticking out of it. Quite obviously no one had been up here recently. The dust that lay thickly everywhere was devoid of any footmark. Peter returned to the ground floor and went out into the porch. The cold fresh air was pleasant after the stuffy smelliness of the cottage. He took out a cigarette and lit it. He was halfway through his third cigarette when Ann returned with the police.

2

Ann had been lucky. She had met a labourer on the outskirts of the village who had directed her to the little police station, and she arrived almost coincident with the return of Colonel Shoredust and Superintendent Odds from a rest after their activities of the night. To them she hastily explained the reason for her visit, which had the effect of reducing the Chief Constable to a state of babbling incoherency, and the still weary Odds to a kind of astonished, but apathetic, resignation. When these immediate results had partially worn off, Colonel Shoredust became intensely energetic and began issuing orders at a prodigious rate, most of which the superintendent tactfully ignored. There ensued a chaotic confusion from which Ann emerged to find herself, without quite knowing how it had been achieved, wedged in the back of Peter's car between the Chief Constable and Doctor Culpepper, with Superintendent Odds and Sergeant Quilt occupying the front seats. During the short journey back, Colonel Shoredust indulged in a staccato conversation with all four of them, punctuated with many pauses as he adjusted his normal vocabulary to suit the presence of Ann. She was never able to remember what he talked about, and none of the others appeared in the slightest degree interested.

Doctor Culpepper, looking rather tired and grave, said nothing at all, and Superintendent Odds gave all his attention to driving. Twice Sergeant Quilt remarked 'yes, sir,' but it sounded purely mechanical, and Ann was quite certain that he had only the vaguest idea of what the Colonel had said.

Peter hailed them from the porch, when at last they drew up outside the cottage, with a warning to be careful of the footprints in the snow. They joined him, and he gave them a brief but more detailed account of the discovery which he and Ann had made.

'I recognized Miss Courtland because I

met her at dinner last night at my aunt's,' he concluded. 'But I don't know who the other three people are. No doubt you will be able to identify them.'

He led the way into the narrow passage and the others crowded behind him. Colonel Shoredust looked into the room through the open door, and expelled his breath sharply through his teeth with a sound like the sudden escape of steam. Superintendent Odds uttered a little strangled grunt. Sergeant Quilt made no sound at all, but his eyes stared fixedly as though he had been hypnotized. Doctor Culpepper, peering between Odds and the Chief Constable, pursed his lips and frowned.

'Rather ghastly, isn't it?' said Peter.

For a long moment none of them answered him, and then Colonel Shore-dust gave a shuddering sigh.

'Horrible,' he muttered. 'Horrible!'

'Horrible, and also very extraordinary,' said Doctor Culpepper, still frowning into the room. 'Laura Courtland, Robin Mallory, Fay Bennett and André Severac. What could have induced them to come here in the first place . . . ?'

'You can identify these people, sir?' asked the superintendent.

The doctor nodded a trifle impatiently.

'Yes, yes, I know them all quite well,' he answered.

'The fifth person is the most important to identify, I think,' said Peter, softly. 'The person who occupied the vacant place at the head of the table.'

'Perhaps nobody occupied it,' grunted Colonel Shoredust.

'Then who,' said Peter, with a gesture towards the table, 'was responsible for *that*?'

'There's no absolute proof that it was murder, is there, sir?' said Superintendent Odds. 'These people may have committed suicide . . . '

'A sort of pact, eh?' broke in the Chief Constable. 'Now that's poss . . . '

'Look at their faces,' interrupted Peter, curtly. 'Do they look as if they had *expected* to die?'

Colonel Shoredust looked, and very quickly looked away again.

'They received some kind of shock just

before they died,' went on Peter. 'Something so unexpected and horrible that its effect remained stamped on their faces . . . '

'You're not suggesting that they died of fright, are you?' said the Chief Constable, and Peter shook his head.

'No,' he replied. 'I think they were poisoned.'

'The doctor'll be able to tell us about that,' put in Superintendent Odds, practically. 'Will you make your examination, sir, and then we can get busy . . . '

Doctor Culpepper squeezed past Colonel Shoredust and entered the room. He carefully examined each of the grotesque figures at the table, peered at the remains of the food on the plates, and sniffed at the wine in the glasses.

'I think Mr. Chard is right,' he remarked, when he had finished. 'These people have undoubtedly been poisoned. The poison was administered in the wine, I believe, and, judging from the leaden, bluish tinge of their skins, I should say that it was some form of cyanide, probably potassium cyanide. I cannot be more definite than that until after the post-mortem, and an analysis has been made of the wine.'

'At what time did death take place, sir?' asked the superintendent, and Doctor Culpepper pursed his lips.

'Somewhere in the region of midnight,' he answered after a pause. 'Certainly not later than two o'clock this morning. I'm afraid it's impossible to be more exact than that. The conditions are difficult. Last night's intense cold would make a difference to the advance of rigor mortis and other signs . . . '

'But we can take it that it happened between twelve o'clock and two o'clock in the morning?' said Odds.

'Yes,' Doctor Culpepper nodded. 'Nearer twelve than two would be my personal opinion.'

'And this poison you mentioned — would that act quickly?'

'Very quickly,' answered Doctor Culpepper. 'It would only be a matter of minutes, depending, of course, to a great extent on the quantity administered. By the appearance of the bodies I should say the quantity was quite large.'

'Blasted queer business,' muttered Colonel Shoredust, rubbing his nose. 'What was the idea of coming here to have a meal? Damned unpleasant place. Can't understand it.'

His remark was received in silence.

Superintendent Odds had begun methodically exploring the room for anything that might help to explain this nightmare party. When he had finished with the room he went through the pockets of the two overcoats hanging on the nail by the fireplace. From one he brought out a white silk handkerchief, a pair of gloves, and a packet of cigarettes. From the other a box of matches, another pair of gloves, and a bunch of keys. That was all. The pockets in the dead men's clothing yielded another bunch of keys and the normal articles that might be expected.

'Nothing helpful at all, sir,' he said, disappointedly, looking at the Chief Constable. 'Maybe there's something here.' He picked up one of the two small evening handbags that lay beside the plates of the dead women, and carefully emptied it. It proved to contain nothing except the usual flapjack, lipstick, handkerchief, and purse. The other, which had belonged to Laura Courtland, was also devoid of anything unusual or interesting. Odds sighed, and put the bags gently down.

'Well, that's that,' he remarked. 'Absolutely nothing. The ambulance should be here soon, and then, if you agree, doctor, the bodies can be removed.'

Doctor Culpepper nodded.

'There's no reason why not,' he said. 'I shall want the wine, you know. Both what remains in the glasses and the bottles as well.'

'I'll attend to that, sir,' said the superintendent. The light was beginning to fade. The shadows in the corners of the room were spreading and thickening. 'I'll just have a look through the rest of this place,' Odds went on, 'and then see if those prints in the snow outside can tell us anything.'

'You'll find mine and my wife's mixed up with them,' said Peter, 'just to make it more difficult . . . '

'How's that, sir?' asked the superintendent sharply. 'I understood that you had been careful not to . . . '

'The prints I am referring to,' explained Peter, 'were made yesterday afternoon . . . ' He told the interested Odds about their visit to the cottage during their enforced walk to Fendyke St. Mary.

'Oh, I see, sir,' said Odds, looking as though he did nothing of the kind. 'What made you come back here this afternoon?'

'That was my idea,' put in Ann. 'My husband's aunt, Miss Wymondham, was telling us about the history of the place — this cottage, I mean — and I was curious to see it again . . . '

'When we were here yesterday there were no other footprints but our own,' said Peter. 'When we saw all these others, today, leading to the door of an empty cottage, which we had been given to understand had an evil reputation, and which people were supposed to avoid like the plague, we were naturally curious.'

The superintendent's face cleared and he nodded understandingly.

126

'I see, sir,' he said again, and this time he sounded as if he meant it. 'Well, it shouldn't be difficult to distinguish your prints, and Mrs. Chard's, from these others. Come on, Quilt, let's have a look at the rest of the place.'

'You know,' remarked Doctor Culpepper, thoughtfully, when Odds and the sergeant had disappeared into the rear of the cottage, 'somebody went to an enormous amount of trouble. I can't quite see the purpose . . . '

'What d'you mean?' grunted Colonel Shoredust, frowning at him.

'All this,' said the doctor, waving a podgy hand round the darkening room. 'All this china and glass and linen . . . It wasn't here, you know. It had to be *brought*. And the food, too. That wasn't cooked here. It was cooked elsewhere and heated up on that hot-plate . . . '

'See what you mean,' said the Chief Constable, fingering his moustache and nodding jerkily. 'It's da . . . er — dashed extraordinary . . . '

'Do you think,' said Ann, 'that it could have been some kind of freak party?'

127

'It was definitely a freak party,' said Peter, a little grimly. 'But what kind of freak party? What was the motive for killing all these people . . . ?'

'Must there *be* a motive?' broke in Doctor Culpepper. 'We already know there is a maniac killer in the district somewhere. Why shouldn't this be his handiwork too?'

Colonel Shoredust looked startled.

'You're not suggesting that . . . that this has anything to do with the other bl — beastly business?' he exclaimed.

'Why not?' Doctor Culpepper's shrewd black eyes surveyed him steadily through his spectacles. 'You can't call any of this *sane*, can you? A supper party in a dirty, cold, empty house, and four people poisoned? Can you think of anything more like the outcome of a deranged mind?'

'It had occurred to me that it was an extension of the same thing,' said Peter.

'I don't think there's any doubt of it,' declared Doctor Culpepper, emphatically.

'Is there any news of the little girl?' asked Ann, and the Chief Constable shook his head.

'No,' he answered, gloomily. 'My men are still searching . . . '

'You'll have to do something, Shoredust,' said Doctor Culpepper, curtly. 'This can't go on indefinitely, you know. The person responsible has *got* to be found and stopped.'

'I had already decided to call in the assistance of Scotland Yard,' answered Colonel Shoredust, stiffly. 'I am telephoning this evening . . . '

'I think you're wise,' said the doctor, shortly.

Superintendent Odds and the sergeant returned from their excursion to the back at that moment and went noisily up the staircase. There was a silence. The Chief Constable was obviously resentful of the doctor's criticism, although there was no gainsaying the truth of what he had said. Colonel Shoredust, thought Peter, may have been an admirable soldier, but he was very definitely not cut out for police work, or, at any rate, this kind of police work. He was probably quite capable of dealing with the ordinary normal routine cases that came his way, but this was something different. This required to be handled with imagination and brains, and Shoredust was evidently quite devoid of the former, and only very sparingly supplied with the latter. Neither did Odds and the sergeant impress Peter as being very intelligent men. Plodding, painstaking, and conscientious, perhaps, but that was all. It had not occurred to any of them, apparently, to wonder how the four dead people had got here from Fendyke St. Mary, and, if they had come by car, what had happened to the car. He thought that it was a very wise decision indeed on the Chief Constable's part to call in Scotland Yard. It seemed a great pity that he had not done so before.

Odds and Sergeant Quilt came down from upstairs to report that they had found nothing. Armed with a shoe from each of the four dead people, they turned their attention to the tracks in the snow. Peter and Ann were called to identify theirs, and then returned to the porch to watch the proceedings with Doctor Culpepper and Colonel Shoredust. For twenty minutes or so, the superintendent and Quilt worked busily, comparing and sorting the confused jumble of prints, and when they had finished there was a puzzled look on their faces.

'Excluding Mr. and Mrs. Chard's, sir,' said Odds to the Chief Constable, 'there are four sets of prints, each made by one of the people in there.' He jerked his head towards the open door of the cottage.

'Only *four* sets?' exclaimed Peter, incredulously. 'Surely you must have made a mistake, superintendent . . . '

Odds shook his head.

'No, sir,' he answered, 'I haven't. I've accounted for every footprint . . . '

'But,' cried Peter, 'what about the person who occupied the *fifth* chair . . . The chair at the head of the table . . . ?'

The superintendent shrugged his shoulders.

'There are only *four* sets,' he repeated, emphatically. 'There's no track of any *fifth* person having come here at all, sir.'

3

They stood in the rapidly gathering dusk of that cold November afternoon and stared at the smudged tracks in the snow that led from the gap in the low stone wall to the porch. For some time nobody spoke, and then Doctor Culpepper cleared his throat.

'It looks,' he remarked, 'as if there hadn't been a fifth person after all.'

'But there must have been,' exclaimed Peter. 'You've seen those people in there? They are all staring at that empty chair at the head of the table . . . '

'That doesn't prove there was anybody in it,' grunted Colonel Shoredust.

'It does to me,' answered Peter, quickly. 'Their expressions prove it. They were looking at someone . . . '

'Well, I don't know how the 'someone' got here, sir,' broke in Superintendent Odds, wearily. 'There are only four sets of footprints, not counting yours and Mrs.

Chard's, and they were made by the four people in that room. I'd be willing to swear that anywhere . . . '

'Couldn't this . . . this other person have come a different way?' suggested Ann, but the superintendent shook his head.

'The only other way he could have got in is by the back,' he said, 'and the door is bolted on the inside. It's covered with old spider's webs, and I shouldn't think it had been opened for years. The same thing applies to the window . . . '

'I don't think there's any evidence to show that there *was* a fifth person,' interrupted Colonel Shoredust. 'In fact, what evidence there is, is to the contrary. The plate, and glass, haven't been used in front of that chair. You can't go by expressions. There *was* to have been a fifth person, but he, or she, didn't turn up.'

'Then who killed these people?' asked Peter, bluntly.

'Whoever it was didn't necessarily have to be present,' replied Shoredust. 'This isn't a shooting or stabbing affair. It's a poisoning, and the poison could have been put in the wine *before* it was brought here. That's only bla — blessed well sense, isn't it?' He appealed to Doctor Culpepper.

'Yes, it could have happened like that,' agreed the doctor.

'There you are,' said the Chief Constable, triumphantly. 'This stuff cyanide acts d — dashed quickly, doesn't it? Well then, when they'd drunk the wine and realized it was poisoned, they guessed who'd done it; the person who should have occupied the chair at the head of the table. That was their last thought before they died, an' that's why they are all looking at that empty place.' He looked from one to the other for approbation for this astute explanation.

'And who locked the door?' said Peter, quietly. 'The door was locked, and I had to break it open . . . '

'Any one of them could have locked the door,' said Colonel Shoredust, dismissing this objection with a summary gesture. 'There's nothing in *that*.'

'There's a great deal in it,' retorted

Peter. 'Because if any of those four people had locked the door, the key would have been in the lock on the inside, or, at least, in the room. And it wasn't, and it isn't.'

His words acted on Colonel Shoredust's complacent satisfaction over his own theory like a sudden douche of ice-cold water. His thickish lips parted and his eyes became more prominent. Even he could see the force of this argument. None of those four people seated at the table could have locked the door on the outside and taken away the key, which meant that there must have been a *fifth* person in the cottage . . .

'Those keys,' he said, turning swiftly on Odds. 'The two bunches you found . . . Does one of 'em fit the door?'

The superintendent went inside and, after a short interval, came back shaking his head.

'None of them fits the lock, sir,' he said.

'So it would appear,' remarked Peter, rather pleased with himself, 'that we are faced with two impossibilities from which to choose. (*a*) That in some mysterious fashion the door locked itself. (*b*) That there *was* a fifth person present who, in some equally mysterious fashion, was able to transport himself without leaving any tracks in the snow.'

Superintendent Odds looked at Colonel Shoredust. Colonel Shoredust looked at Superintendent Odds. Peter looked at them both with what Ann told him later was 'one of the most objectionable expressions of smug complacency that she had ever seen.' He was enjoying himself hugely.

'Wait a minute. Wait a minute,' grunted the Chief Constable, having got, as it were, his second wind. 'What about this, eh? Supposing this other person was already in the place? I mean supposing he came before the blas — before the snow stopped falling and *stayed* until the others arrived? How's that, eh? The snow would have covered any tracks he made then . . . '

'Oh,' exclaimed Ann, suddenly. 'Peter! Do you remember . . . ? That queer feeling I had yesterday afternoon when we came here? As if somebody was *watching* . . . '

'You thought there was somebody watching, eh?' said Colonel Shoredust, pouncing on this confirmation of his idea with avidity. 'You were probably right, madam. There *was* somebody in the place then, and . . . '

'It's no good, Colonel,' said Peter, shaking his head. 'Even if this person *was* in the house then, it doesn't get over the difficulty.'

'Eh?' said the Chief Constable. 'What's that? Doesn't . . . what the deuce d'you mean?'

'He still had to *leave*,' explained Peter, patiently. 'He had to lock the door and leave, taking the key with him, *after* these four people had arrived, presumably after they were dead. And he still had to do it *without leaving any tracks*.'

Colonel Shoredust's face slowly suffused with blood.

'It's blasted impossible!' he exploded, throwing politeness to the four winds.

'I entirely agree with you,' said Peter. 'But there it is.'

'Here comes the ambulance,' broke in Superintendent Odds.

4

When the remains of Laura Courtland, Robin Mallory, Fay Bennett, and André Severac had, with difficulty, been transferred to the ambulance — with difficulty because of the extreme rigidity of the bodies — and it had driven away to the mortuary, taking with it, at his own request, Doctor Culpepper, Superintendent Odds also prepared to take his departure. Leaving the reluctant Police Constable Cropps, who had arrived with the ambulance, to guard the cottage, with the strictest instructions that he was not on any account to enter the room where the deaths had taken place, or to touch anything, and to remain at his post until another constable could be sent over from Hinton to relieve him, the superintendent requested that Peter would drive Colonel Shoredust, Sergeant Quilt, and himself, back to the police station at Fendyke St. Mary. Peter readily agreed, and once

138

more Ann found herself squeezed in the back of the car, only this time she was between Odds and the Chief Constable, which was more comfortable, because the superintendent was not so stout as Doctor Culpepper. On this trip, too, Colonel Shoredust did not try to 'tire the sun' with talking. He remained completely silent, and Ann thought he was thinking deeply until a sudden and completely unexpected snore disillusioned her.

When they arrived at the police station, Colonel Shoredust announced his intention of going home. He lived, apparently, at Hinton, which was the nearest town to Fendyke St. Mary, and from which Superintendent Odds and Sergeant Quilt also came. Odds made no effort to dissuade him. Indeed, he seemed to be considerably relieved that he was going, and after arranging for the superintendent to report immediately by telephone should any fresh developments take place, the Colonel departed in a rakish-looking two-seater coupé.

'Well, sir,' said Odds, when he had

gone, and heralding his remark with a sound that was suspiciously like a sigh of relief, 'I don't think I need detain you and your wife any longer. I understand that you are staying at Wymondham Lodge and are likely to be there for some time, so I can get in touch with you if the occasion should arise. Of course, you'll be required to attend the inquest, but you'll be notified of that in due course.'

Peter was reluctant to be dismissed so easily. The strangeness of the whole business had taken hold of his imagination and whetted his appetite to know more — a lot more. These people who had died in such extraordinary circumstances were merely names to him at present. He wanted to learn more about them — their backgrounds, habits, interests, friends, all the things that made up their essential personalities. The only one with whom he had come in actual contact during life was Laura Courtland, and, although she had not impressed him very favourably, she was, at least, real. The others were only lay figures.

'I suppose, superintendent, you have a

lot of work to do before you can call it a day?' he said, conversationally.

'You're right there, sir,' replied Odds, feelingly. 'My wife won't be seeing me this side o' midnight, I don't suppose. And I was out all last night, too. Oh, well, I managed to snatch two or three hours' sleep earlier on today, an' it's a lucky thing I did by the look of things.'

'What's the next move?' asked Peter, 'or is that a police secret?'

The superintendent's tired face relaxed into a slight smile.

'There's nothing very secret about it, sir,' he said. 'I'm going along with Sergeant Quilt to where those four people lived to see if there's anything to be picked up that'll throw a light on this business . . . '

'Look here,' said Peter, grasping the nettle firmly, and hoping that he'd get away without too bad a sting, 'would you mind if I came with you?'

Odds was surprised, and looked it. He considered for a moment and then he shook his head.

'Well,' he replied, slowly, 'I don't see

why you shouldn't, sir.'

Peter, who had not expected such an easy victory, was delighted.

'Good!' he exclaimed. 'I'll just run my wife to Wymondham Lodge and come back. Will that be all right?'

'Yes, sir,' said Odds. 'I was thinking of having a cup of tea before setting out, and I've got to ring up the station at Hinton to get them to send a man over to relieve Cropps, an' see to one or two other things. I don't mind admitting that your car 'ull come in very handy,' he added. 'I came over from Hinton in the Chief Constable's and . . .'

'I'll drive you anywhere you want to go,' promised Peter, realizing why the victory had been so easy. 'Come along, darling.' He took Ann by the arm and hurried her out to the car.

'Well. I *do* think you're mean, Peter,' she said indignantly, as he opened the door for her to get in. 'Why can't I come, too?'

'Because I don't think Odds would have stood for both of us,' he answered.

'He's only standing for you because of

the car,' she said.

'I know that,' he answered. 'Look, darling, there's something I wish you'd do. Find out from Aunt Helen all you can about those four people, Fay Bennett, Mallory, André Severac, and Laura Courtland . . . '

'I shall dream about that room,' she said, as he started the car. 'It was horrible, Peter. The four of them sitting there round that beastly table — like dummies . . . ' She broke off and shivered.

'The whole thing is horrible,' he said. 'The lambs and the children . . . all of it.'

'Peter, do you think it's connected?' she asked. 'All part of one thing?'

'Yes, I do,' he answered. 'I don't know how, or why, or anything, but I'm certain of it.'

'What were they all staring at in that chair?' said Ann. 'What was there, Peter, that came and went without leaving any marks in the snow . . . '

'You are not suggesting that it was something supernatural, are you, darling?' said Peter, looking at her sideways.

'I'd believe almost anything,' she

answered, with a queer little laugh. 'That house is steeped in something that's evil — hideously and horribly evil. It envelops you like a fog when you cross the threshhold . . . '

'Association of ideas,' he commented, but she shook her head.

'No. it isn't — not altogether,' she said. 'I felt it before I knew anything about the history of the place . . . Yesterday afternoon. I told you . . . '

'Whatever unsavoury reputation the place had in the past, this business is going to add to it with a vengeance,' said Peter, 'and more than half the village'll range themselves on the side of the supernatural. They still believe in witchcraft in these parts, the majority of them . . . ' He broke off abruptly, braked, and gave a sharp twist to the wheel. The car swerved and Ann was thrown violently against him.

'Did you see that damned fool?' exclaimed Peter, angrily, swinging the car back into the straight. 'Stepping off the pavement, like that, almost under my wheels . . . '

'Yes,' gasped Ann, rubbing her arm. 'I

shall have a huge bruise, Peter, and people will think that you knock me about . . . '

'I just caught a glimpse of his face when he turned,' went on Peter, ignoring her remark. 'A great, vacant, moon-like face . . . I believe it was that chap that Culpepper was talking about, what's-his-name? The village idiot . . . '

'Twist,' said Ann.

'Yes, that's it,' said Peter. 'I'm sure it must have been he . . . '

'Does it matter?' asked Ann, resentfully. Her arm had come in contact with the hard curve of the bucket seat and it hurt. She was a little annoyed at Peter's lack of sympathy.

'Well, no, I suppose it doesn't a great deal,' he said, bringing the car to a halt at the gate of Wymondham Lodge. 'Will you explain everything to Aunt Helen?' He got out, came round to the other side of the car and opened the door for her. 'And don't forget to ask her all she knows about those four people, will you? It won't be difficult. Once she gets started you'll only have to listen . . . '

'How long do you think you'll be?' she

asked, as he helped her out.

'I don't know,' he answered. 'Not longer than I can help, but don't wait dinner for me, darling. I'll have a sandwich or something when I get back . . . '

'Peter, you *will* be careful, won't you?' she said, anxiously

'Of course.' He kissed her and held open the gate. 'Now you run along. I'll be back as soon as I can.'

He waited until she had disappeared in the gloom of the drive, and then he returned to the car and drove back to the police station.

5

Prior's Keep was about a mile and a half outside the village in the direction of Hinton, and when Peter and Superintendent Odds reached it, Sergeant Quilt had been sent back to Witch's House to collect the remains of the food and wine for analysis, it was so dark that very little of the old house was visible. From what he could see, Peter judged it to be a fair-sized mansion and came to the conclusion, subsequently confirmed by the appointments of the interior, that whatever else the Courtlands might lack it was not money. The big hall, to which they were presently admitted by the expressionless Pitt, was furnished expensively if not quite in the best of taste. Everything was very good, but it gave the impression that *cost* had been the predominant factor in the choice rather than suitability. Peter could imagine whoever had been responsible saying:

'Yes, that piece of furniture is very nice, but there is a piece over there that is four times the price. I'll have *that*.'

Superintendent Odds, less sensitive to such things, was obviously impressed. Having introduced himself and requested to see the master of the house, he waited beside Peter while the butler disappeared upstairs. He had been reluctant to disturb Mr. Courtland, who, he informed them, was confined to his bed with a severe cold, and only the superintendent's rank, and his assurance that the matter was of the utmost urgency, had persuaded him to do so. He returned after the lapse of a few minutes, said: 'Will you come this way, please?' and conducted them up the great carved staircase to a large bedroom that was furnished with the same opulence as the hall. Mr. Courtland, reclining in the huge bed, and propped up against many pillows, looked, Peter thought, rather out of place amid all his luxurious surroundings. It was like finding the dustman stretched on a settee in the drawing room, reading the newspaper.

'Well?' said Mr. Courtland, hoarsely and thickly, dismissing the butler with a wave of a fat, hirsute hand. 'What do you want? Pitt said it was something urgent, or I wouldn't have seen you. What is it?'

His small eyes flickered from one to the other with rather a hostile expression.

Prefaced by a preliminary clearing of his throat, Odds explained. As he proceeded, Peter saw an expression of shocked astonishment come into the flabby face of the man in the bed. But, to his surprise, no sign of grief. He was startled and horrified, but that was all.

'This . . . this is terrible news,' he muttered, when the superintendent had finished his brief recital of the discovery. 'Dreadful! I can scarcely believe it. Some kind of poison, you say . . . ?'

'Yes, sir,' said Odds. 'I'm given to understand that it was a form of cyanide. We shall know more about that when the doctors have made their examination. In the meanwhile, I should be glad if you could give me any information, sir, that might help to throw a light on this business.'

Mr. Courtland's immediate reply to this rather stilted request was to reach for his handkerchief and blow his nose violently. When, by this means, he had partially cleared his head, he shook it slowly.

'I don't understand it,' he declared. 'It's . . . it's incredible . . . '

'Can you suggest why your daughter went to this place — Witch's House, I believe, is the local name for it — with these people, sir?'

Again Mr. Courtland's bald head moved from side to side on the pillow.

'I've no idea at all,' he answered. 'You say they had all partaken of a meal of some sort?'

'Yes, sir.'

'Then I can only suggest that it was some kind of freak party. My daughter was very fond of anything unusual.'

'What sort of freak party, sir?'

'I can't tell you that. I'm only suggesting that that's what it was. I have no definite knowledge concerning it. My daughter said nothing about it to me. She very seldom discussed her plans with me.

I was under the impression that she was dining at Wymondham Lodge and returning home afterwards. If she had made other arrangements I was not aware of them.'

'But when you found Miss Courtland had not returned, surely you wondered what had happened, sir?'

'I naturally wondered where she had gone, but I wasn't disturbed or worried. My daughter had a habit of going off to all sorts of places at the shortest possible notice.'

'Regarding these other three people, sir,' went on the superintendent, consulting his notebook. 'Miss Fay Bennett, Mr. Robin Mallory, and Monsieur André Severac.' He boggled at the pronunciation. 'Were they particular friends of your daughter's?'

'I don't know,' said Courtland. 'I knew she was acquainted with Mallory — she invited him here to dinner one night. Quite an innocuous young man, I thought, though rather full of his own importance. So far as the other two people you mention are concerned, I didn't even know she knew them. She had a number of friends and acquaintances that I knew nothing about.' He paused and his small eyes flickered from Odds to Peter and back again, a curious habit he had. 'My daughter's ideas of enjoying herself were rather . . . well, rather modern, if you understand me. I'm afraid that we did not always agree on quite a number of things. The result was that she went her way and I went mine, which were in totally opposite directions.'

Superintendent Odds moistened his lips with the tip of his tongue and regarded the man in the bed a little dubiously. The emotionless way in which he had received the news of his daughter's death and his apparent complete lack of knowledge concerning her affairs, obviously disconcerted him.

'It seems, sir,' he remarked, disappointedly, 'that you can't help me very much.'

'I'm afraid I can't,' agreed Courtland. 'As I've told you, my daughter lived her own life, and it seldom came in contact with mine. We lived under the same roof and, occasionally, had our meals together, but apart from that we were almost strangers.'

'You know of no one who had threatened your daughter, sir, or would in any way benefit by her death?'

Courtland shook his head.

'No,' he replied. 'My daughter had no money or property of her own. I made her an allowance, but that, of course, ceases now. I can imagine quite a number of people disliking her intensely, but none who would go to the length of killing her.'

'There was no love-affair that had gone wrong, sir?' suggested the superintendent, valliantly trying everything.

'There were many,' said Courtland, candidly. 'My daughter was always involved with some man or other . . . '

Odd pricked up his ears. It was a worn-out expression, but Peter thought it was the only way to describe the change that came over him.

'Oh, indeed, sir,' he said. 'Now that . . . '

'I shouldn't rely on anything there,' broke in Courtland, dashing his rising hopes. 'There was nothing serious about any of 'em. Usually they resulted in a weekend or two, and that was all. My daughter was, I regret to say, er — promiscuous.'

Odds looked slightly shocked.

'Oh, I see, sir,' he murmured. 'Perhaps something more serious may have developed on the part of one of her — er — friends?'

'That I can't possibly say,' said Courtland. 'I should think it was very unlikely, however. Anyway, how would these other people be affected? They were poisoned, too, weren't they? If you are looking for a motive, surely you've got to find one that will cover them as well?'

'I think the most important thing to find out,' said Peter, speaking for the first time, 'is why these four people went to that empty cottage late at night to eat a meal. If we could discover that, I believe we should be two-thirds of the way towards understanding everything.'

'That is a most extraordinary thing,' said Mr. Courtland, frowning. 'The only explanation I can see is what I suggested, a freak party . . . '

'A freak party, certainly,' said Peter.

'But what *kind* of freak party? What was its object? Whose idea was it, and who arranged it? And why was that particular rendezvous chosen? A place that has the reputation of being haunted and which nobody in the village will go near . . . '

'Perhaps that's why it *was* chosen,' interrupted Courtland. 'Perhaps they wanted to make certain that they wouldn't be disturbed. I suppose there's no doubt that this *was* murder . . . ?'

'Not any, sir, I don't think,' said the superintendent. 'If you were thinking of suicide . . . '

'I wasn't,' said the man in the bed, shortly. 'Laura was too fond of life for anything like that. I was just wondering if they might not have been experimenting with some sort of drug . . . '

'Had Miss Courtland ever been addicted to drugs, sir?' broke in Odds, quickly.

'No,' said Courtland, calmly. 'Not so far as I know. But she'd try anything once, if it was likely to offer an unusual thrill.'

'It's hardly likely that anybody sane would experiment with cyanide,' remarked Peter. 'Most people are aware that it is a particularly deadly poison and quite use-less as a means of furnishing the sensations which the drug addict seeks.'

'I suppose there's some truth in that,' said Courtland. 'It seems to me that Laura must have got herself mixed up with some-thing very strange and queer . . . '

'Maybe there's something among her effects, sir,' said the superintendent, hope-fully, 'that'll explain why they all went to this cottage. Have you any objection to my looking through her apartment?'

'Not in the least,' said Courtland. 'It wouldn't be much good if I had, would it?'

He leaned over and pressed a bell-push beside the bed. 'Perhaps you'd both like a drink? I feel that I could do with a pretty stiff brandy myself . . . No? Well, please yourselves. Laura has a suite of two rooms. I'll get Pitt to take you. You'll probably find them in an incredible state of untidiness. I've never been there myself, but the servants are always complaining . . . Come in.'

Pitt appeared, following his preliminary tap on the door, expressionless and correct.

'Take these gentlemen to Miss Laura's apartments,' ordered his master, 'and then bring me some brandy.'

The butler bowed. Not a flicker of curiosity stirred the impassiveness of his face as he turned and led the way along the thickly carpeted corridor. And yet he must *be* curious, thought Peter. He can't be human and not wonder what all this is about.

Laura Courtland's suite was on the other side of the house. Pitt opened the door and ushered them into a large room that was furnished with all the luxuriant ornateness that characterized the rest of the house. The colour scheme was in lilac, cream, and gold, and the room was, as Courtland had said it might be, incredibly untidy. In some queer way, too, which Peter was quite unable to fathom, it gave out an atmosphere of decadence.

'That door over there leads into the bedroom, sir,' said the butler, nodding slightly towards it, 'and the bathroom opens off the bedroom.' He bowed again and softly withdrew, closing the door behind him.

'That man is uncanny,' remarked Peter. 'He displays not the slightest interest regarding the reason for our visit, and yet he knows that you are a police officer and, therefore, something pretty serious must have happened. It's unnatural.'

Superintendent Odds grunted.

'It's not the only thing unnatural about this house, sir, if you ask me,' he said, while his eyes travelled slowly about the room. 'What about Mr. Courtland's attitude? Is it natural to receive the news that your daughter's been murdered like that? Whatever she may have been. I've got a girl of my own, and she's a pretty good girl too, thank the Lord, but, if she was as bad as could be, I wouldn't be taking her sudden death as a matter of course, an' I don't think there's many as would. Callous an' unfeeling *I* call it.'

Peter was inclined to agree with him, though he thought there might possibly be extenuating circumstances in Mr. Courtland's favour. Laura had not been the type to inspire affection, at any rate not paternal affection. He was not prepared to argue this out with Odds just then and, anyway, the superintendent had already begun his inspection of the sitting room. Peter, therefore, left him to it and prowled around on his own account. There were magazines and books scattered all over the place and trails of cigarette-ash everywhere. Laura Courtland seemed to have had a habit of never putting anything back in its proper place. He found a bookcase and examined the contents with interest. The books were mostly novels. An unexpurgated edition of *Lady Chatterley's Lover* stood next to two novels by James Hadley Chase. He saw that the rest were nearly all of the same type, which was an interesting signpost to the dead woman's character. On the lower shelf, thrust between a rather nice edition of the *Decameron* and a copy of Oscar Wilde's poems, was a book by Montague Summers, which rather surprised him. It was hardly the sort of thing he would have expected to find there, judging by Laura's rather bawdy taste in literature. Superintendent Odds had come to an anchor by a small writing bureau, which he had opened (it had not been locked) and was going carefully and methodically through the contents. It was as untidy as the rest of the room. The pigeonholes were stuffed with letters, and bills, and old theatre programmes, some of which had overflowed on to the blotting-pad. Odds looked round at Peter and his eyebrows went up.

'There's no doubt that she was pretty hot stuff, sir,' he remarked, shaking his head in disapproval. 'Some of these letters don't leave much to the imagination, I must say. Perhaps you'd give me a hand, Mr. Chard? I don't want to wade through all this muck unless it's got some bearing on the murders . . . '

Peter wasn't too keen to pry into the dead woman's private correspondence, but he realized that it was necessary and came over to help Odds sort them out. He very soon found that what the superintendent had said was something of an understatement. He had never seen such letters before, and he felt a curious sense of embarrassment at seeing them now. It was like suddenly surprising the dead girl, herself, in the nude. They were nearly all from different men, signed for the most part with Christian name only, but in some cases just an initial, and they left no doubt regarding Laura's chief interest in life. There was nothing, however, which could remotely have any bearing on her death. The majority bore London addresses, and the dates covered a period of many months. When they had examined the last one and had a look in all the drawers, the superintendent sighed disappointedly.

'Well, sir,' he said, 'there's nothing there, is there? We'd best try the bedroom.'

The bedroom was in a worse litter than the sitting room. Articles of wearing apparel lay all over the place — stockings, underclothes, dresses, and shoes. It was evident that the room had not been tidied since Laura Courtland had last used it, and Peter rather wondered at this. He discovered some time later that she had disliked the servants in her rooms unless she was there to see what they did. The dressing-table, laden with perfumes and toilet preparations, yielded nothing of interest. A jewel-case, which was unlocked, contained several pieces of expensive jewellery, among which was a rather pretty brooch of platinum with the initial L in rubies, which, Peter thought, was rather attractive.

At the end of a thorough search, which included the very handsomely appointed bathroom adjoining, they were forced to the conclusion that they were no wiser than when they had started. There was nothing at all to suggest why Laura Courtland had gone to the derelict cottage on the previous night in company, or to meet, those other three, or why in the course of that weird meal she had met her death.

Superintendent Odds looked at his watch.

'It's just half-past seven, sir,' he said. 'If you're agreeable, we'll go back to Fendyke St. Mary. I'd rather like to pay a visit to Miss Fay Bennett's house. Maybe we'll be luckier there than we have been here.'

6

Rose opened the door to Superintendent Odd's knock and stared at them with wide and rather frightened eyes.

'Miss Bennett isn't at home . . . ' she began, but the superintendent cut her short.

'I know that, miss,' he said, gravely. 'I'm afraid that your mistress won't *be* coming home. I'm Superintendent Odds of the County Police, and I'd like a word with you. May I come in?'

Rose gasped, goggled, and swallowed. Her face flushed with excitement.

'Has . . . has there been an accident?' she stammered.

'I'm afraid there has,' answered the superintendent.

'Oh, my goodness!' cried the girl, excitedly, as he and Peter stepped into the hall. 'I'll call Mrs. Bossom . . . '

But there was no need to call Mrs. Bossom. That lady appeared of her own accord, her eyes snapping with eager curiosity.

'What's the matter? What's 'appened?' she demanded, turning her shining red face from one to the other.

'There's been an accident . . . ' began Rose, but Mrs. Bossom ignored her completely and addressed her remarks to Odds.

'What's 'appened?' she repeated. 'What's it all about . . . ?'

'May I ask your name, ma'am?' interrupted the superintendent.

'You may,' replied Mrs. Bossom, instantly adopting a tone of defensive belligerency. 'It's Lucy Bossom — Mrs. Lucy Bossom — an' I ain't ashamed of it . . . '

'What position do you occupy in this household?' asked Odds.

'Cook-'ousekeeper,' answered Mrs. Bossom, 'an' I'd like to know . . . '

'Did Miss Bennett live here alone?' went on the superintendent, without giving her time to state what it was she was so anxious to know.

'No, me an' Rose lives in,' said Mrs. Bossom. 'An' what I . . . '

'I mean apart from you and Rose,' said Odds, driving ruthlessly through her attempts to take hold of the conversation. 'Did any of Miss Bennet's relations live with her . . . ?'

'Relations?' cried Mrs. Bossom, shrilly. 'I know nothin' about no relations. There's no one else livin' 'ere 'cept me an' Rose an' Miss Bennett. Now what . . . ?'

'What time did Miss Bennett go out last night?' continued the superintendent.

'I'm answerin' no more questions till I know what it's all about,' declared Mrs. Bossom, planting her hands firmly on her substantial hips and glaring at him truculently. 'It's a fine thing to come burstin' into people's 'ouses an' firin' off questions without tellin' 'em nothin' . . . '

'Now, now, there's no need to get upset,' said Odds, soothingly. 'You may as well know now as later. Your mistress's body was found this afternoon in circumstances which suggest she was murdered . . . '

Rose gave a startled cry and clapped a hand to her mouth, while her eyes went round with horrified astonishment. Mrs. Bossom gaped foolishly, all her previous belligerency wiped away.

'Well, I do declare,' she gasped, inadequately. 'Whoever could 'ave done such a thing . . . ?'

'We don't know yet,' said Odds. 'Now, if you will answer a few questions . . . '

'I don't know nuthin',' said Mrs. Bossom, instantly back on the defensive. 'I've never been mixed up in anything . . . '

'I'm quite sure you haven't.' Odd's voice was smooth and conciliatory. 'But it may be helpful if you will tell us something about Miss Bennett's movements during the past forty-eight hours. What time did she go out last night?'

'It'd be round about half-past eight,' said Mrs. Bossom, frowning. 'She 'ad 'er dinner at seven an' then she dressed . . . Yes, it'd be about 'alf-past eight.'

'Did she say where she was going?' asked the superintendent, and Mrs. Bossom gave one of her expressive sniffs.

' 'Er say where she was goin'?' she repeated, scornfully. 'No, that was a thing she never did. No consid'ration for other people *she* 'adn't. Lyin' in bed 'alf the day an' wantin' meals at all hours . . . '

'So you have no idea where she went?' said Odds.

'No.'

'Did she go out alone. I mean, did anyone call for her?'

'So far as I know she went alone. Nobody called, did they, Rose?'

'No,' said Rose, shaking her head. 'No one came yesterday at all.'

'Did she have many visitors as a rule?' asked the superintendent.

'Visitors!' said Mrs. Bossom, tossing her head. 'I should say she did. Always droppin' in at all hours, they was. And she'd receive 'em sometimes in a flimsy wrap that was more suitable to the bathroom than the drawin' room, if you ask me, an' gentlemen at that! Some people don't 'ave no sense of modesty . . .'

'Were Mr. Mallory, Monsieur Severac, and Miss Courtland, among Miss Bennett's friends?' said Odds, breaking in on Mrs. Bossom's virtuous indignation.

'Yes, they was,' answered Mrs. Bossom. 'Mr. Mallory was always poppin' in an' out, and so was Miss Courtland. Monsieur Severac didn't come so often as the other two, but he called once or twice.'

'What were the names of the other people who came to see Miss Bennett?'

'Rose can tell you more about that than I can. She used ter answer the door to 'em, an' a pretty dance it give 'er sometimes. I 'ad all my work cut out ter look after the kitchen . . . '

The superintendent looked at Rose questioningly, and she puckered up her face in an effort of memory.

'Well, there was Mr. Gourley,' she said, after a pause. ' 'E used ter come quite a lot. 'E lives up by the Green. An' then there was the Reverend Gilbert Ray, the curate — 'e only come once . . . '

'I should think so, indeed,' put in Mrs. Bossom, with another sniff.

'There was quite a lot of names I can't remember,' Rose continued, apologetically. 'I didn't take much account of 'em, reely, an' the names 'as gone out of me 'ead . . . '

'If you should remember any of them,' said Odds, 'will you put them down and let me know? I'm anxious to find everybody who was acquainted with Miss Bennett . . . '

'That Miss Courtland's the one you want to talk to,' said Mrs. Bossom, decisively. 'Bosom pals, as you might say, *they* was. Birds of a feather, if you want my opinion, an' neither any better than what they should be . . . '

It was fairly obvious, thought Peter, that Fay Bennett's reputation, so far as Mrs. Bossom was concerned, was anything but good. He realized that this really meant very little. The Mrs. Bossoms of this world are only too apt to see bad in everybody whose station in life is a little bit better than their own. At the same time there was probably something in what she said about 'birds of a feather.' Laura Courtland, on her own father's admission, had been, to put it very mildly indeed, fast, and if she and Fay Bennett had been such friends it was only reasonable to conclude that the latter was of the same genus.

'How long,' he asked, 'have you and Rose been in Miss Bennett's employ?'

Mrs. Bossom gave him a look that said plainly: 'And who might *you* be, I'd like to know,' but she answered civilly enough:

'Two an' a half years, come this month. We both came together when she took the 'ouse.'

'Where was she living before?' inquired the superintendent.

Mrs. Bossom shook her head.

'That's more than what I can tell you,' she said. 'She wasn't given to talking about 'erself — leastways not ter me an' Rose. The only time she spoke to us was ter give orders . . . '

'And you don't know whether she had any relations living?' said Odds, and Mrs. Bossom declared 'she didn't know nuthin' about her late mistress at all.'

The superintendent asked several other questions, for the most part repetitive, but he failed to extract any further information, and this was quite evidently because neither Mrs. Bossom nor Rose — whose other name, it appeared, was Higgs — were in possession of any. They were both bursting with curiosity to learn the circumstances in which their mistress had come by her death, but Odds made no effort to satisfy this ghoulish eagerness. He requested to be shown over the house, and Mrs. Bossom took both he and Peter on a personally conducted tour, with Rose lingering in the rear. It was not a very large house, but it was furnished in a way that showed that the dead woman had been exceedingly well off. Everything was very modern and of the best. Odds gave the most attention to Fay Bennett's bedroom, and the drawing room which, Mrs. Bossom assured him, she had principally used. He found nothing whatever to reward him for his trouble, and it was Peter who made the only discovery worth mentioning. He was drifting rather aimlessly about the bedroom, while the superintendent conducted his search, and happened to look into a small silver trinket-box that stood on the mantelpiece. It was empty except for a brooch, and the brooch was a replica of the one he had seen in Laura Courtland's bedroom at Prior's Keep. The same filigree work in platinum; the same initial L in rubies. Peter examined it curiously and frowned. If it had been the same with the initial F instead of L, he would not have given it a second thought, but why should Fay Bennett have had a brooch, and an expensive brooch, with an initial that was not her own? He called Odds and showed him the brooch, but the superintendent did not seem to attach much importance to it.

'Most likely Miss Courtland had two of 'em,' he said, 'and dropped one when she was here sometime. I understand ladies wear these things in hats and turbans . . . '

Peter thought that *might* be an explanation, but he wasn't satisfied with it. It seemed to him rather unlikely that Laura would have possessed two brooches that were exactly alike. There was some other explanation, and he felt that the brooch was somehow important. When nobody was looking he dropped it into his pocket . . .

7

It was too late by the time Odds had finished at Fay Bennett's to do anything more that night, and Peter offered to drive him to his home at Hinton, a little over two miles away; an offer that was gratefully accepted.

'I'd just like to step into the police station here on the way, sir,' said Odds, 'and get Sergeant Quilt's report. He's been to Mr. Mallory's house, and Severac's, and he may have found something. And, if you have no objection,' he added, 'we might take him along with us . . .'

They found Sergeant Quilt seated at the battered desk drinking coffee and munching sandwiches, both of which had been prepared by Police Constable Cropps who had, with great relief, handed over his duties at Witch's House to the man from Hinton, and was now, being off duty until the following day, having his supper and taking his ease in his shirt sleeves. He provided Odds and Peter with coffee, and while they drank it they listened to Sergeant Quilt's report. It was brief and disappointing.

On the superintendent's instructions he had attended to the collection of the remnants of food and the remains of the wine from the cottage and taken the sealed containers to Doctor Culpepper. After that he had gone to Robin Mallory's house and let himself in with the key which the superintendent had taken from the dead man's pocket and given him for that purpose. He had searched the place thoroughly but had found absolutely nothing that could have any bearing on the investigations. He had then gone to André Severac's house and repeated his procedure with the same unedifying result. That was all, except that Colonel Shoredust had rung through to say that he had been in communication with Scotland Yard, and that a detective-inspector and a detective-sergeant were arriving on the following afternoon and there would be a conference at four o'clock at the police station at Hinton.

'Well, I can't say I'm sorry,' grunted Odds. 'Maybe they'll perform a few miracles and clear the whole business up, and, anyhow, it relieves us of a lot of responsibility. Is there any news of that poor kid, Joan Coxen?'

Quilt shook his head.

'No. sir, nothing,' he replied. 'They're still searching.'

The superintendent set down his empty coffee-cup and gave a prodigious yawn. 'If you're ready, sir, I think we'll go,' he said, looking at Peter. 'I've got to be on the job pretty early in the morning. There'll be the doctor's reports to collect, and I'll have to see the Coroner and arrange for the inquest. Mr. Chard is going to run us back to Hinton, Quilt.'

'That's very kind of you, sir,' said the sergeant.

They went out to the car. Quilt offered to direct Peter, and took his place in front, while Odds climbed wearily into the back. It showed how worn out he was when he almost immediately fell asleep and remained asleep until they woke him at the door of his house in Hinton.

It was nearly eleven o'clock when Peter got back to Wymondham Lodge. Ann was alone in the drawing room. Miss Wymondham had, apparently, not been feeling very well and had gone to bed.

'She's caught a cold, I think,' explained Ann. 'Darling, you must be starving! There are chicken sandwiches on that tray and a bottle of Johnny Walker. Sit down by the fire and get warm and I'll pour you out a drink . . .'

She went over to the tray and mixed a whisky and soda and brought it back to him, together with a plate of sandwiches. Peter took a long drink and gasped.

'My God,' he said, 'that's nearly neat . . .'

'It'll do you good,' said his wife, curling herself up on the settee and lighting a cigarette. 'Now, tell me all about it.'

'I'm afraid there isn't much to tell,' he replied. He told her what there was while he ate and drank. 'Scotland Yard are arriving tomorrow,' he concluded, 'and Odds seems more relieved than anything else. I rather like him. He's a damned hard worker, even if he doesn't get much result. I suppose you weren't able to get anything out of Aunt Helen about these people if she wasn't feeling well . . . ?'

'Oh,' said Ann, laughing, 'she wasn't too ill to talk. In fact it was I who eventually insisted that she should go to bed. She would never have gone on her own account. She's wildly excited about the whole thing, and I had no difficulty at all in getting her to tell me all she knew about those four people. Felix Courtland, it appears, was in the cinema business. He owned a string of provincial picture theatres which, about four years ago, he sold, lock, stock, and barrel to one of the big combines. He's rolling in money, and, although he's virtually retired, he still dabbles in 'deals,' which bring him in more. Laura's mother died when Laura was quite a child, and Courtland seems to have always been too busy to give the girl much attention. The result being that she has always done pretty much as she liked . . . '

'Which, from what her father says, seems to have been a bit hectic,' remarked Peter, getting up and pouring himself out another drink.

'You got that, too, did you?' said Ann. 'That's what I gathered from Aunt Helen, though I don't think she knows very much. She seems to think that Laura was more to be pitied than blamed and that it wasn't altogether her fault . . . '

'*I* think she was a thoroughly bad lot,' said Peter. 'And I don't mean as regards her morals. They just didn't exist, of course, but there are quite a lot of girls who are completely immoral — I'm referring to the accepted sense of the term — who are otherwise good sorts. I believe there was something about Laura, however, that was *really* — evil . . . '

'I got the same impression,' said Ann, nodding quickly. 'Something that was rather . . . unwholesome . . . '

'That's it,' agreed Peter. 'That's an admirable description.'

'I don't know what gave me the impression,' she went on, 'but I felt it directly I met her . . . before I knew anything about her . . . I'd like a drink, too, darling, please.'

He brought her a whisky and soda.

'What about the others?' he asked. 'Did

you learn anything about them?'

'M'm.' Ann took a sip of her drink. 'They all appear to have belonged to the same set. Plenty of money, nothing to do, and endlessly seeking some new way of having a good time. You know the type? Rather decadent and depraved and constantly searching for a fresh thrill. It's unusual to find them in a village like this, but there are dozens like them in the West End of London. Robin Mallory was an artist, and, Aunt Helen says, was supposed to be a pretty good one. His father left him a fortune, so he had no need to earn his living by painting, which was probably a pity. He came to live here about three years ago and there were rumours that he'd got into some kind of trouble in London and had to clear out. Aunt Helen was very vague about it, and I gathered that there may be no truth in it at all. Since he has lived here he's conducted himself quite well. He used to throw parties now and again which went on until the small hours, and everybody got very tight, but that was all. Fay Bennett was a bit of a mystery, and nobody, again according to your aunt, knew very much about her. More rumours went round — that she was the co-respondent in a divorce case; that she was married and had left her husband; that she had been a film actress; all the usual malicious stories that people invent when they don't know the truth.' Ann paused and took another sip of her drink. 'There seems to be no foundation of fact for any of them,' she went on. 'She appears to have had plenty of money and a host of friends — people were always coming to see her — and she quickly got friendly with Laura Courtland, Robin Mallory, and André Severac. They had the same outlook, tastes, and habits, so, I suppose, it was only natural that they should drift together. Severac was living here before any of the others. He was also rich, idle, and something of a dilettante. He dabbled in literature, painting, music, and God knows what else. His origin is also a little obscure. It is generally supposed that he was the son of a French marquis and that he had a row with his family through marrying an English girl against their wishes, who subsequently died. This is, again, nothing but pure speculation, but I'm including all the gossip true or otherwise. He appears to have been very friendly with our curate — you know, the man we met this morning who looked like a foreigner — but that may be because they were both of French extraction. It seems hardly likely they could have had much else in common. Well, there you are, darling, that's the best I could do.' Ann finished her drink and looked at him, turning the empty glass round in her fingers.

'I think it's pretty good,' remarked Peter. 'At least these people are beginning to emerge from the shadows and become real. We don't know very much about them yet, but we do know something. We know that they were all of the same stamp. As Mrs. Bossom so pertinently remarked, 'they was birds of a feather,' and the plumage seems to have been a bit draggled. Oh, by the way, what do you make of this?' He went over to his coat and took from the pocket the brooch which he had found at Fay Bennett's.

Ann set down her glass and examined the little piece of jewellery with interest.

'It's beautifully made,' she said, 'and quite expensive, I should think. The rubies are very good. Where did you get it?'

'I found it on the mantelpiece in Fay Bennett's bedroom,' he answered. 'In a little silver box. The curious thing is that there was a brooch exactly like it in Laura Courtland's jewel-case in *her* bedroom.'

'Not with the same initial, surely?' she said, and he nodded.

'Yes, that's the curious thing,' he replied. 'In Laura's case the initial fits. Odds suggests that she had two of these brooches, and lost one while at Fay Bennett's house, but somehow I can't see a woman having two brooches exactly alike. What do you think?'

'It would be very unusual,' said Ann.

'Then why should Fay Bennett have possessed a brooch which bears an initial that is obviously not her own?' he demanded.

Ann frowned, pursing her lips and staring thoughtfully at the little trinket in her hand.

'It couldn't be a badge of some kind, could it?' she said suddenly, looking up.

'I believe you've hit it!' exclaimed Peter. 'Why didn't *I* think of that . . . '

'Well, now that *I've* thought of it instead,' she said, 'where does it get us?'

'It shows that they must have both belonged to the same thing, whatever it is,' he answered. 'Some kind of society . . . '

'Peter!' she interrupted, with a mischievous twinkle. 'You are not going to suggest that these four people were members of a secret society, are you, darling?'

'Well, no. Perhaps not exactly a secret society . . . '

'I'm very glad to hear it,' Ann continued, smiling. 'Because I really couldn't believe anything that sounds as if it had come straight out of the pages of a thriller. A secret society that holds its meetings in a haunted cottage is really too perfect to be true. It just *couldn't* happen . . . '

'Something happened,' said Peter, seriously. 'Something that might equally well have come straight out of the pages of a thriller. Those four people *did* meet at the haunted cottage, as you call it, and they *were* killed . . . '

'And there was a fifth person,' said Ann, the laughter fading from her eyes. 'A fifth person who came and went without leaving any marks in the snow . . . Yes, Peter, something happened — something inexplicable and . . . and uncanny . . . and horrible . . . ' She stopped with a little shiver and held out the brooch, which he took. Something had come into that quiet, warm, cosy room — a disturbing, unpleasant something, as though a door had been partially opened and through the crack had come writhing abominable and hideous things from an unnameable hell . . .

Peter slid the brooch into his pocket.

'Let's go to bed, shall we?' he said, soberly. 'I think I've had enough horrors for one day . . . '

8

Miss Wymondham did not appear at breakfast. Roberts informed them that she was feeling far from well, and when Ann went in to see her she found her with a high temperature and all the symptoms of a severe cold. Peter telephoned to Doctor Culpepper, who promised to come along at the first available opportunity.

'Have you heard the news?' he said. 'They've found little Joan Coxen, or rather what's left of her . . . '

'When?' demanded Peter.

'In the early hours of this morning,' answered the doctor. 'The body was in a clump of reeds, quite naked, and the child had been dead for over forty-eight hours . . . '

'How did she die?' asked Peter.

'The same way as the others,' replied Doctor Culpepper, grimly. 'Tell Miss Wymondham to stay in bed and keep warm and I'll come and see her as soon as I possibly can.'

Peter hung up the receiver and went to find Ann in a cold rage.

'Poor little mite,' she said, when he told her. 'Peter, it's dreadful! It can't be allowed to go on happening . . . '

'Scotland Yard will be here today,' he said, gruffly. 'Perhaps *they* will be able to find this unspeakable swine who's responsible . . . It's ghastly, darling . . . Ghastly and meaningless . . . ' Abruptly he pulled out a packet of Players and lit one.

'I'd like a cigarette, too, please, Peter,' said Ann, gently.

'I'm sorry, dear.' He gave her one and lit it for her. 'This has rather upset me . . . '

'I know,' she laid a hand on his arm affectionately. 'I don't think I've ever seen you look so . . . so grimly pugnacious before, Peter . . . '

'Isn't it enough to make *anyone* pugnacious?' growled Peter. 'Think of that poor little kid . . . and those other poor kids, too . . . I'd like to strangle the brute who did it with my own hands . . . '

'You've got to find him first, Peter,' she said, quietly.

'Yes, rather putting the cart before the horse, aren't I?' he said. He looked at his watch. 'I think I'll walk down to the village. I want some more cigarettes, and I'd like to get the local reaction to all this. Are you coming?'

She shook her head.

'No, I think I ought to stay here in case I can do anything for Aunt Helen,' she said.

'I suppose you ought,' he agreed. 'Would you rather I didn't . . . '

'Oh, no, Peter,' she said, quickly. 'You go. I shall be quite all right . . . '

'Well, I won't be longer than I can help.' She followed him out into the hall and watched him while he put on his overcoat. 'Is there anything you want me to bring back?'

'No, I don't think so.' She shook her head. 'Except yourself . . . ' She came close to him and caught hold of the lapels of his coat, looking up into his face seriously. 'You will be careful, Peter?'

'Why do you keep saying that?' he

asked, smiling down at her.

'Because I don't want anything to happen to you,' she answered.

'Darling, nothing's *going* to happen to me,' he said. 'What *could* happen?'

'I don't know. But you're dabbling with something that might be dangerous,' she said, 'and if you *did* find out anything — or if the person who's doing all these beastly things thought that you *might* . . . ' She broke off as Peter kissed her.

'Don't worry, darling,' he said, lightly. 'I'll take care of myself, both from 'the pestilence that walketh in darkness' and 'the destruction that wasteth at noonday'. '

'Don't joke, Peter,' she admonished, gravely. 'I'm serious.'

'I know you are,' he replied, 'but . . . '

'If you insist on quoting the Old Testament,' she said, 'don't forget 'the prudent man looketh well to his going . . . ' '

'All right, I'll be prudent,' said Peter. 'And I'd better be looking well to my going.'

He kissed her again, picked up his gloves, and set out for the village. It was a fine morning and there were signs that a thaw was imminent. The wind had changed and there was less of a bite in the air, and the snow under his feet was no longer dry and powdery but beginning to clot. His first port of call was the little tobacconist, sweet-shop, and newsagent's in the High Street, kept by Miss Tittleton and her brother. They were both in the dark, rather poky shop when he entered accompanied by the jangle of a bell from above the door; Mr. Tittleton poised precariously on a pair of steps and dusting, under the direction of his sister, an upper shelf containing a row of large, almost empty, sweet jars. He was a small man with weak-looking eyes and a straggling moustache of a washed-out ginger colour. A fringe of hair of the some indeterminate shade surrounded his bald head and he had a large, beak-like nose that wasn't quite straight and gave his thin face a lopsided appearance.

Miss Tittleton was almost exactly like her brother. Her hair was the same shade; her eyes were weak and watery; and her nose, even larger than Mr. Tittleton's, deviated from the perpendicular in exactly the same degree. In fact the only superficial difference between them was that she was not bald and her upper lip showed only an incipient growth of hair. Peter learned afterwards that they were twins. They both ceased what they were doing at his entrance and turned inquiring stares on him.

'Good morning,' he said, pleasantly. 'Have you any Players cigarettes? I should like two boxes of a hundred, if you have them.'

'We've plenty of tens and twenties, sir,' said Mr. Tittleton in a high, thin tenor, 'but I don't think we has any 'undreds . . . '

'There are two boxes of fifty, somewhere,' put in Miss Tittleton. 'I remember . . . '

'I sold them two boxes the week afore last,' interrupted her brother.

'You never told *me*,' she snapped, crossly. 'Why don't you . . . '

'That I did,' said Mr. Tittleton. 'I told you direc'ly you come in . . . '

'I don't mind taking two hundred in twenties,' said Peter, quickly, to avoid the argument that seemed likely to ensue.

'Perhaps you will be getting some hundreds in? I am staying with my aunt, Miss Wymondham, at Wymondham Lodge, for a month, and both my wife and I are pretty heavy smokers . . . '

'Oh!' Mr. Tittleton uttered the exclamation and looked significantly at his sister. She returned his look and then regarded Peter with curiosity and added interest.

'We'd be pleased to get some 'undreds for you.' she said. 'We don't have much call for 'undreds, not usually.'

'I suppose you don't,' said Peter.

'Mostly tens and twenties in these parts,' said Mr. Tittleton from aloft. 'Wasn't you . . . ' he hesitated, 'wasn't you the gentleman what found the . . . the bodies of them people at Witch's 'Ouse . . . ?'

'I was,' said Peter, nodding. 'A very mysterious and nasty business.'

'Ah!' said Mr. Tittleton and shook his head.

'And not the only mysterious and nasty business in the district from what I hear,' went on Peter, conversationally.

'That it isn't,' said Miss Tittleton, busily counting packets of cigarettes. 'If you mean about the poor little children . . . ?'

'Yes, I did mean that,' assented Peter. 'Altogether horrible, isn't it? I heard that Joan Coxen was found early this morning?'

'Ah,' remarked Mr. Tittleton, nodding and drawing the duster back and forth through his bony fingers.

'I understand,' Peter continued, 'that she makes the fifth victim. It's dreadful that these things should be allowed to happen. I really think that the police should have done more about finding the person responsible . . . '

Miss Tittleton paused in her counting and looked up at him.

'Maybe it isn't a thing for the p'lice,' she said, meaningly.

'Now, now, Aggie,' warned Mr. Tittleton. 'Don't you go gettin' on to that agin . . . '

'Why not?' she demanded. 'Why shouldn't I say what I think?'

'Quite right,' agreed Peter. 'Freedom of speech is one of the advantages of this country. You mean you think it's more a case for a doctor . . . ?'

'No, I don't,' said Miss Tittleton, snappishly. 'Doctor, indeed! What good would a doctor be . . . ?'

'If the person responsible is a lunatic,' said Peter, 'a doctor . . . '

'I never said anythin' about a lunatic,' interrupted Miss Tittleton.

'Oh, but surely,' protested Peter, 'only a lunatic could be capable of perpetrating such horrible atrocities . . . '

'That's what I says, sir,' broke in Mr. Tittleton, eagerly, coming down two steps. 'I . . . '

'You only say it to be different to me,' snapped Miss Tittleton. 'It ain't what you think — not really. You think the same as most of us do.'

'What *do* most of you think?' asked Peter, before Mr. Tittleton could reply to this accusation.

Miss Tittleton brought forth a piece of brown paper and string from beneath the counter and began to make a neat parcel of the ten packets of cigarettes she had counted out.

'There's some things that can't be accounted for by natural means,' she muttered. 'It's my belief, an' the belief of a lot more other people, too, in these parts, that witchcraft's at the bottom of it. This place was a hot-bed of it at one time an' some people think that the old forces are workin' again as they did then.'

'Do you seriously believe that witch-craft is capable of kidnapping children and murdering them?' asked Peter, with a faintly incredulous smile.

'That I do,' declared Miss Tittleton, emphatically. 'And why not? If people make pacts with the Devil there's nothing they wouldn't be capable o' doin', is there? They put spells on children an' cattle, yes, and on people too, in the old days, an' who's to say it can't be done today . . . ?'

'Who do you believe has made a pact with the Devil in Fendyke St. Mary?' said Peter, quickly.

'That I wouldn't like to say,' answered Miss Tittleton. 'But there's someone round 'ere who has, you mark my words. I know it's the fashion to laugh and scoff at such things these days, but there's more in it than what a lot thinks.'

'Well,' remarked Peter, shaking his head, 'I like to keep an open mind about most things, but I find it very difficult to believe that witchcraft can have been responsible for this outbreak of murder. It seems to me much more likely to be the work of a homicidal maniac.'

'I'm not asking you to believe anything,' said Miss Tittleton. 'I'm only giving my opinion, that's all. But you'll find I'm right.' She tied a final knot in the string and pushed the parcel across the counter towards Peter.

'Thank you.' He took out his notecase and tendered a pound-note. 'Have you any basis for your opinion?' he asked. 'Other than your own conviction.'

'Ted Belton saw the Black Man,' she answered, seriously, searching in the till for change, 'on All-Hallows' Eve . . . '

'The Black Man?' Peter raised his eyebrows inquiringly.

'That's what they used to call the Devil in olden times,' she explained. 'That's what they still call him round 'ere. Ted

Belton saw him the night before last close by Mother Knap's old cottage . . . '

'That's right, sir,' put in Mr. Tittleton, who had come down from his perch on the steps by easy stages and had now joined his sister behind the counter. 'Full of it 'e was the next day. A great black figure, 'e said it were — nigh on ten feet 'igh . . . '

'Near Mother Knap's cottage?' said Peter, with interest. 'That's the place they call Witch's House, isn't it?'

'That's right,' answered Mr. Tittleton. 'Where you found them people, sir . . . '

'What time was it when he saw this black man?' asked Peter. Here was something, if the information could be relied on, that might be of importance.

'As near midnight as makes no difference,' said Miss Tittleton. 'He'd been over to 'Inton earlier on, on his bicycle, and 'ad an accident coming back . . . '

'Skid it was,' broke in Mr. Tittleton. 'Buckled 'is front wheel and he 'ad to leave the machine an' walk the rest o' the way 'ome. Nigh on seven mile. 'E was close to the old cottage when 'e see this 'uge black figure. 'E says it seemed to grow outer the side of the building and glide away in the darkness. Those was the very words 'e used, wasn't they, Aggie?'

Miss Tittleton nodded, putting Peter's change down on the counter. 'Twice the 'eight of a normal man, he said it was,' she supplemented.

'The beer must be very strong in Hinton,' said Peter, sceptically.

'Ted Belton don't drink,' said Miss Tittleton, curtly. 'He's barely turned seventeen . . . '

'There was a queer sort o' light, too, shinin' from the window,' said Mr. Tittleton. 'Dim an' faint-like, he said it was. Proper scared 'e was, an' took to his 'eels and run.'

The light, thought Peter, must have come from the candles in that silver candelabra — the candles that had burned until they had guttered out. Ted Belton had not imagined *that* part of his story anyway, but what about the rest? A man ten feet high was absurd, but had he seen someone and allowed his imagination to run riot over the rest? He decided that Ted Belton might be interviewed with possible profit.

'It's an extraordinary story — particularly in view of what's happened at the cottage,' he said. 'I suppose it's your opinion that this black man was the Devil himself?'

'Everyone's entitled to think what they please,' said Miss Tittleton with a slight jerk of one shoulder to indicate that whatever Peter liked to think was entirely his own affair.

'I believe,' he said, 'that this place, Witch's House, has always had rather a bad reputation, hasn't it? Don't you think it possible that, knowing the legend concerning it, Ted Belton may have imagined he saw something?'

'I've told you what *I* think,' replied Miss Tittleton, 'and I'm not the only one what thinks the same.'

'I admit to being very interested and I should like to hear the story at first hand,' said Peter. 'Where can Belton be found?'

' 'E works for Tom Acheson, sir,' answered Mr. Tittleton. 'At the garidge. He's there most times up to six o'clock . . . '

'Thank you,' said Peter, picking up his change and his parcel. 'I've been very interested in what you've told me. You won't forget to try and get those Players, will you? I'll call in again in a few days' time.'

He left the shop, setting the discordant bell jangling again.

The Tittletons stared after him for a moment and then turned and stared at each other.

'Pleasant sort o' gentleman,' said Mr. Tittleton.

'Pleasant enough,' agreed his sister.

''E don't believe Ted Belton seen anything,' said Mr. Tittleton, preparing to reascend the steps.

'He wouldn't believe anythin' that he couldn't explain,' replied Miss Tittleton. 'An' there's some things that can't *be* explained — leastways not by means *he'd* understand. Maybe he'll 'ave cause to change his mind, though, if he stays here very long.'

She began to rearrange the stock on one of the lower shelves . . .

9

Ted Belton was a lanky youth with a mop of dark hair and intelligent eyes. When Peter found him he was engaged in greasing a car, an operation which appeared to have had the effect of distributing a goodly portion of the grease about his own person. He was more than willing to discuss his adventure of All-Hallows' Eve, and he told his story with a straightforward directness that impressed Peter favourably. There seemed no doubt at all that he had seen something that night and no amount of questioning would alter the original account he had given, which corresponded almost exactly with what the Tittletons had said. He had been coming down the road, very tired from his long tramp in the snow, and also very cold and hungry, when he had seen a glow of light from the window of the cottage. It had startled him because he had forgotten that the place even existed until the light reminded him, his entire attention being taken up by thoughts of home and food and bed. The sight of that light glowing in the darkness, and coming from a house that ought to be empty and deserted, scared him badly. All the old stories concerning Witch's House came crowding into his mind and he felt himself seized with a sudden panic. It had a curious effect of partially paralysing his legs and filled him with an intense dread of passing the place. He had to force himself to move at all, and then it was only slowly, as though he had suddenly stumbled into a patch of wet tar so that his feet clung reluctantly to the roadway. He managed to overcome this a little, and he was almost level with the cottage when he saw something move away from it . . .

'Like a great dark shadow, it were,' he said, rubbing a lump of oily cotton waste between his greasy hands. 'An' it sort o' came outer the wall, an' floated away into the darkness. It looked like a man dressed all in black, but taller than what any 'uman being could 'ave been, sir. More'n twice my 'eight an' I'm nigh on six foot . . . '

'If it was so dark, how were you able to see it?' asked Peter.

'Well, sir,' answered Belton, 'the light from the winder was thrown back, like, from the snow. It was only dim an' I only caught a sort o' glimpse of it . . . ' He gave a half sheepish grin. 'I didn't wait no longer,' he added, 'I just run like hell.'

'You're quite sure you weren't mistaken?' said Peter. 'Perhaps it was only the shadow of something . . . '

Belton shook his tousled head emphatically.

'No, sir,' he declared. 'It weren't no shadder. It was too solid, and it moved. It sort o' drifted away . . . '

'And you're quite sure of the height?' persisted Peter.

'Yes, sir. It was a good ten foot. It weren't nothin' 'uman, sir. I'd take me dyin' oath on that . . . '

'In fact,' said Peter, with a smile, 'you're convinced that this huge black figure you saw was the Devil. Isn't that right?'

Belton rubbed the back of his hand across his forehead, thereby adding a fresh streak of grimy oil to the rest.

'Well, yes, sir,' he said, candidly.

Peter left him to get on with his work, the richer for a ten-shilling note, and stopped on his way out to have a word with Tom Acheson, a bow-legged little man with sparse grey hair and small, very bright black eyes. There was no doubt at all that Acheson firmly believed in the truth of the story told by his employee. Belton was a lad with a very good character and a reputation for veracity. Neither was he given to imagining things or exaggerating what he experienced. Without admitting it in so many words, Acheson made it quite clear that he was of the same opinion as Miss Tittleton regarding the baby killing.

As he came out of the garage, Peter met Anthony Sherwood. He looked rather tired and drawn, and a little grim, but his face cleared as he saw Peter, and he greeted him pleasantly. After inquiring about Miss Wymondham and Ann and answering Peter's reciprocal inquiry concerning April, he said abruptly:

'You've heard about Joan Coxen, of course?'

Peter nodded.

'Shocking, isn't it?' said Sherwood, his face darkening. 'It's incredible that such things can be allowed to happen in this so-called enlightened age . . . '

'Colonel Shoredust has called in Scotland Yard,' said Peter. 'Two detectives are arriving today, I believe, so perhaps we shall get some results.'

'Perhaps,' remarked Sherwood, gloomily. 'I'm rather doubtful if this is the sort of thing in which the police'll be much good . . . '

'Don't tell me,' said Peter, raising his eyebrows and looking at the other quizzically, 'that you belong to the great majority?'

'What do you mean?'

'The general opinion appears to be that all this violence and sudden death is the result of a survival of witchcraft,' said Peter. 'I've just been talking to a youth who claims to have seen the Devil himself on the Eve of All-Hallows, lurking in the vicinity of that old cottage they call Witch's House ... ' He related Ted Belton's adventure.

'H'm, queer,' said Sherwood. 'Particularly when you come to think of what happened to those four people ... '

'You've heard about that too, have you?' remarked Peter. 'I must say news travels fast in this district.'

Sherwood smiled.

'No faster than any other village,' he said. 'You tell one person and they pass it on to another, and so on ... I heard about it, and about poor little Joan, from the milkman ... '

'Did you know Mallory, Fay Bennett, and Severac?' asked Peter.

'Not very well,' replied Sherwood, 'but well enough to be sure that the world has suffered no very great loss ... You found them, didn't you, Chard?'

Peter nodded.

'Is it true that they were poisoned?'

'Yes. Doctor Culpepper thought with some form of cyanide ... '

'Strange business altogether,' said Sherwood, musingly, caressing his chin. 'What in the world made them all go to that old cottage? And at that hour of the night? Laura must have gone there almost directly after she left your aunt's . . . What do you make of it?'

'I don't,' said Peter. 'It's inexplicable to me. There was an old table there laid for a meal and they were all seated round it . . . It was weird and rather horrible . . . ' He gave a brief description of the scene as it had appeared to him when he had burst open the locked door.

'No wonder the people in the district believe it's witchcraft,' commented Sherwood. 'You can't really blame them . . . '

'Do you believe that witchcraft has anything to do with it?' asked Peter, pointedly.

'I?' Sherwood laughed, and shrugged his shoulders. 'No, but then I'm not a native of these parts. My grandfather was the proprietor of a circus, and I was born in a tent, but most of the families in Fendyke St. Mary have lived here for generations. Their forefathers go right back to the Middle Ages when witchcraft was regarded as an everyday occurrence, and the belief in it has been handed down from father to son. It's like a belief in God. After all, if you believe in God it's a natural corollary that you should believe in the Devil, and all witchcraft is founded on a belief in the Devil. The witch entered into a pact with the Black Man and in exchange for her soul received abnormal powers . . . '

'You seem to know a lot about it,' said Peter, rather surprised that he should, though he couldn't have said why.

'I do know a certain amount,' answered Sherwood. 'I've always been very interested and I've read all the books I could get hold of about the subject. This particular district was steeped in it. The abominable orgies of the Witches' Sabbath were regularly practised in the place where Lucifer's Stone stands now, and Fendyke St. Mary had a particularly virulent coven of its own of which Catherine Knap, the original tenant of Witch's House, was a leading light. Brought up, soaked in all this tradition, it's not to be wondered at that the inhabitants are only too ready to explain anything strange and inexplicable by witchcraft.'

'No, I suppose not,' agreed Peter. 'I'd no idea that you had made such a study of the subject . . . '

'I haven't made a really serious study,' said Sherwood, quickly. 'But I've got one or two books that might interest you, which I've picked up at odd times. Why don't you and your wife come and have dinner with us tomorrow night and I'll show them to you?'

'We'd like to very much,' said Peter.

'Good,' exclaimed Sherwood. 'Then we'll expect you about seven-thirty. I must push off now . . . Promised April I'd be back before eleven . . . ' He shook hands and hurried away, leaving Peter to walk slowly up the High Street . . .

10

Doctor Culpepper had been and gone when Peter eventually got back to Wymondham Lodge. Miss Wymondham was suffering from nothing more serious than a severe cold in the head, and he had prescribed some medicine and told her to remain in bed.

'She's fuming and fretting because she can't get up,' said Ann, 'and thoroughly annoyed with herself. I think you might go in and talk to her for a bit presently, darling. She's bursting with curiosity to know what's going on . . . By the way, Superintendent Odds rang up just before you came in. Colonel Shoredust wants you to attend the conference at Hinton this afternoon . . . '

'Me?' said Peter, in surprise, and she nodded.

'Yes. The detectives from Scotland Yard will be there and he wants you to give a first-hand account of how you found those people in the cottage . . . '

'Oh, I see,' said Peter.

'The conference is at four o'clock at the police station,' she continued. 'How did you get on this morning, darling?'

He told her, repeating his conversation with the Tittletons, and his interview with Ted Belton.

'Do you think he really saw something?' she asked.

'I'm sure he thinks he did,' answered Peter. 'He wasn't just making up a story for the sake of causing a sensation. He genuinely believes in the absolute truth of what he says . . . '

'But he couldn't have seen what he says he saw,' she exclaimed. 'It's impossible, Peter. What could this thing be that was ten feet high?'

Peter shrugged his shoulders.

'Don't ask me, darling,' he said. 'Belton is convinced that it was the Devil . . . '

'It couldn't have been the fifth person, could it?' she said, wrinkling her brows.

'Not unless you are prepared to admit that there's a giant concealed somewhere in the district who can walk across snow without leaving a mark,' said Peter. He lit a cigarette. 'I met Anthony Sherwood as I left the garage,' he went on. 'He wants us to go and dine with them tomorrow evening. I said we would. Is that all right with you?'

'Yes, if you think we ought to leave Aunt Helen,' said Ann.

'I'm sure she won't mind,' he said. 'I think I'll go along and see how she is . . .'

Miss Wymondham was lying in bed, propped up with pillows, and knitting industriously. She greeted her nephew with obvious delight and burst into a flow of speech.

'My dear, I can't tell you how sorry I am that this should have happened just now,' she said. 'So stupid and inconvenient. I told Doctor Culpepper that it was perfectly ridiculous of him to insist on my staying in bed, but he was quite adamant about it. I'm sure it isn't really necessary at all. However, it will only be for a day or two, and you mustn't let it interfere with any of your arrangements. Ann has been so very sweet, my dear. I think you're very lucky to have such a lovely and charming wife, Peter. She really is one of the dearest girls . . . '

'I entirely agree with you,' said Peter. 'That's why I married her.'

'And so you ought,' said Miss Wymondham, searching under her pillows for a handkerchief. 'Oh, dear, how very unpleasant a cold can be . . . I feel exactly as if my head was stuffed with suet pudding and *hot* pudding, too. Such a nasty sensation, my dear . . . Now sit down and tell me *all* about everything . . . When Ann came back and told me what you'd found at that horrible cottage — Laura and the other three sitting round that table, and all dead — I could scarcely believe it possible, and yet the strangest things *do* happen, my dear, don't they? Now sit down there, on the side of the bed, and tell me all about it, but don't come too near in case you catch my cold . . . '

Peter complied, to the accompaniment of a running commentary of exclamations and clucking of teeth from Miss Wymondham.

'Well, really, my dear,' said the old lady,

when he had finished, 'it sounds incredible. What *could* those unfortunate people have wanted to go to a place like that for? And to eat a meal, too. It seems to me a crazy thing to do, but people really do the maddest things these days, and there seems to be no accounting at all for some of them . . . Why do you think they went there, Peter? I can't imagine any sensible reason at all . . . Oh, dear, where *has* my handkerchief got to? I had it here only a moment ago . . . '

Peter found the handkerchief and Aunt Helen blew her nose.

'The people in the village seem to believe that it's all the result of witchcraft,' he said.

'Of course they would, my dear,' said Miss Wymondham. 'The whole district is absolutely reeking with superstition — always has been and always will be. The mentality of the people hasn't advanced very much since the dark ages . . . they still believe in spells, and about two years ago Mrs. Wigtree — such a queer name, don't you think? — was found sticking pins into a wax image of Miss Overy, who keeps the dairy, because she thought she had given her short measure of something or other . . . '

'And what happened to Miss Overy?'

'Well, now, that was a very funny thing,' said Miss Wymondham. 'Of course it was nothing more than a coincidence, but she was taken ill with a very bad bilious attack. Everybody swore it was due to Mrs. Wigtree and her wax image but, of course, it was nothing of the kind. However, it just shows you what these people round here are like . . . '

'Well, they seem to have some excuse for their beliefs,' said Peter, thinking of what Sherwood had said. 'After all, if you have been brought up to believe in a certain thing it takes a lot to eradicate it from the system. And they *may* be right. Perhaps there *is* something in it . . . '

'Rubbish!' declared Miss Wymondham. 'I'm surprised that you of all people should suggest such a thing. You were always brought up a good Christian . . . '

'There you are, you see,' said Peter, laughing. 'I was brought up to believe in the Christian faith and therefore I do. But

214

I've no proof in the existence of God any more than these people have in the existence of witchcraft. It all boils down to a question of faith — something that you were taught by somebody else to believe.'

'Nonsense,' said Miss Wymondham. 'Everybody has a mind of their own, I should hope. What they like to believe depends on themselves entirely . . . '

'There are very few people,' said Peter, 'who take the trouble to think for themselves. They accept what they read, or are told, as a fundamental truth. For example, everyone has been told the principles of the solar system, but how many, do you suppose, have tried to prove the truth of it for themselves? Not one in a million, I should think. They just accept it as a truth . . . '

'Have *you*, my dear?' demanded Miss Wymondham.

'No, I haven't,' retorted Peter, 'but if it ever became important to me I should want to test the truth of it.'

The argument might have developed, there was a glint of battle in Miss

215

Wymondham's blue eyes that suggested she was preparing to launch an attack, but at that moment Roberts appeared with a laden tray and informed Peter that luncheon was waiting. He retreated, therefore, in good order and undefeated, a result that he was not at all sure would have been achieved if the interruption had not taken place.

* * *

It was five minutes to four when he arrived at the police station in Hinton and was shown into the superintendent's office. Colonel Shoredust sat behind the desk, and grouped about him, so that the none too spacious room seemed uncomfortably crowded, were Superintendent Odds, Sergeant Quilt, Doctor Culpepper, and three other men who were strangers to Peter. The Chief Constable introduced them respectively as Doctor Mipplin, the police surgeon, Detective-Inspector Donaldson, from Scotland Yard, and Detective-Sergeant Porter, also from Scotland Yard. Doctor Mipplin was a large, bony man with a high forehead and very little hair; the detective-inspector dark, quiet, rather thick-set, and possessed of a pair of shrewd grey eyes; Detective-Sergeant Porter thin, mouse-coloured, and almost nondescript. Peter took stock of them as he sat down in the chair which Superintendent Odds indicated. Colonel Shoredust cleared his throat, looked round the gathering, cleared it again, and opened the proceedings.

'We are here, gentlemen,' he said, 'to investigate not only the deaths of four people which took place under very extraordinary circumstances on the night of October the thirty-first, or in the very early hours of November the first, but also a series of brutal murders which have been spread over a period of eighteen months. It may be that there is a connection between these happenings. It may be not. That has got to be decided. I have asked Mr. Chard to attend this conference because he found the bodies of the four people I have already mentioned, and will be able to give you a firsthand account of the circumstances. Except for the barest outline, you two fellers know damn-all, so I think we'd better start by Superintendent Odds giving you a summary of all the details in his possession.'

Detective-Inspector Donaldson nodded.

'I think that would be best, sir,' he said in a quiet, unassuming way. 'Beginning with the series of murders that started eighteen months ago.'

'Yes, of course.' Colonel Shoredust looked at Odds. 'Ready?' he demanded.

'Yes, sir,' answered the superintendent. He glanced down at a note-book balanced on his knee, and began. Peter had not heard a complete and detailed account of the affair before, and he listened with interest and growing disgust and indignation. Each case was practically identical, and differed very little from that of Joan Coxen. He saw Inspector Donaldson's jaw tighten as Odds proceeded, and his face grow set.

'A very nasty and unpleasant business, sir,' he remarked to the Chief Constable, when the superintendent had completed his recital. 'You've discovered nothing likely to lead to the person concerned?'

'Nothing at all,' said Colonel Shoredust. 'We've done our best, but we haven't been able to find a blasted thing.'

'There doesn't seem much doubt it's a homicidal maniac we've got to look for,' murmured Donaldson, pinching the tip of his nose. 'There can't be any other reason for killing these poor children that I can see. That makes it a very difficult job, sir. There's none of the usual things to help — motive and such-like.'

'That's what we found,' grunted the Colonel. 'We've done everything blasted-well possible . . . '

'Did you ever set a trap for the murderer?' inquired the inspector.

'Trap? What d'you mean?' asked Colonel Shoredust.

'Leave some child in a place, alone, where it would have been easy to get at it,' explained Donaldson, 'and keep a vigilant watch. I think I should have been inclined to try that, sir. It might not have come off the first time, or even the second and third, but there's a good chance of it being successful in the long run.'

'That's a blasted good idea,' exclaimed Colonel Shoredust. 'Wonder *I* never thought of that. Like the old hunter's trick, eh? Tethered kid to attract the lion . . . '

Peter saw the inspector look sharply at the Chief Constable and guessed that, like himself, he had been momentarily under the impression that Colonel Shoredust had made an intentional pun. But a glance at the Colonel's face showed that he was quite unconscious of anything of the sort.

'I think it would be worth trying,' said Donaldson. 'Now I should like to hear about these other deaths, if you please.'

'Your turn, Chard,' said Colonel Shoredust, and Peter described in detail how he and Ann had made the discovery. The inspector listened with the closest attention and without interruption, while Detective-Sergeant Porter took the whole thing down, verbatim, in shorthand as he had with Odds's narrative.

'Well,' commented Donaldson, when Peter came to the end of his story, 'there doesn't seem to be much room for doubt that it was murder. The locked door and the missing key prove that all right. The next thing is how were these people killed?' He looked interrogatively at Colonel Shoredust, and Colonel Shoredust looked at Doctor Culpepper and Doctor Mipplin.

'You tell him,' he said, briefly.

Doctor Mipplin acted as spokesman. He had, he stated, made a post-mortem examination of the bodies, in conjunction with Doctor Culpepper, and in all four cases death had been caused by the swallowing of a large quantity of potassium cyanide. It was a very quick-acting poison and, judging from the amount found in the stomachs of the deceased persons, death must have taken place almost instantly after the act of swallowing — certainly within two minutes. An analysis of the remains of the wine left in the glasses showed the presence of potassium cyanide in considerable quantities. It was also present in the dregs of one of the opened bottles of wine, but not in the other. There was no poison of any sort in the unopened bottles of wine. There was no poison of any sort in the food. The appearance of the bodies was compatible with cyanide poisoning. Death had taken place, in the opinion of himself and Doctor Culpepper, between midnight and one o'clock in the morning. Doctor Mipplin's voice was dry, rasping, and utterly lacking in any sort of emotion. When he had finished what he had to say he stopped abruptly, like a clock that has suddenly run down. Doctor Culpepper very briefly confirmed everything his colleague had said, and for a moment there was a silence. Then Inspector Donaldson said:

'Well, sir, I think I've got the hang of the case. Eighteen months ago a number of lambs were found at periodic intervals with their throats cut, and this was followed by the disappearance and subsequent murder, of five children, ending with the discovery of the murdered body of the child, Joan Coxen, in the early hours of this morning. They were all killed in the same manner — by having had their throats cut. The suggestion is that someone in the district is a homicidal maniac who kills for the sake of blood-lust, but there is no clue to the identity of this person. On the night of October the thirty-first a Miss Laura Courtland with Mr. Robin Mallory, Miss Fay Bennett, and a French gentleman, André Severac, went, for some reason at present unknown, to an empty cottage known locally as Witch's House, where they ate a meal, transported there for the purpose. During this meal they all died from the effects of poison, namely, cyanide of potassium, which had been introduced into the wine which they drank. A fifth place was laid at the table, but the plate and glass at this place had not been used. The evidence of the locked door and the missing key suggests, however, that there *was* a fifth person present and that this fifth person, after the others were dead, locked the door, took away the key, and, in some extraordinary manner, succeeded in escaping from the cottage without leaving any tracks in the snow. It seems only reasonable to suppose that this fifth person was responsible for the introduction of the poison into the wine, but there is nothing to prove this. No fingerprints, other than those of the dead persons, were found on anything in the room. There is no evidence to suggest, either, who this person might be, or what motive prompted the killing of the other four, nor is there any evidence to connect the poisoning with the slaughter of the lambs and the murder of the children . . . '

'No,' grunted Colonel Shoredust.

'Therefore,' continued Donaldson, quietly, 'until such evidence should come to hand, I think the two cases should be treated as separate and distinct.'

'Quite agree,' said the Chief Constable, nodding.

'I shall have inquiries made into the past histories of the four dead people,' said the inspector. 'Something may be discovered there that will help us. I gather,' he looked at Odds, 'that you have arranged for the inquest, superintendent?'

Odds nodded.

'Tomorrow morning at ten o'clock,' he

answered, 'in the village hall. I suggested to the Coroner that it should only consist of evidence of identification, and the medical evidence, and then be adjourned for a fortnight . . . '

Donaldson remarked that he thought this was a good idea.

'I shall have to see him again, now,' went on Odds, with a sigh, 'about Joan Coxen . . . '

'Yes, of course,' said the inspector. 'Well, sir, unless you have anything further to suggest, I think that's all for the present. I should like to chew over what you've told me and . . . '

'There is just one other thing,' interrupted Peter. 'Something I heard this morning which might be of importance . . . ' He told them about the adventure of Ted Belton. Colonel Shoredust was sceptical.

'Boy imagined it,' he declared. 'They blasted-well imagine anything in this district . . . '

'I don't think he did,' said Peter. 'He struck me as being a particularly truthful lad. I'm not saying he actually saw a man

225

ten feet high, but I'm sure he saw *something* . . . '

'Well, it's worth remembering,' said Inspector Donaldson, who had listened with great interest. 'I'm much obliged to you, Mr. Chard, for the information. I suppose there's been the usual local gossip about all this? What's the general opinion?'

'The general opinion,' said Doctor Culpepper, slowly, 'is that Fendyke St. Mary is suffering from a revival of witchcraft . . . '

'Blasted lot of nonsense,' growled Colonel Shoredust, angrily.

'Belton is convinced,' said Peter, 'that the thing he saw was the Devil . . . '

'Is that so, sir?' said Inspector Donaldson, and he did not smile as might have been expected. 'Well, I've come up against a few minor devils in my time, but never the Old Gentleman himself. That'd be an entirely new experience . . . '

'And, probably, rather dangerous,' remarked Doctor Culpepper.

PART THREE

THE COVEN

'We have made a covenant with death,
and with hell are we at agreement.'

Isaiah xxviii. 15.

1

The inquest brought everybody in the district, who was able to get there, flocking to the village hall on the following morning. It brought, also, a sprinkling of people who were not of the district: several newspaper reporters and two elderly, grave-faced solicitors whose names the industrious Odds had discovered among the effects of the late Robin Mallory and Fay Bennett, respectively, and notified by telephone of the tragic deaths of their clients. He had been unable to do the same in the case of André Severac for the simple reason that he had either not employed a lawyer, or had kept no record of his name and address. Mrs. Sowerby was there looking very important in her Sunday best, tightly clutching her subpœna and whispering volubly to Mrs. Bossom and Rose Higgs. Felix Courtland, in a heavy fur-lined overcoat, and muffled up to the eyes, was there, looking as though he would rather be anywhere else, and the Reverend Gilbert Ray was there. Inspector Donaldson was there with Superintendent Odds, but there was no sign of the nondescript Sergeant Porter, or Sergeant Quilt. Peter, who had got there early with Ann so that he could watch the inhabitants arrive, saw Mr. and Miss Tittleton come in and almost immediately after them a shambling figure with a head that appeared several sizes too big for it and wearing an overcoat that reached down to its heels. The vacant, foolish face turned towards him, and he nudged Ann.

'Look,' he whispered, 'that's the chap who nearly walked under the wheels of my car. It must be Twist . . . '

'That was Colonel Shoredust's chief suspect, wasn't it?' she murmured, and he nodded.

'Yes. What do you think of him?'

'I feel rather sorry for him,' she answered, watching the ungainly figure. 'I always feel sorry for people like that. There's no reason to, I believe. They are usually quite happy — far happier than anyone with a normal intellect. But it seems rather sad, I think — a grown man, or woman, with the mind of a child. I wouldn't say *he* was the person you're looking for, Peter. It's not *that* type of lunacy that murders children . . . '

'I think I agree with you,' said Peter. 'There's Sherwood and his wife . . . ' He signalled to them and they came over.

'I hear you are coming to dinner tonight?' said April, smiling, and looking very pretty in a short fur coat over a black suit. 'Anthony told me he'd invited you both . . . '

'We're looking forward to it,' said Ann. She had taken an instant liking to this dark girl with the grave eyes and the humorous mouth when she had first met her at Miss Wymondham's, in the same way as she had taken an instant dislike to Laura Courtland. There was something very genuine and sincere about April Sherwood. She took the trouble to think for herself and did not merely reproduce the ideas and opinions of others, which was a refreshing change in this age of standardization and mass production where the majority thought, acted, and even looked, like so many peas in a pod. She possessed the rapidly vanishing quality of individuality.

'Who,' said Peter, suddenly, 'is that extra-ordinary-looking woman who's just come in?'

Anthony Sherwood followed the direction of his eyes and smiled.

'That is our chief exhibit,' he remarked. 'Isn't she, April?'

His wife nodded, her eyes dancing.

'Exhibit is right,' said Peter, watching the woman who had aroused his interest with astonished eyes. 'Good Lord! She must be fifty if she's a day . . . '

'Darling, I think you're being very rude,' broke in Ann, admonishingly. 'The poor woman can't help her age . . . '

'She can help trying to look as though she were seventeen,' said Peter. 'My God, just look at her hair . . . '

'Miss Flitterwyke is still under the impression that she's both youthful and attractive,' murmured Anthony. 'She's the terror of every man in Fendyke St. Mary. That's Miss Overy from the dairy she's talking to . . . '

Peter looked at the two women curiously. Miss Flitterwyke was tall and very thin. Her long bony face was framed in a mass of very fluffy, very yellow hair, and as she talked she had a habit of fluttering her eyelids and simpering. In a young girl it would have been irritating enough, but in Miss Flitterwyke's case the result was ghastly — rather like an Egyptian mummy trying to be coy. Miss Overy was a little, fat, pleasant-faced, grey-haired woman who looked acutely embarrassed at having been singled out for Miss Flitterwyke's girlish attentions, and kept edging away in a desperate and futile attempt to evade her. Miss Flitterwyke, however, was not to be evaded. As fast as her victim retreated, she pressed forward with coy determination, fluttering like a butterfly, until finally Miss Overy was brought to a stop against the wall, and pinned there, and had to resign herself to the inevitable. Peter's amused contemplation of this little comedy was distracted by the arrival of a newcomer; a tall, lean man with a dark, saturnine face that was deeply scored with lines. His thin mouth was turned down at the corners and his eyes glowered from under rather bushy brows. His whole face was a sneer, embittered and unpleasant, as though the world in general had done him some serious and unforgivable injury. Peter pointed him out to Sherwood and inquired who he was.

'That's Gourley,' said Sherwood, 'Ralph Gourley. Gruff, unfriendly-looking chap, isn't he? Nobody likes him and I don't think he likes anybody . . . '

'He was a friend of Fay Bennett's,' said Peter, watching the man take up a position as far away from everybody else as he could.

'Was he?' Sherwood raised his eyebrows. 'Well, that surprises me. I shouldn't have thought he was friendly with anybody. He usually ignores any attempt in that direction. He always gives me the impression that, at some period or other, he'd been through a lot of trouble and suffered pretty badly. But that may be just imagination on my part. Perhaps he's one of those people who are naturally sour and taciturn.'

The arrival of the coroner, a genial-looking little man, who reminded Peter of Mr. Pickwick, put an end to any further discussion concerning the disagreeable Mr. Gourley for the moment. The jury were sworn, and the coroner opened the proceedings. He explained the reason for the inquiry in a speech that was admirable for its brevity, and then took the evidence of identification. Felix Courtland was the first witness called and he gave his evidence in a voice that was still thick and hoarse from cold. The reason for the presence of the Reverend Gilbert Ray became plain when he was next called to the stand and identified the body of André Severac. One of the solicitors, with the appropriate name of Laws, was next. He identified the body of Robin Mallory, and the other, a man named Taplow, completed that part of the business by identifying the body of Fay Bennett. The medical evidence followed. Doctor Mipplin repeated, at greater length and in more technical language, what he had said at the Chief Constable's conference on the previous day. Doctor

Culpepper confirmed his statement, and then Peter was called. He explained how he had come to find the four bodies in the empty house and described the circumstances surrounding his discovery in detail. The coroner asked one or two questions that did not seem very important, and then Peter was dismissed and Ann took his place. Her story was, naturally, almost a repetition of Peter's, and she was followed by Superintendent Odds. He briefly related how he had been called to Witch's House by Mrs. Chard, and gave an account of what he had found there, ending by asking that the inquiry should be adjourned for a fortnight in order to give the police time to collect further evidence. The coroner, who had obviously been well primed beforehand, made no demur, and the proceedings terminated. It was all very tame and, to judge from the expressions on their faces, very disappointing to the onlookers who had evidently been expecting to see, and hear, something sensational.

Peter, on his way out with Ann,

Anthony Sherwood, and April, found himself next to Detective-Inspector Donaldson.

'Good morning,' he said, pleasantly.

'Good morning, sir,' answered the inspector, a little curtly, he thought.

'How is the investigation going?' asked Peter.

'It's a very strange business, sir; very strange altogether, and that's a fact.' Donaldson looked quickly round. Ann and the Sherwoods had gone on ahead and there was nobody near them. The coroner was still collecting his papers and talking to Superintendent Odds. 'I've had a look round at the cottage,' the inspector went on, dropping his voice.

'Did you find anything fresh?' inquired Peter with interest. 'Anything to show how that fifth person came and went without marking the snow?'

The inspector looked at him. It was a steady, calculating look, and it made Peter feel suddenly uneasy.

'There were some marks near a clump of reeds,' he answered. 'The snow was all churned up as though somebody had stood there for some time. But the place was a good fifty yards away. So it couldn't have had anything to do with this unknown fifth person who locked those four dead people in that room and took away the key . . . '

'There must be *some* explanation,' said Peter. 'A person can't walk over soft snow without leaving any trace . . . '

'No, sir,' interrupted the inspector, 'and, therefore, there's only *one* explanation that I can see at the moment. There were six sets of footprints — Miss Courtland's, Miss Bennett's, Mr. Mallory's, Mr. Severac's, and your own and Mrs. Chard's . . . '

'Well?' said Peter, as he paused, but he guessed what was coming.

'They were the *only* ones,' continued Donaldson, quietly. 'Not counting, of course, the ones made later by the Chief Constable, Superintendent Odds, Sergeant Quilt, and the constables. So it would seem, sir, that the only people who *could* have locked that door and removed the key were you, or Mrs. Chard . . . '

2

So he's seen it, thought Peter. Somebody was bound to before very long. He'd been wondering who would be the first to suggest that solution, for, of course, it was the obvious one. It was surprising that it had not occurred to Superintendent Odds, or Colonel Shoredust. It was the logical conclusion to reach from the evidence available, but, although he had been expecting it, it startled him none the less to hear it put so bluntly.

'I suppose,' he remarked, speaking as calmly as he could, 'that *is* what one would be driven to think. I can assure you, however, that you're quite wrong. Neither I, nor my wife, locked the door, took away the key, or administered the poison which killed those four people. In fact we neither of us know any more about it than we have said.'

'I haven't accused you, sir,' replied the inspector. 'I merely said that it would seem . . . '

'That,' interrupted Peter, 'is pure quibbling. Now isn't it?'

'Well, no, sir,' said Donaldson, shaking his head. 'I'm not saying you or Mrs. Chard actually *did* any of the things you deny having done. I'm only offering an explanation for an apparent impossibility. Can you suggest an alternative one?'

'No,' admitted Peter, candidly. 'I can't. But there must be one, because the one you suggest is wrong. Why on earth do you imagine that either my wife or I should want to kill four people who were utter and complete strangers? It doesn't make sense . . .'

'No, sir,' agreed the inspector, 'it *doesn't* make sense as *you* put it . . .'

'There's no other way to put it,' said Peter, sharply. 'You'll have to find another solution, inspector.'

'Maybe we shall, sir,' said Donaldson. 'I understand that you and Mrs. Chard will be staying here for some time?' He looked hard at Peter as he spoke and there was no mistaking what he meant.

'Until the end of the month,' answered Peter. 'You needn't worry that we're likely to run away . . . '

'I'm not worrying about *that*, sir,' said the inspector, and his tone suggested that it wouldn't be much good if they tried. 'Well, I must be getting along. I've got a lot to do . . . '

'Don't waste your time chasing wild geese,' said Peter, shortly, and went to join Ann and the Sherwoods, who were waiting for him at the door of the hall.

'Who was that you were talking to, Peter?' asked Ann, curiously.

'That was Donaldson, the detective from Scotland Yard,' he replied. 'He's just informed me that you and I are the chief suspects . . . '

'What?' exclaimed Ann, incredulously. 'The man must be crazy . . . '

'Oh, no, he's anything but crazy,' said Peter, shaking his head. 'From his point of view he's particularly sane. The wonder to me is that nobody else thought of it. I did . . . ' He repeated his conversation with the inspector as they all walked up the street together. 'The only thing that prevents him detaining us both on suspicion is that he can't find any reason

241

why we should have killed those people,'
he concluded.

'It's ridiculous!' said April, indignantly.
'Absolutely ridiculous.'

'Yes, but I can see his angle,' said her
husband, frowning.

'So can anybody,' put in Peter. 'It's the
natural conclusion to come to on the
evidence of those footprints. We know
that he's wrong, because we know that we
had nothing to do with it, but he can't be
expected to know that . . . '

'Peter,' said Ann, 'you don't think we're
likely to be arrested, do you?' She looked
at him in dismay, and her expression was
so ludicrous that he laughed.

'No,' he answered, 'not until he can
find some fresh evidence to confirm his
theory . . . '

She gave a sigh of relief.

'Oh, well, that's all right, then,' she
said, lightly. 'He can't do that so we've
nothing to worry about . . . '

'Of course you haven't,' said Anthony
Sherwood, reassuringly. 'It would be
interesting to know, though, just how
anybody did enter and leave that cottage

242

without making any tracks in the snow.'

'It would,' declared Peter, emphatically. 'I've puzzled over it for hours, but I can't see how. Unless you accept the general theory in the village that it was the Devil . . . '

'I might even accept *that*,' said Sherwood, 'but I doubt if Scotland Yard would . . . '

'It's no more absurd than thinking that Ann and Peter could have had anything to do with killing those people,' put in April. 'That's just silly.'

'Thank you, April,' said Peter, smiling. 'I take that as a great compliment . . . '

'Well, it *is* silly,' she declared. 'I think the police are a lot of dunderheads. I've always said so, haven't I, Tony? Look at the way they messed about over all those child murders, and what good did they do? They still went on . . . '

'The police are all right so long as they have ordinary, straightforward crime to deal with,' said Sherwood, 'but put 'em up against something that's out of the ordinary . . . something that they don't understand, and they're out of their depth. They've nothing to go on. They can't consult fingerprint registers and dossiers and run through the usual routine. Don't you agree, Chard?'

'Partly, but not altogether,' said Peter. 'It may take them longer to adjust their methods to something new, but they succeed in the long run . . . '

'It's been a jolly long run over those baby killings,' said April, indignantly. 'Over eighteen months and they've done nothing . . . '

'But Scotland Yard hasn't been handling it all that time,' said Peter. 'They've only just started . . . '

'Well, I don't think they've started very well, if suspecting *us* is an example,' remarked Ann.

'They don't suspect us of having anything to do with the child murders,' answered Peter. 'They're treating the two things as separate cases . . . '

'Don't *you* believe they are separate cases?' asked Sherwood, quickly.

'Personally I don't,' said Peter. 'It's no good asking me *why* I don't. I couldn't tell you. I don't even know myself. But it

seems to me that they must be connected . . . '

'I don't see how,' said April, turning a
questioning face to him.

'Neither do I,' said Peter. 'It's just that I
can't imagine that in a small place like
this there could be two separate murderers . . . '

'That's not a very convincing reason,
darling,' observed Ann.

'I know it isn't,' agreed Peter. 'It really
isn't a reason at all. It's just my feeling in
the matter.'

They had reached the *Red Lion*, and
Anthony Sherwood suggested a drink.
The suggestion seemed agreeable to
everybody and they went in. The place
was very full. Apparently quite a fair
proportion of the people who had
attended the inquest had come along to
refresh themselves and discuss the matter.
Several of the newspaper reporters were
drinking beer and chatting at the bar, and
Peter saw the nondescript figure of
Detective-Sergeant Porter standing aloof
in a corner, staring into a pint tankard,
and taking no notice at all of what was

going on around him.

Sherwood made his way to the bar, after finding out what they would drink, and was greeted with a beaming smile from the buxom landlady. Peter and Ann came in for some curious and interested glances, but the hostility which they had sensed before was no longer there. They had evidently been accepted as part of the community.

Sherwood came over with two gins and Italians for Ann and April, and went back to fetch beer for himself and Peter.

'The beer here is very good,' said Peter, after sampling the contents of his tankard. 'I discovered that the other morning.'

'It's draught Bass,' said Sherwood, 'but it's mostly the way it's kept. The best beer can be ruined if it isn't looked after properly. Old Ruddock is an expert . . . '

'Is that the landlord?' asked Peter.

Sherwood nodded.

'Yes,' he replied. 'You don't often see him about in the daytime. He leaves it to his wife. He comes out at night like the evening primrose . . . '

'Anything less like a primrose than Sam

Ruddock would be difficult to find,' remarked April. 'You're not very good at simile, Tony.'

'You seem to know everybody round here pretty well,' said Peter, laughing. 'Have you lived here long?'

'Quite a while,' answered Sherwood. 'Must be getting on for five years now . . . '

'It's more than that, dear,' interposed April. 'We came here just after we were married, and we've been married six years . . . '

'It doesn't seem as long as that,' he said, smiling at her affectionately. 'We like this part of the country, you know. It's not to everybody's taste, but it suits us, doesn't it, darling? I've got a wherry at Hinton, and when the weather's fine we go off, for weeks at a stretch sometimes, exploring the Broads . . . '

'That must be lovely,' said Ann. 'I should like that.'

'I don't think there's anything to beat it,' said Sherwood, with enthusiasm. 'Give me a boat and you can have all the cars that were ever made.' He drained his tankard and looked at his watch. 'I say, we must be going,' he added, hastily. 'I've got an appointment at twelve . . . '

'Have another drink before you go?' said Peter, but he shook his head.

'Not for me, thanks,' he said. 'But don't let that stop *you*. Come along, April . . . '

'Cheerio,' said his wife, with a smile. 'We'll see you both tonight. Seven-thirty, and don't be late . . . '

'I like those two,' observed Peter, when they had gone. 'There's something very nice about them.'

'Very nice,' agreed Ann. 'Are you going to have another drink, darling?'

'Well,' he raised his eyebrows slightly and smiled down at her, 'it *might* be a good idea, don't you think?'

She sighed and held out her empty glass.

'To think that I am tied for life to a dipsomaniac,' she said, dramatically. 'I'll have another gin and 'it', please, darling . . . and make it a large one . . . '

3

Detective-Inspector Donaldson laid aside the transcript of Detective-Sergeant Porter's shorthand notes, which he had been studying, and sat back with a sigh in the uncomfortable chair behind the battered desk in Fendyke St. Mary's inadequate police station. He was quite alone in the small cottage. Police Constable Cropps was on duty, and Sergeant Porter had been entrusted with certain inquiries which would keep him occupied for quite a considerable time. Superintendent Odds, having arranged with the coroner for the inquest on the body of poor little Joan Coxen, had gone to Hinton with Sergeant Quilt, to attend to some routine work that was waiting to be cleared up, and to report the result of the inquest that morning to Colonel Shoredust.

Detective-Inspector Donaldson was not averse to being alone. In fact, he rather welcomed the opportunity it gave him to collect and arrange his ideas. It was, he thought, as he smoked a cigarette and stared at a discoloured patch of damp on the opposite wall, the very devil of a case, or rather *two* cases, for, up to the present, he could see no possible connection between the murders of the children and the poisoning of those four people in the empty cottage. Since his arrival at Hinton on the previous day he had been pretty busy. He had interviewed Mrs. Sowerby, Mrs. Bossom, Rose Higgs, and Felix Courtland and, with the help of Sergeant Porter, had made a meticulous search of the belongings of the four dead people. He had interviewed the bank manager of the branch at Hinton — there was no bank in Fendyke St. Mary — which carried Fay Bennett's account, and also the manager of the other bank which carried Robin Mallory's, André Severac's, and Laura Courtland's accounts. All four accounts had been in perfect order — he had been a little surprised at the large amount of money to their various credits — and there was nothing whatever to arouse the smallest suspicion. No irregularities, nothing at all. They had all spent money freely, but they were in a position to do so, and the source of their wealth was quite open and above board. There was nothing there to explain why they had died. Neither had the two solicitors, Mr. Laws and Mr. Taplow, who had arrived to take charge of the affairs of Robin Mallory and Fay Bennett, respectively, and whom he had questioned before the inquest, been able to suggest anything helpful. The lives of the four dead people may have been discreditable from a purely moral point of view; it was evident that they had all led a pretty fast and hectic existence, but otherwise irreproachable. There were no scandals, no hint of possible blackmail, nothing at all to suggest a motive for the murders, or who had committed them. There was the possibility, of course, that something *might* come to light, later.

He had asked Scotland Yard to make a rigorous inquiry into the past history of all four, and the result might produce just the kind of information he was seeking. It might. On the other hand it might not. The whole circumstance of the murders was queer. It seemed to him completely insane that four grown people should have dressed themselves up in evening-dress and gone on a freezing cold night, with the ground thick with snow, to a dirty old cottage to eat a meal. There must have been a reason for that, but what was it? His long experience at the Yard had inured him to some of the mad things that the 'smart set' *would* get up to for a new thrill, but this was the craziest he had ever struck. And where did the thrill come in, eating an uncomfortable meal in a cold, dirty, and draughty old cottage? Perhaps there was something more to it than that? Were these four people mixed up in some kind of a conspiracy, and using the cottage as a meeting-place because it was isolated and they would be unlikely to be disturbed? That was all right so far as it went, but what sort of a conspiracy, and why did they have to eat there? Why go to all the trouble and inconvenience of transporting food and drink when they could have had a meal in comfort in their own homes before they went? In the case of Laura

Courtland she *had* had a meal. She'd had dinner at Wymondham Lodge with that fellow Chard and his wife . . . Nice looking girl, *she* was, with a good figure that was neither too thin nor too fat, but curved in the right places. And her hair was lovely. A real, deep chestnut . . .

His wife had hair that was something of the same colour, going a bit grey now, though, here and there . . . It was the colour of her hair that had first attracted him . . . A good few years ago that was . . . Young Alice had got it too, and a figure to go with it . . . There'd be a lot of heart throbs when *she* got a bit older . . . Donaldson gave himself a mental shake. This kind of thinking wasn't getting him anywhere. No good letting his mind drift away on his family . . . There was plenty to do before he'd see *them* again. Now where had he got to? Oh, yes, this fellow Chard . . . Well, now, what about him? The evidence of those footprints in the snow was damned queer, say what you would. He and his wife *were* the only people who could have come and gone from that cottage, unless somebody had performed a miracle . . . And they had admitted being there the day before they had made the discovery . . . *Their* footprints were all over the place . . . And there were *no others*, except those that had been accounted for . . . Come to think of it, too, that excuse for their first visit to the cottage was a bit thin, now wasn't it? There was nothing to prove that the car *had* broken down. It was quite possible that it had been *put* out of order deliberately, just to make the story ring true . . . Would anybody have stopped for a cup of tea? It must have been pretty obvious that the place was empty . . .

Taking it all round there seemed to be a fairly good reason for suspecting Chard and his wife of being mixed up with the deaths of these people, but why . . . ? Yes . . . Why? That was the fly in the ointment — a whole bunch of flies in fact . . . Inspector Donaldson crushed out the stub of his cigarette and thoughtfully rubbed his nose. If only some sort of a connection could be established between the Chards and those four people . . . that'd help things a lot. Something

that'd supply even the trace of a motive
. . . As things were he hadn't the ghost of
a case against them, but, if they *hadn't*
had anything to do with it, how the devil
had someone locked that door and left
the cottage with the key without leaving
any tracks in the snow? It was a complete
and utter impossibility . . . Hello, just a
minute, though. There was no *proof* other
than Chard's word that the door *had*
been locked and that the key was missing
. . . Supposing . . . but that only led back
to Chard being implicated in the
business. Was it possible that he and his
wife were shielding someone . . . That
only brought up that ever-recurring
question — why?

Chard affirmed that neither he, nor
Mrs. Chard, had ever seen these people
until they had found them dead — or, at
least, three of them. That might not be
the truth, of course, but there was
nothing to show that it wasn't . . . But for
that confounded impossibility of the
snow-tracks he would never have thought
of suspecting Chard. He had to admit
that . . . He wasn't the type of man likely

to poison anybody. Poison wasn't usually a man's weapon, either. It was mostly women who used poison . . . Now was there something in that . . . ? Mustn't go too fast here, he thought. Supposing *Mrs. Chard* had been the poisoner. How did *that* work out? There was the original snag of motive to start with . . . But leaving that for the moment . . . ? Her husband would naturally try and cover *her* up . . . and there was nothing to show that they had made those footprints in the snow *together* . . . they could have been made on separate occasions.

Inspector Donaldson lit another cigarette and blew the smoke towards the ceiling, following it with troubled eyes. Yes . . . she could have gone to the cottage *by herself* . . . . Supposing there had been no visit on the afternoon when the car had broken down; supposing that the breakdown had been genuine, but they had never stopped at the cottage on their walk to Fendyke St. Mary; supposing the *first* time Mrs. Chard had gone there had been in company with Laura Courtland, Robin Mallory, André

Severac, and Fay Bennett . . . She could have slipped out from Wymondham Lodge and joined them somewhere . . . or couldn't she? Not without her husband knowing, perhaps . . . and that brought him into it again . . . It was a teaser whichever way you tried to twist it, and there wasn't really anything substantial to go on . . . Maybe he was wrong about the Chards. Maybe they *hadn't* had anything to do with it . . . Then how could you explain away the fact that there were no other footprints . . . ? You came up against a blank wall either way . . .

How about approaching the thing from another angle . . . ? The reason *why* those people had all gone to the cottage and eaten that meal. If the reason for that could be discovered it would most likely go a long way towards clearing up all the rest . . . And the poison . . . ? How had the murderer come by that? You couldn't just walk into a chemist's shop and buy cyanide of potassium like toothpaste . . . It would be very difficult to get hold of, and quite a large quantity had been used. There was a possibility there . . . The poison and the reason for that queer meal . . . If he went to work along those lines it might uncover the whole thing . . . Better leave the Chards to stew for the time being and, anyway, he had nothing on them really. Only those confounded footprints . . . Well, so much for that. Now what about the other business? All those children who had been killed so brutally . . . That was nasty, that was . . . A great deal more beastly and horrible than the poisoning. So far as he could make out the four people who had died in Witch's House wouldn't be much loss. Rather a degenerate and decadent crew from all accounts . . .

Of course that didn't excuse murder, but somehow he felt more strongly about those poor bloody kids . . . That seemed to be just wanton slaughter — some perverted brute with a kink — and that was going to make it all the more difficult . . . They'd properly landed him with a packet this time, and no mistake . . . Odds had had eighteen months of it and hadn't got very far, and *he* knew the district, and the people, like the back of his hand . . .

Well, he could only do his best and he'd need to, too, if he was going to make anything of it . . . The Chief Constable was about as much use as a sick headache, and likely to give you one if you had much of him, but Odds was willing to be helpful . . . No resentment at the Yard sticking its nose in, like there was with so many of these local chaps . . . Jolly glad to shelve some of the responsibility, probably, and he didn't blame him . . .

Inspector Donaldson sighed, yawned, and shifted a little on his hard chair. His cogitations hadn't got him very far, he thought ruefully. He was settling down for a further session when the telephone bell rang and the voice of Superintendent Odds informed him over the wire, in a harsh, distorted whisper, that Laura Courtland's car had been found, abandoned, in the middle of a thick clump of reeds on the edge of a lonely part of Hinton Broad . . .

4

Peter suggested, after lunch, that they should take advantage of the Reverend Amos Benskill's invitation and pay a visit to the vicarage, a suggestion which Ann received with only partial enthusiasm.

'Must we?' she said, a little dubiously. 'We're going to the Sherwoods this evening and, I think, I'd rather stay here and read . . . '

'All right, darling, if you'd prefer it,' said Peter. 'I'll go by myself . . . '

'Why are you so keen?' she asked.

'Information,' he answered, promptly. 'I want to learn all I can about this place, and its people, and Benskill struck me that he'd be a regular old gossip once he got started . . . '

Ann sighed and looked regretfully at the deep-cushioned settee beside the fire on which she had contemplated spending the afternoon.

'In that case,' she said. 'I suppose I'd

better come . . . '

'There's no need unless you really want to,' began Peter.

'I'm not going to miss anything,' she declared. 'I'll just go upstairs and change my dress and powder my nose and then I'll be ready . . . '

They reached the vicarage just before half-past three and were admitted by a grey-haired woman whose face was so wrinkled that it looked like the map of some strange country. The Reverend Amos Benskill was sitting before the fire in his study, a huge, untidy room full of books, and he rose to greet them with obvious pleasure.

'Really this is most kind of you both,' he said. '*Most* kind. A pleasure all the more delightful because it is unexpected. Do sit down, Mrs. Chard, you will find that chair most comfortable. It may not look it, but I assure you that it is. You will stay and have some tea, of course? Mrs. Dilly, my housekeeper, makes the most delicious scones . . . '

'That sounds very tempting,' said Ann, sinking into a shabby leather chair that was all the vicar had said about it.

'With cream and home-made straw-berry jam,' said Mr. Benskill, with all the delighted anticipation of a small boy.

'Quite irresistible,' remarked Peter. 'How is your cold, vicar? Better, I hope?'

'A little — a little, I'm glad to say,' replied the old man. 'I hear, though, that your aunt has — er — succumbed to the prevalent malady . . . '

'I'm afraid she's got it rather badly,' said Ann. 'Doctor Culpepper insists that she stays in bed for a few days . . . '

'Dear me, I'm very sorry — very sorry indeed,' said Mr. Benskill. 'I sincerely trust that she will soon be better. A cold is a most unpleasant thing. I am usually fairly immune from the wretched things, I'm happy to say. A cigarette, Mrs. Chard?' He brought over a carved wooden box from a littered writing-table and held it out to her.

'Thank you,' said Ann, taking a ciga-rette. 'You don't disapprove of women smoking, then?'

'Bless my soul, why should I?' exclaimed the vicar, offering the box to Peter. 'A harmless pleasure. I smoke like a chimney myself.' He put down the box and striking a match held it to her cigarette and then to Peter's. 'I remember the time when it was considered a terrible thing,' he said, with a chuckle, throwing the used match into the fire, 'but, happily, we have outgrown such nonsense.'

'There's quite a lot we haven't outgrown,' said Peter. 'One thing in particular that I very much doubt if we ever shall.'

'To what do you refer?' inquired Mr. Benskill. He sat down and produced from the pocket of his shabby jacket a battered pipe and a leather pouch.

'Violence,' replied Peter, quickly. 'Violence in all its many forms. War, murder . . . '

'Ah, yes.' The vicar nodded and began to fill his pipe industriously. 'I agree. Civilization has still a long way to go, I fear . . . '

'Civilization hasn't started until you eradicate violence as a means of settling disputes, both between nations and individuals,' said Peter. 'Human nature, when you scratch the surface, hasn't changed much for all its boasted progress . . . '

'Oh, come, come,' said Mr. Benskill, in mild remonstrance. 'Surely that is a rather sweeping statement? We have advanced from the days of savagery . . . '

'Yes,' retorted Peter, 'instead of flint-headed arrows and stone hammers we use bullets, bombs, shells, and guns. We have advanced considerably in the science of wholesale slaughter. Personally I don't call that an advance . . . '

'Nature is red in tooth and claw,' said Mr. Benskill, lighting his pipe.

'In the raw,' said Peter. 'But surely *human* nature should have got beyond the raw state by now? What is the use of education if it can't achieve that?'

'It could,' broke in Ann, 'if it was the *right* kind of education.'

'What would you call the right kind, Mrs. Chard?' inquired the vicar, interestedly.

'A kind that goes further than teaching the multiplication table,' she replied quickly; 'that goes deeper than history, and geography, and all the usual curriculum. A form of education that would teach an appreciation of *beauty* . . . '

'You can't teach that,' said Peter, shaking his head. 'An appreciation of beauty is an instinct . . . '

'I think it *could* be taught,' declared Ann. 'If the right method was found . . . '

'And if it could be taught to the multitude,' said the Reverend Amos Benskill, 'do you think that an appreciation of beauty would eradicate violence from the world?'

'I think it would go a very long way towards it,' said Peter.

'Doesn't it rather depend on what you mean by the word 'beauty'?' said the vicar, with a twinkle in his eyes. 'The appreciation of a beautiful woman, for instance, has often led to a great deal of violence . . . '

'Not the appreciation,' said Peter. 'The desire for, yes . . . Violence cannot exist where there is a true and fundamental love of beauty in the abstract . . . '

'To a great extent you are right,' conceded Mr. Benskill, cautiously, 'but I cannot entirely agree with your premise. I do, however, agree that this fundamental love of beauty cannot be taught . . . '

'Why can't it?' demanded Ann. 'I'll admit that it would require a revolutionary revision of the existing methods of education, and that it would probably take three or four generations before the full effect could be achieved, but would that matter if it was eventually successful?'

'But I don't believe that it *would* be successful,' argued Peter. 'The vast majority of people haven't the slightest sense of the beautiful in them, and it cannot be inculcated. It either exists, or it doesn't. For instance, take a hundred people from a slum in the East End and transport them to clean and lovely surroundings and watch the result. In ninety-nine cases they will instantly, and energetically, proceed to try and reproduce the squalor and ugliness of the slum they came from . . . '

'Simply because they've never been taught to appreciate anything better,' retorted Ann.

'No, simply because that is their nature,' said Peter.

'You believe that heredity is more powerful than environment?' remarked the vicar.

'Yes, I do,' asserted Peter.

'I think I'm inclined to agree with you,' murmured the Reverend Amos Benskill. 'Except, of course, in one or two exceptional instances. While we are on the subject of violence, it was you and your wife who made that appalling discovery at Witch's House, was it not?'

Peter nodded. Whether the vicar had deliberately introduced the subject in order to avoid further argument he was uncertain, but he was quite content that the conversation should turn in that direction.

'A dreadful thing,' went on Mr. Benskill, shaking his head sorrowfully. 'There have, I fear, been some terrible happenings in this part of the world during the past months. Violence? Yes, indeed. Awful, appalling violence. My curate tells me that the local police have called in the assistance of Scotland Yard

— a very sensible procedure in my opinion. Have they formed any theory, do you know?'

'They have,' answered Peter, a little grimly. 'They have decided that the only possible people who can be guilty are my wife and I!'

The vicar looked genuinely startled.

'My dear Mr. Chard!' he expostulated. 'You are joking, surely?'

'I assure you I'm doing nothing of the kind,' said Peter. 'That is Inspector Donaldson's brilliant idea. He told me so himself . . . '

'But on what grounds does he base such a preposterous belief?' asked Mr. Benskill, and Peter told him. The vicar listened with the greatest interest and attention.

'I can quite see the inspector's reason for thinking as he does,' he commented, when Peter had finished, 'of course it's absurd and ridiculous to suppose that either of you had anything to do with this terrible tragedy, but the absence of other footprints *would* point to that conclusion . . . '

'I know,' agreed Peter. 'I saw that myself almost at once. But since we didn't have any hand in the killing of those four people and, since there was, undoubtedly, a fifth person present that night who did, the problem resolves itself into how was it managed?'

'And a very puzzling problem, too,' remarked Mr. Benskill, frowning. 'Yes, very, very puzzling. I am a great reader of detective stories and I always prefer those which have come to be known, I believe, as 'the sealed room' variety. It has given me many hours of pleasure to pit my wits against the author's and try and anticipate the solution. In one or two cases I have, I am proud to say, been successful . . . '

'I wish you could find a solution to this,' said Peter. 'I've racked my brains but *I* can't.'

'These things are usually very simple when you discover the 'how,' ' said the vicar. 'Like all the better type of conjuring trick, which relies on directing the attention of the beholder elsewhere at the crucial moment. This particular problem pivots on *one* apparently impossible happening — that someone was able to lock a door and escape with the key from a house surrounded by snow without leaving any tracks. That is the situation?'

'Yes,' said Peter, 'that is the situation. Also, unless this person arrived at the cottage *before* the snow had ceased falling, he, or she, would have had to do the trick *twice*, coming and going.'

'H'm,' murmured Mr. Benskill. 'It is certainly a remarkable proposition and an extremely interesting one. There were no marks of *any* kind in the snow?'

'Other than the footprints that could be accounted for, none.'

'I once read of a man who wore shoes,' said the vicar, reminiscently, 'with soles in the shape of hooves . . . '

'There was nothing like that in this case,' broke in Peter. '*I* thought of that. Neither were stilts used. I thought of *that* too. Anything of that nature would have made marks of *some* sort.'

The Reverend Amos Benskill rubbed his head gently.

'Very remarkable,' he said, 'very, very remarkable . . . '

'Your parishioners are convinced that it was the Devil,' said Ann.

'Due to the story of a lad named Belton,' said Peter, 'who was passing the cottage at midnight and saw, what he describes as, a black figure ten feet high float away into the night . . . '

'*Float?*' queried the vicar, raising his eyebrows.

'That's what he said,' replied Peter. 'I believe he really did see something . . . '

'Float?' repeated Mr. Benskill, musingly. 'Could there be something in that? Could this person have, perhaps, swung himself over the snow on the end of a rope . . . ?'

'There is nothing he could have attached the other end to,' said Peter, shaking his head. 'There's no tree, or anything, near enough to the cottage.'

'Dear me,' said the vicar, disappointedly. 'It really seems that there are some grounds for my parishioners thinking that the Devil must have had a hand in it . . . '

The arrival of tea, brought in by Mrs. Dilly on a large tray, put a stop for the moment to further discussion of the subject. The housekeeper set the tray on a low table before the fire, and Mr. Benskill invited Ann to officiate. She had just poured out three cups of tea when the Reverend Gilbert Ray came in, looking cold and rather tired. He seemed surprised to find visitors.

'You're just in time, my dear fellow,' greeted the vicar. 'Ask Mrs. Dilly for another cup and saucer and find yourself a chair. You know Mr. and Mrs. Chard?'

The curate bowed.

'Come over by the fire, Mr. Ray,' said Ann, pleasantly. 'You look frozen.'

'It *is* rather cold,' said Ray, crossing and ringing the bell by the mantelpiece. 'But not quite so cold as it has been. The snow is thawing rapidly ... ' His voice was deep and musical with only the faintest trace of an accent, and his manner charming, but Peter was conscious of an intense feeling of dislike. There was something about the man that was unpleasant, though he would have been hard put to it to say what. It was nothing tangible. Nothing that could be cata-logued; more of an atmosphere than anything else, and yet that was not quite the right description . . .

'Bring another cup, please, Mrs. Dilly,' said Ray, when the housekeeper answered the bell, and, pulling forward a chair, sat down between Peter and Ann.

'How is Mrs. Close?' asked the vicar, sipping his tea.

'Better,' replied the curate, 'and, in consequence, rather irritable. I think she was annoyed that I should have visited her instead of you.' There was a touch of amusement in his dark eyes.

Mr. Benksill chuckled, and began to spread jam thickly on a buttered scone.

'She would be,' he declared, 'and when *I* visit her, she's annoyed because it isn't the Bishop! Mrs. Close is nearly ninety,' he explained for the benefit of Peter and Ann, 'and is firmly under the impression that she ought to be one of the Almighty's especial favourites. Why, I cannot imagine, because she's a most cantankerous old woman with a tongue like vitriol . . . '

'She declares that all the terrible things that have happened in the village are a judgment,' remarked the Reverend Gilbert Ray, helping himself to a sandwich, 'and prophesies that there is even worse in store . . . Thank you, Mrs. Dilly . . . '

The housekeeper came in silently, set the extra cup and saucer on the tray and withdrew.

'Sugar?' asked Ann.

'Thank you — two lumps, please, Mrs. Chard,' said Ray. He took the cup she held out to him and stirred the tea gently. 'Most of the villagers are convinced that witchcraft is at the bottom of everything,' he continued, smiling. 'They seem to think that Ralph Gourley is responsible . . . '

'Why?' asked Peter, and the curate gave a slight shrug.

'For no particular reason, except that he's unpopular,' he answered. 'If this idea gets a stronger hold, I'm afraid it may quite easily lead to a lot of trouble. The whole village is on the verge of a panic . . . '

'Do you mean trouble for Mr. Gourley?' asked Ann.

'Yes,' answered Ray, between mouthfuls

of his sandwich. 'You see, the attitude of the village people is this: a revival of witchcraft is at the root of all these outrages, and the police are quite incapable of coping with it. The murders will go on until the person responsible for the bewitchment is found, and dealt with in the appropriate way. Their belief has been strengthened by the fact that young Tom Belton swears he saw the Devil on All-Hallows' Eve . . . '

'Mr. Chard has just been telling me about that,' remarked the vicar. 'Really, this is very worrying and distressing . . . '

'But why,' persisted Peter, 'should they have hit on Gourley? There must be *some* reason . . . '

'I think the reason possibly lies in the fact that his hobby is chemistry,' said Mr. Benskill, quietly. 'He is engaged in some kind of research work, I believe. He used to be a doctor, but about seven years ago there was some scandal and he was struck off the register. That was when he came to live here. I know nothing of the details; I believe it was rather an unsavoury business, but he came to live here for quietness and seclusion. He is, I am given to understand, a very clever man . . . ' He shook his head and held out his cup to Ann for more tea.

'What form does his research take?' asked Peter. Here was something that might be significant. Those four people had been poisoned, and Gourley was a chemist . . .

'I've no idea,' replied the vicar. 'I don't imagine that anyone has, except himself. He's very taciturn and, well — uncouth is the word, I think. There was some trouble two years ago with the anti-vivisection people . . . '

'Do you mean he experiments on animals?' broke in Ann. 'How horrible!'

'The trouble was over some cats,' said Mr. Benskill. 'There was quite a respectable size row about it . . . Thank you, my dear . . . '

Significant? thought Peter. Yes, very. Supposing the cats had been followed by lambs and, perhaps . . . children . . . ?

5

'I don't believe it,' said Ann, obstinately, when they were dressing that evening to go to the Sherwoods. 'It's too much like a Boris Karloff film . . . '

'I suppose it is, really,' admitted Peter. 'Unless, of course, this fellow Gourley, *is* mad. Then it would be possible.'

'I'm not saying it isn't *possible*,' she said, delicately applying a film of pink varnish to the nail of her right middle finger. 'I just don't believe in it as an explanation, that's all. It's . . . it's too *unreal* . . . '

'Whenever you do that,' remarked Peter, 'I'm always reminded of Miss Coggleton. She kept the sweet-shop where I lived when I was a small boy and she sold large and luscious peardrops for which I had a consuming passion. She had very thick black eyebrows and an incipient moustache. I can always see her whenever I smell that stuff . . . '

'It sounds a most unpleasant memory.' Ann looked round and laughed. 'Or was your youthful passion for Miss Coggleton and not for the peardrops.'

'I was scared to death of her,' said Peter, fervently. 'Somebody told me that she was an ogress and ate babies, whereas I believe she was a very high-minded, Christian woman, and a leading light of the local chapel.' He came behind her and began to tie his tie, looking into the mirror over her head. 'Talking of chapels, why is it that that fellow Ray inspires me with such a dislike? He does, but there's no reason for it that I can fathom.'

'I don't like him, either,' said Ann, transferring her attention to the next fingernail.

'Why?' demanded Peter. 'That's what I'm trying to get at.'

She thought for a moment, and then she shook her head.

'I don't know,' she confessed. 'There isn't always a reason for that sort of thing, is there? Not a tangible one, I mean.'

'You can generally find *some* basis for disliking a person,' said Peter. 'Damn this tie! I've made a mess of it . . . '

He pulled it loose and began again. 'He's good-looking, well-mannered, talks well, and yet there's *something* about him that's distinctly unpleasant. I wish I could place it . . . '

'Unwholesome?' suggested Ann. 'That's the impression he gives me. He's much *too* good-looking, he talks *too* well, and his manners are *too* good. He turns on the charm at the main and overdoes it. Probably it's only his stock-in-trade. A curate has to try and make himself popular, and the women, particularly the older women, love that sort of thing.'

'And underneath it all there's a different man?' Peter nodded, gingerly trying to persuade one end of his tie to go through the right loop. 'You never *see* anything of that other man, but you can sense him . . . That what you mean?'

'Yes . . . A little cruel, more than a little sensual . . . '

'And altogether nasty,' he ended. 'The sort of fellow who eventually turns up in the *News of The World* . . . '

She laughed, waggling her fingers in

the air to dry the nail varnish.

'We're probably being very unfair and even slanderous,' she said. 'He may be quite a nice person, really. It's purely our imagination, isn't it?'

'I think instinct is the better word,' said Peter. He patted his tie into place and stared at it critically. 'Most people's instincts are generally right, only they smother them with reason. It's always been a theory of mine that if instinct could be properly cultivated it would become a very reliable sixth sense . . . '

'You're probably quite right,' said Ann, 'but how are you going to cultivate it?'

'By accepting an impression without trying to reason about it,' replied Peter, putting on his waistcoat.

'But that's practically impossible,' she declared. 'You start reasoning automatically . . . '

'I know it is,' said Peter, 'but the theory holds good just the same. Where did I put my cigarette-case?'

'I haven't the least idea, darling,' said Ann, frowning intently at her shining nails. 'Why don't you remember where you leave your things . . . ?'

'All right, I've got it,' he said. 'The trouble is I so seldom use a case. I much prefer the packet. How long are you going to be?'

'At least half an hour,' she answered. 'There's plenty of time. It's only just a quarter to seven. Give me a cigarette while my nails are drying . . . '

He lit one and brought it over to her, and then went back and sat on the side of the bed.

'Have you got any ideas about this business?' she asked, breaking a short silence.

'No, darling,' he confessed. 'Not a solitary, single idea.'

'Great detective admits to being completely baffled,' said his wife. She turned round and looked at him quizzically.

'I'm afraid he does,' said Peter. 'Perhaps there's a lot in that rather hackneyed expression about the cobbler sticking to his last. After all, my job is writing books . . . '

'Peter! You're not giving up, are you?' she answered.

'It's not so much giving up as getting started,' he said. 'I can't make bricks without straw . . . '

'Darling,' said Ann, reproachfully, 'two cliches in less than a minute . . . ?'

'Well, they were both perfectly descriptive of the situation.'

'But you might have found a better way of expressing it. Look here, do you think it would be possible to get the dates on which each of the four children, before Joan Coxen, disappeared? We know when *she* did . . . '

'Why?' asked Peter, quickly. 'Have *you* got an idea?'

'I've got something,' she answered. 'I don't think you could call it an idea. It's far too vague and hazy. It might be the nucleus of an idea, though . . . '

'What is it?' he demanded, but she shook her head.

'I don't think I'm going to tell you,' she said. 'Not yet. It's rather fantastic. You'd probably think it was ridiculous . . . '

'Well, give me a chance,' pleaded Peter.

'No,' she replied, firmly, turning back to face the mirror and examining her reflection critically. 'I'd really rather not, darling, if you don't mind. Perhaps, after you've got hold of those dates . . . '

'What have they got to do with it?'

'They've got everything to do with it,' she answered, seriously. 'Oh, Peter, if I'm right, it's horrible — unbelievably, incredibly horrible . . . ' She gave a little shiver.

'Look here,' said Peter, with determination. 'You're not getting away with this. You're not going to work me up into a frenzy of curiosity and then let me down flat. Speak, woman, and tell me all.'

'That's just it,' she said. 'There's so little I *can* tell you. Only a — a nebulous notion . . . '

'Don't be alliterative. It's infinitely worse than using cliches,' interrupted Peter. 'Just tell me what's on your mind. After all, two heads . . . '

'Not *another* cliché, Peter, please,' she said. 'Look here, if I do tell you, will you promise not to laugh?'

'Is there anything humorous in your idea?'

'No, nothing,' she answered. 'It's hideous and . . . and terrible . . . My

283

God, Peter, if it's true it's dreadful . . . '

'Tell me,' he said, gravely. 'I promise I won't laugh . . . '

'All right,' she said, and hesitantly, and rather uncertainly, she began. It did not take very long. As she had said, there was very little to tell. Only the embryo of a vague theory. She spoke with reluctance and an unusual diffidence, as though she expected to be scoffed at, but Peter felt far from scoffing. The trace of a cold sweat moistened his forehead, and into his eyes, steadily watching her reflection in the mirror, crept a look of sheer horror.

'Well?' she said, a little defiantly, when she had finished. 'There it is. You can say it's incredible, fantastic, absurd . . . anything you like.'

'I'm not going to say any of those things,' he broke in, quietly. 'Because it's nothing of the sort. What you suggest *does* go on. There have been cases in London, and Brighton, and in France — recent cases, too. Perhaps not carried to such extremes . . . '

'Then you don't think the idea stupid?' said Ann.

He shook his head.

'No,' he replied. 'I think you may very likely be right. There's nothing fictional or problematical about the basis of your idea, darling. It's cold, hard fact, though I'll admit very few people know that such things take place. The only problematical side to it is whether this is a case in point . . . '

'If it should be it's . . . beastly,' she said.

'It's worse than that. It's loathsome, and hideous, and diabolically abominable,' said Peter, with a set face. 'We've got to find the person responsible and stamp the whole thing out. There may be any number of people involved, but there must be one who *runs* the whole horrid business. I think the police should be in on this . . . '

'Don't you think they'd laugh?' said Ann, doubtfully.

'Possibly,' answered Peter, grimly. 'But, whether they laugh or not, I'm going to put the matter up to Donaldson in the morning. Now we'd better get a move on, hadn't we, or we shall be late at the Sherwoods' . . . ?'

6

Peter would have enjoyed the evening at the Sherwoods better if his mind had not kept niggling at Ann's theory. The conversation ebbed and flowed around him, but he only heard parts of it. The Sherwoods must have noticed his abstraction, but they said nothing, neither did Ann, though she knew the cause of it. Only once did Peter give his wholehearted attention to what was going on, and that was when Anthony took him to see the collection of rare books on witchcraft he had accumulated. There were between forty and fifty, and they covered every conceivable aspect of the subject. There were two which interested Peter immensely, and he asked if he might be allowed to borrow them for a day or two. Sherwood gave his permission readily, and when, getting on for midnight, he and Ann took their departure, the two

bulky volumes by Doctor Montague
Summers went with them. Peter sat up
for the greater part of the night dipping
into the contents . . .

7

Detective-Inspector Donaldson was surprised to receive a visit from Peter on the following morning. His surprise showed in his eyes, mingled with a questioning look that said: 'Hello. What's the idea, I wonder?' What he actually did say was:

'Good morning, sir. Sit down, please.'

Peter sat down in the chair which he indicated.

'I haven't come to make a confession,' he said, remembering the last time he had seen the inspector.

'No, sir?' remarked Donaldson, stolidly. 'I didn't really think that you had, sir . . . '

'I've come,' said Peter, 'to offer a suggestion. You'll probably think that it's wildly ridiculous, but it's my opinion that there's something in it . . . '

'I'm prepared to listen to anything you have to say, sir,' said the inspector, politely. Peter offered him a cigarette, took one himself, and began to talk. He talked without interruption for nearly fifteen minutes while Donaldson listened. Contrary to his expectations, the inspector did not treat the idea as ridiculous, or fantastic. When Peter had finished, he looked at him gravely for a moment in silence.

'You know, sir,' he said, at last, 'I've had some experience of this thing you mention. There was a case in the West End of London about three years ago, and I was in charge of it. Nasty business it was, though it was a mild form to this, if what you suggest is right, and I'm inclined to believe it may be. The whole thing was hushed up because there were some pretty well-known names involved . . . '

'I believe it is still practised more than people think,' said Peter. 'Particularly on the Continent — France and Germany, and some of the Balkan states. There's been one or two cases in America also.'

The inspector nodded.

'Quite a lot of it isn't the genuine article at all,' he said. 'This case I mentioned to you just now wasn't. It was quite near enough, all the same, to make your flesh creep and leave a very nasty taste in your mouth.' He passed the tip of his tongue over his lips as though some of the nasty taste still remained. 'I was very glad to get shot of it, I can tell you. We consulted an authority on the subject at the time, and he told me all about it. It's a horrid, filthy business and I can't understand anyone getting mixed up in it, but they do, and the chief people concerned make quite a lot of money out of it . . . '

'To a certain type it would provide a tremendous thrill,' said Peter. 'The traditional rites of the cult cover a multitude of sins, among the least of which is the opportunity for unbridled obscenity and sensual indulgence. That is the appeal which the foul, black cult of Satan-worship has for the morally corrupt. There are, I should imagine, very few genuine Satanists belonging to these — covens is, I believe, the right word — and by genuine Satanist I mean a person who really believes in, and worships, the Devil. The majority of the devotees are attracted because the cult provides an excuse for advanced sexual orgies — all the wild abandon and obscene orgies associated with the traditional Witches' Sabbath and the horrible, abominable ritual of the Black Mass. In other words, the cult of Devil-worship offers vice in a new form: vice in fancy dress, coupled with the thrill of sheer diabolical wickedness for its own sake . . . '

'Just the kind of thing, in fact, that would have appealed to the four people who were murdered, sir,' said Inspector Donaldson, quietly. 'They were, from what I have gathered so far, the ideal types. And, talking of genuine Satanists, you realize, Mr. Chard, that if this theory of yours is correct, and we're not quite letting our imagination run away with us, there *must* be a genuine Satanist mixed up with it? If this *is* the reason for the lambs and the children, the ritual employed is the genuine article . . . '

'Yes,' agreed Peter. 'Of course I realize that.'

'Whoever is running this outfit,' said the inspector, his face very stern and hard, 'has gone the whole hog . . . ' He pulled a sheet of paper towards him and picked up a pencil. Taking a small diary from his pocket he consulted it, comparing certain pages in it with the transcript of Sergeant Porter's notes which had been taken at the conference with the Chief Constable. Rapidly he jotted down some dates and looked up at Peter.

'A bit significant, sir,' he said, slowly. 'These dates are what you asked for — when the children disappeared . . . ' He pushed the paper across the desk, and Peter picked it up. The first disappearance had taken place on the day before Good Friday, the second on the day before the eve of St. Michael and all Angels, the third two days before Midsummer Eve, or the Vigil of the Feast of St. John, the fourth on Christmas Eve, and the fifth, and last, little Joan Coxen, on the day before the Eve of All-Hallows.

'This goes a long way to confirm the Satanist theory,' said Peter. 'These dates all coincide with a high festival of the Church. According to Doctor Montague Summers they are also dates associated with particularly vile and frenzied rites of the cult of Satan.'

'Yes, sir,' said Donaldson. 'Strange that you should mention Doctor Montague Summers. I'll show you something.' He opened a drawer in the desk and brought out a book. 'This arrived by registered post for André Severac. It was never delivered, because on the morning it reached here, he was already dead.' He handed the book across to Peter and he read in gilt lettering on the spine: *Demonology and Witchcraft* by Montague Summers.

'There was another book by Summers in the bookcase in Laura Courtland's sitting room,' remarked Peter. '*The History of Witchcraft* . . . '

'Yes, sir,' said the inspector, 'I saw it . . . '

'It all adds up, doesn't it?' said Peter, and Donaldson nodded.

'Yes,' he answered. 'Let's see what sort of a total we can get. It's your opinion, and I must say that it's getting to be mine, too, that there's a coven of Satanists, or Devil-worshippers, in the district, to which Laura Courtland, Robin

Mallory, Fay Bennett, and André Severac belonged. That, whether these people really believed in the Devil, or merely adopted the cult because it provided a new sensation, we are of the opinion that the *full* ritual was practised in all its ghastliness and hideousness, and that the disappearance and subsequent murders of five young children are the direct result of these horrible rites. Unfortunately, we've very little evidence to support this theory. We have no actual knowledge that such a coven exists, or that these people belonged to it. We don't know of anybody else who may have belonged to it, or who the person is who is running it. All we have to go on is that such a theory provides an adequate motive for the murders of these children; that their various disappearances took place on dates that correspond with such a theory; that there was a book on witchcraft in the possession of Laura Courtland, and another book on the same subject, and by the same author, arrived by post from a firm of booksellers for André Severac. That's all . . . '

'Not quite,' interrupted Peter. 'In the possession of both Laura Courtland and Fay Bennett was a brooch of platinum set with rubies . . . ' He produced the brooch from his pocket and explained how he had come by it.

'This is the first I've heard about it,' grunted Donaldson, examining the brooch with interest. 'You'd no right to have removed this, sir, but we'll let that go. What's your idea about this?'

'I think that the L stands for Lucifer,' replied Peter, 'and that it was a kind of badge of membership . . . '

'H'm, that's quite probable,' said the inspector. 'In which case there should be something similar for the men . . . '

'Didn't you find anything of the sort?' asked Peter.

'No,' answered Donaldson. 'Sergeant Porter made the search of their belongings and I don't suppose, even if he had found anything of the sort, it would have conveyed much to him. In view of this I'll have another look myself.' He put the little brooch down on the desk in front of him. 'You know,' he went on, 'this theory may be an explanation for what you might call one half of the case, but it doesn't explain the other half; the finding of those four people, dead from poison, in that old cottage . . . '

'Or how somebody walked over the snow without leaving any marks,' remarked Peter, looking quizzically at him. 'If you still have any lurking suspicion that it was me, or my wife, you'd better put the idea out of your mind once and for all . . . '

'I've never actually accused either of you, sir,' said Donaldson, noncommittally. 'You must understand that I'm investigating a murder case, and it's my job to look at it from every angle. That apparent impossibility of the snow has *got* to be explained, you know, sir. Until we can show *how* the person, whoever it was, did the trick, we couldn't take the case before a jury — even if we knew his identity. By the way, we've found the car . . . '

'Laura Courtland's car?' asked Peter, and the inspector nodded.

'Abandoned in a clump of reeds by Hinton Broad,' he said. 'There was nothing in it to help us . . . '

'Hinton Broad is a good way away from Witch's House,' said Peter. 'The murderer must have driven it there.' Again Donaldson nodded. 'Laura Courtland probably called for the other three,' went on Peter, thoughtfully, 'and drove them to the place where they all got out and walked to the cottage . . . '

'She didn't call for the woman,' interjected the inspector.

'Fay Bennett, you mean?' said Peter. 'She may have gone round to Severac's, or Mallory's, and been picked up there. You know I'm beginning to understand that meal. Do you remember *what* the food consisted of?'

'Kidneys and liver,' said Donaldson.

'Offal,' said Peter, significantly. 'Offal, inspector. And offal was the staple diet at the old Witches' Sabbaths . . . '

'By the Lord Harry, you're right!' ejaculated Donaldson, in startled agreement. 'I remember reading about that when I was looking the subject up for this other case I was telling you about. Well, that's another point in confirmation of your theory, Mr. Chard. D'you suppose this meeting at the cottage was a kind of Witches' Sabbath?'

Peter shook his head.

'No, not entirely,' he answered. 'I should say that it was more likely a sort of side party, hatched up between the four of them and the unknown fifth person. But I'm inclined to agree that it had the same objective. Since it was All-Hallows' Eve, the main bulk of the Coven would be meeting in strength elsewhere. The cottage is quite unsuitable for the full ritual of the Black Mass, which they would scarcely omit to celebrate on such an occasion. I think the party at Witch's House was arranged between them, unknown to the rest of the Satanic cult.'

Inspector Donaldson fumbled in his pocket and rather absently withdrew a packet of cigarettes. He stuck a cigarette between his lips and searched in the same absent-minded manner for his matches. Peter pulled out his lighter and flicked it into flame.

'Oh, thanks,' said the inspector. 'Will you have a cigarette . . . ?'

Peter took one and lit it.

'I'm sorry,' Donaldson went on. 'I was thinking . . . ' He blew out a cloud of smoke. 'Isn't it essential for the full rites of the Black Mass to have a real, properly ordained clergyman . . . ?'

'Yes,' said Peter, 'or at least a properly consecrated Host, stolen from a Catholic church.'

Donaldson, with a puckered brow, pursed his lips.

'That makes it a bit difficult, sir, doesn't it?' he remarked.

'No, I don't think so,' said Peter. He looked at the glowing tip of his cigarette and then steadily at the detective. 'I think I can suggest a person who *might* fit the bill.'

'Yes, sir?' said the inspector.

'The Reverend Gilbert Ray,' said Peter.

8

Detective-Inspector Donaldson deposited a cylinder of ash in a tray on his desk, very deliberately and carefully.

'Have you,' he said, after a pause, 'any sound basis for that suggestion, sir?'

Peter shook his head.

'Not that you would call sound,' he answered. 'Nothing that could be measured, or produced as evidence. My reasons are — well, not quite what would be designated psychological, but near enough to be described by that ill-used word.'

'That's a pity,' said Donaldson. 'But still it's a pointer. Maybe we can find evidence if we have an idea in which direction to look. You think that the Reverend Gilbert Ray is at the head of this coven?'

'I said *might* be,' corrected Peter. 'It isn't without precedent, you know. There was the Reverend George Burroughs, the Abbé Guibourg . . . quite a number of depraved parsons in the history of witchcraft who held similar positions . . . '

'It's a very serious accusation . . . ' began Donaldson.

'Suggestion,' broke in Peter.

'Well, then, suggestion, if you prefer it,' said the detective. 'It's a very serious suggestion, and we shall have to move very carefully and make *quite* sure that there is no mistake. This fellow's of French extraction, isn't he?'

'I believe so,' said Peter.

'Well, now,' murmured Donaldson, pinching his chin, musingly, 'let's see where we've got to . . . ' He fixed his eyes on a corner of the ceiling and went on: 'It's your opinion that there's a bunch of Satanists operating in the district and that Laura Courtland, Mallory, Severac, and Fay Bennett were members of the coven. You further suggest that the leading light in this bunch of devil-worshippers is the Reverend Gilbert Ray, curate of St. Mary's. You believe that these people, in company with a number of others unknown, were responsible for the murder of these children and the killing of the lambs. Is that right?'

'Baldly, yes,' agreed Peter.

'Then let's see what evidence we've got to substantiate this theory,' said Donaldson. He ticked off each point on his fingers as he continued, 'One: Broadly it accounts for nearly all the facts as we know them. Two: The brooches belonging to Laura Courtland and Fay Bennett tend to confirm the supposition that they were members of a club or organization and the initial L on them could stand for Lucifer, another name for Satan. If anything similar is found among the belongings of the two men this supposition will be strengthened. Three: The meeting at the empty cottage took place on All-Hallows' Eve, one of the great festivals associated with the Witches' Sabbath. Four: At this meeting a meal was eaten consisting of offal, the staple food at all Satanistic orgies. Five: The dates on which the children disappeared correspond with a high festival of the Church on which there would be a full meeting of the coven and wild orgies from midnight to cockcrow. Six: The children were all killed in the same way, by the shedding of blood, which is necessary for the full rites of the Black Mass ... It's quite a formidable list, sir.'

'Yes,' said Peter. 'I don't think there's much doubt that Satanism is at the bottom of it ... '

'No more do I,' said the Inspector. 'But the difficulty is going to be to prove it. You realize that these four people being killed is going to put a stop to all the cult's activities? They won't dare go on with their hideous and abominable practices — at least not until the whole thing has died down.'

'I suppose not,' said Peter. 'That's one of the things that don't fit, you know. Why were those four people killed?'

Donaldson pursed his lips.

'Perhaps they were contemplating getting out,' he said. 'Once anybody has been initiated into a cult of this sort they have to *stop* in. They dare not let 'em go, because they know too much. They've seen things that the normal person would shrink away from in horror ... I can tell you, Mr. Chard, that when I was working on that London case, some of the things I

303

found made me feel physically sick and ill, and in comparison to this they were only playing at it. There's a big money end to this kind of thing, you know, sir. The people who run it make a pretty packet. Membership is restricted to people with pots of money, and they have to pay heavily for their beastly pleasure . . . '

'Which means that to be a successful proposition for the promoters, the membership of the coven must be fairly large,' remarked Peter. 'I say, wouldn't there be a list of members, somewhere?'

'Oh, yes,' Donaldson nodded. 'But where? You can bet that *that's* been very carefully hidden. These people have to take the most elaborate precautions against betrayal, for they deal in crimes and abominations completely unknown to the average person. The greatest hold that the High Priest of Satanism has over his followers is blackmail. If they betray *him*, they betray themselves . . . '

'All the same,' said Peter, '*if* anybody contemplated betrayal, and this intention became known to the others, it would provide a very strong motive for killing them, wouldn't it?'

'Yes,' agreed Donaldson. 'But if you are thinking of those four people who were poisoned, I'm not at all sure that *that* was the motive in their case. Why should they suddenly decide that they wanted to leave the cult? It wouldn't have been disgust or horror in their case. They must have become inured to all the beastliness and, besides, they went to Witch's House to carry on a sort of sideline to the main business . . . '

'The meeting at Witch's House might have been suggested and arranged by the murderer.' said Peter, 'so you can't use that as an argument to show that they were not contemplating leaving the coven. They'd have gone in any case. But I don't think they were trying to get out. I believe the motive for the murders was something quite different . . . '

'What?' demanded the inspector.

Peter shrugged his shoulders.

'I don't know.' he answered. 'It'll probably come to light when we discover who arranged the meeting at the cottage . . . '

'Well, sir,' remarked Donaldson, a little dubiously, 'it looks to me as if we got our work cut out to discover anything. I believe your idea is right, but it's all supposition . . . '

'I agree,' interrupted Peter, quickly. 'But at least it gives us a line. The place where they held their ghastly orgies must be somewhere in the district and it 'ud have to be pretty big. If you could find it, there'd probably be a lot of evidence there . . . '

'It's going to be difficult,' said the inspector, shaking his head slowly. 'Very difficult, Mr. Chard. We'll have to go very carefully indeed.'

'Try the past history of Ray,' suggested Peter. 'That might supply some useful information.'

'*If* he's got anything to do with it,' said Donaldson. 'There's not a vestige of anything to show that he has, you know . . . '

'And there's another person it might be worth while to look into,' said Peter. 'Ralph Gourley . . . ' He related what he had heard about Gourley from the Reverend Amos Benskill. 'That cyanide had to come from somewhere.'

'H'm, that *is* something,' said Donaldson. 'I'll get on to that. I don't think I'd say anything to anybody about this theory of yours, Mr. Chard. The fewer people who know about it, the better. I shan't say anything about it. We've got to put in a lot of hard work and get a lot more proof before we dare even admit to ourselves that we're on the right lines. I shall keep it dark even from the Chief Constable . . . '

Peter smiled.

'I doubt if Colonel Shoredust would appreciate it,' he said. 'He'd probably consider it a very highly-coloured flight of the imagination on your part, inspector. Not many people know anything about Satanism . . . '

'I'd probably have treated the idea in the same way, sir,' admitted Donaldson, candidly, 'if I hadn't come up against it, personally, in this other case I was telling you about. To the average person it does sound fantastic and a little ridiculous . . . '

'There's nothing ridiculous about it,' said Peter, grimly. 'The foul, black cult of Satan-worship exists, and has existed, from the earliest times. It offers an excuse for unbridled sensuality and debauchery, and so long as there arc people depraved and corrupt enough to appreciate such things it will continue to flourish in secret. We've come up against a particularly ghastly nest, for if we are right, and I firmly believe we are, the hideous cult was carried to the most horrible and ghastly extremes — the full, bestial ritual of the Satanists . . . '

'Yes, sir,' said Inspector Donaldson, and his expression was very grave and serious. 'Yes, sir. You can be quite sure that *I* realize all that. If such a bunch exists in this district, and I agree with you that it does, we'll stamp it out of existence . . . '

9

'Well,' said Ann, when Peter got back. 'What did Donaldson say? Did he laugh at you . . . ?'

'No, he didn't,' answered Peter. 'He took the idea quite seriously. Luckily he had been engaged on a similar case in London and knew something about it . . . '

'Then he believes that we're right?' she said. 'What's he going to do . . . ?'

'Everything he can,' answered Peter. 'I suggested that possibly the Reverend Gilbert Ray was mixed up in it . . . '

'Peter, you didn't!' she exclaimed, in dismay.
'I did . . . '

'I don't think you should have,' she said. 'There's absolutely nothing at all to connect him with it, except that we don't like him.'

'If this is a real, genuine Satanist outfit — and if it isn't then we're completely wrong,' said Peter, 'there's *got* to be a parson in it . . . '

'But that doesn't mean it's Ray,' protested his wife.

'I know,' replied Peter, 'but I'm a great believer in intuition. There's an unwholesome atmosphere about him — a kind of an evil aura — and there must be some reason for it. There was something of the same kind about Laura Courtland. Perhaps you can't soak yourself in absolute evil and corruption without some sort of emanation . . . Anyway, I believe Ray is the leading light of the abominable cult.'

Ann gave a little shiver.

'The whole thing's horrible,' she said. 'Monstrous and hideous. Every now and again I feel that we *must* be wrong; that such things couldn't happen in this civilized age . . . '

'They couldn't — if this really *was* a civilized age,' said Peter. 'The trouble is that it isn't.'

'I hope they find these people,' said Ann, 'and put an end to them and their obscene, blasphemous, and beastly cult . . . '

'They will, if by 'they' you mean Donaldson,' said Peter. 'He feels just as strongly about it as you do . . . '

10

The days went by, and Inspector Donaldson made no very great headway. A further search of the belongings of Mallory and Severac had, however, brought to light two sets of cufflinks, bearing the initial L in rubies, and exactly alike in appearance, which was one more point in confirmation of the fact that the four dead people had all belonged to some club or sect. Nothing else turned up, although Donaldson was doing his utmost to find evidence in support of the theory which Peter had expounded. The whole thing, as he had said, required very careful and diplomatic handling, for an incautious word, or action, might not only have the effect of destroying all chance of ever discovering the people involved, but lead to a great deal of trouble for him if it should turn out that the idea he was working on was wrong after all. He had written to the *Sûreté* in Paris asking for details concerning the past history of not only Gilbert Ray, but André Severac. As yet, however, he had not received any reply.

The weather had grown milder and the last vestige of snow had melted, filling the swollen dykes and causing the keepers of the locks to watch their straining gates with anxiety. When the thaw was complete, Peter and Ann went one afternoon to look at Witch's House. It looked different without the white covering which had to a great extent softened its harsh and ugly lines. It was possible to see, now, the ravages which time and weather had wrought. Peter and Ann walked round the cottage. There was scarcely any garden at the rear. The place was divided from the flat marshland, that stretched away to the sloping embankment of a dyke, by a wire fence that seemed to be in a better state of repair than the rest of the building. Peter concluded that the land probably belonged to the Conservancy Board and that they were responsible for this. He had come with the intention of trying, once again, to find an answer to the puzzle of how the unknown fifth person had managed to leave the cottage without marking the snow, but, although he and Ann spent a considerable time examining the outside of the dilapidated building, neither of them could find anything that suggested a solution. They left, more than a little disappointed at the fruitlessness of their visit.

In the early hours of the Sunday morning Mrs. Coxen died. Peter was coming back from the post office when he met Doctor Culpepper and heard the news.

'She died from shock and a broken heart,' said the doctor. 'I shall have to put heart failure, aggravated by shock, on the certificate, but what *ought* to be there is the name of the person who killed her child. She was murdered just as certainly as if she'd been stabbed with a knife.'

The woman's death roused the people of the village to an angry indignation. There was, too, an undercurrent of fear that was induced by superstition. Robson, the father of the first child to be murdered, declared openly that someone had put a spell on the whole district. He made his avowal in the bar of the *Red Lion* and Peter and Ann, who had dropped in for a drink, heard him.

'And,' he added, staring at the little group that was gathered round him, 'it wouldn't be difficult to put a name to 'em neither.'

'Meanin' Gourley?' said a small, scraggy-necked man.

'No names, no pack-drill,' warned one of the others, but Robson took no notice.

'Aye, that's the man,' he declared. 'Things ain't never bin the same since 'e come. 'Member them cows bein' took sick an' dying a week arter 'e come?'

There was a general murmur and nodding of heads.

'An' them crops o' beets o' old Jowles. Turned black they did, 'member?'

'Aye, it's true enough, Jim,' agreed the scraggy-necked man. 'There's bin a rare lot o' trouble since 'e come.'

Peter listened with interest. The Reverend Gilbert Ray had been right when he said that there might be trouble. Robson's rugged face was ugly and so were some of his friends'.

'There's queer things goes on at that house of his,' went on Robson. 'Why's there a light burnin' all night. Can any of you tell me that? From dusk to dawn it's lit up. An' why? That's wot I'd like to know. Why?'

Since nobody was able to tell him, nobody answered.

'Did you hear that?' whispered Ann. 'About the house . . . ?'

Peter nodded. He knew what she was thinking. Could Gourley's house be the place where the Satanists met to indulge in their hideous ritual? He answered her thoughts rather than her words. 'He wouldn't have a light *every* night for that,' he said. 'The coven wouldn't meet more than once a month . . . '

'Has Donaldson seen Gourley?' asked Ann.

'Yes,' he answered. 'He made the excuse of wanting to ask him some questions about Fay Bennett. Gourley was very brusque. He said he knew nothing about her whatever . . . '

'But he was one of the people who used to visit her,' broke in Ann.

'That's what Donaldson told him,' said Peter, 'and he answered that his visits were purely of a business nature and refused, point-blank, to discuss the matter further.'

'What kind of business could he have with a woman like that?' asked Ann, and Peter shrugged his shoulders.

'Donaldson would like to know that,' he answered, 'but Gourley isn't talking. Donaldson says that the house is very poorly furnished and indescribably dirty and untidy. He says that it gives the impression of extreme poverty.'

Ann finished the remainder of her gin and Italian. The little group of which Robson formed the nucleus were talking in low voices, their heads almost touching.

'There's going to be trouble, Peter,' she said. 'Unless something is done soon . . .'

Peter agreed with her. These people had reached a pitch of tension which was liable to break out into something serious. For months they had lived in the shadow of a fear which was rapidly developing into a panic. And people in a panic were capable of anything . . .

11

The crisis came suddenly and unexpectedly. Ann developed a slight headache on the following evening and, in consequence, Peter went down to the *Red Lion* alone. It was a clear, rather cold, night, with a thin rind of moon, and he passed several groups of villagers on his way, all whispering animatedly among themselves. It struck him as unusual, and when he reached the *Red Lion* he found something that was more unusual still. The bar was completely deserted.

He attracted the landlord's attention by rapping on the counter, and ordered a pint of bitter.

'What's happened to everybody this evening?' he asked, while Mr. Ruddock was drawing the beer.

'There's a bit of a meetin' on,' answered the landlord in his slow, quiet way. 'Maybe they'll be in presently, sir.'

But he was wrong. Nobody came in.

Peter drank his beer in solitary state and ordered another, and still nobody set foot inside the place. It was extraordinary and made him feel more than a little uneasy. He tried to draw the landlord into a conversation, but Mr. Ruddock only answered in monosyllables and seemed disinclined to talk.

'Where is this meeting you mentioned?' asked Peter.

'Up on the Green,' answered Mr. Ruddock, polishing a glass with extreme deliberation and care. 'An' if you was thinkin' o' going to 'ave a look, sir, I wouldn't, not if I was you . . . '

'Why not?' demanded Peter.

'I wouldn't, not if I was you,' repeated the landlord.

'What's the meeting about?' asked Peter, but Mr. Ruddock appeared to have suddenly gone deaf. With a muttered excuse he disappeared through a door at the back of the bar. Peter's uneasiness increased and so did his curiosity. Something important was going on and he was determined to find out what it was. He swallowed the remainder of his second pint quickly and left the bar, walking rapidly in the direction of the Green. When he reached it he found that it was thick with people. The entire population seemed to be gathered there, and even as he looked, belated stragglers were hurrying to join the rest. A murmur of voices reached him; a wordless murmur that was like the sound of surf upon a beach, and then this suddenly died down and was still. He saw the reason. A man had climbed up on to a bench and was haranguing the crowd. It was Robson. Peter couldn't hear what he was saying at first, but as he got nearer the words became audible.

' . . . stop it for good an' all. We ain't goin' ter stand for no more of it. 'E was at 'is Devil's-work an' witchcraft agin last night. There was a light a-burnin' in the 'ouse until the sun rose. Nobody's goin' to do anythin' about it so we've got ter do it ourselves. Remember my kid, Ivy, an' what 'appened to 'er an' little Joan Coxen, an' Kelvin's baby an' the rest? I say there's only one way to stop it . . . '

An angry mutter drowned the rest of his speech.

'Let's go up to the 'ouse now,' cried a voice, shrilly.

'Aye, to the 'ouse! To the 'ouse!' The cry was taken up and tossed from mouth to mouth until the night rang with it. An ugly and dangerous gathering, thought Peter. There *was* going to be trouble, and serious trouble, unless it could be prevented. He saw with deepening anxiety that every one of that excited mob was armed with stakes and improvised weapons . . .

'Burn it,' screamed a voice. 'Burn the bloody place to the ground.' And there was a roar of approval. A light blazed up, followed by another and another as pitch-soaked rags, wrapped round tree branches, were ignited and waved aloft. The lurid, smoky glare of these hastily made torches lit up the grim faces of the crowd as they began to move in a straggling procession across the Green. A large number of women were present and they kept pace with the uneven column, shouting encouragement. From cottages, from side lanes and by-ways, other men and women came hurrying to join the main throng, and in the rear went Peter, helpless to stem the maddened mob, but hoping that something might yet be done to disperse it before any serious damage resulted. The majority of the people were good, honest working men from the land who had become momentarily imbued with that half-hysterical excitement which is one of the peculiarities of mass psychology. But there was another element, too. Every town and village has its black sheep, and Peter was able to pick out several. These hooligans cared little for the reason for the demonstration. All they were after was the excitement. It was easy to tell them. They were making the most noise and their threatening shouts were louder and wilder. They had worked their way up to the van of the procession and were urging the rest on, and keeping the emotions of the crowd at fever heat. Something ought to be done, thought Peter. In their present mood these people were capable of anything ... And at that moment out of a side turning came the majestic figure of Police Constable Cropps. He stopped, stared at the throng filling the roadway, and then advanced and held up his hand.

' 'Ere,' he demanded, loudly. 'What's all this, eh?'

He was brushed aside like a leaf in a gale.

'It ain't none of your business, Cropps,' shouted Robson. 'We're going ter Gourley's 'ouse, an' no one ain't goin' for to stop us . . . '

'An' lynch 'im!' cried somebody.

'Aye, that's right. Lynch 'im!' screamed a dozen voices.

'Burn down the 'ouse an' lynch 'im . . . '

The crowd pressed on past the astonished and helpless policeman, and with them, now, went murder . . .

Peter caught Cropps by the arm.

'Get hold of Superintendent Odds,' he said, urgently. 'Tell him to bring as many men as he can to Ralph Gourley's house. Hurry, man, for God's sake! There'll be murder done if they don't get here in time . . . '

The constable, still looking a little dazed, departed at a lumbering trot, and Peter set off to catch up with the mob. Gourley's house was an isolated building set amid a small forest of trees, and the crowd swarmed through the gate and clustered in a murmuring mass round the front door.

'Break down the door,' shouted Robson. 'Who's got an axe?'

Peter decided that it was time he took an active hand in the proceedings. Somehow or other these crazy people must be stopped doing anything drastic until Odds had time to arrive. He forced his way through until he reached the porch and then he turned and faced them.

'Stop!' he cried, shouting his loudest to make himself heard above the din. 'Stop, I say!'

His interruption was so unexpected that for a moment they *did* stop. The noise died down, and he took advantage of the lull.

'Listen, all of you,' he said. 'You're going to do something that you'll be sorry for. If you damage this property you'll get into serious trouble . . . '

'Ye'd best not interfere with us, mister,' shouted Robson. 'We've no quarrel with you, but we mean ter 'ave our own way . . . '

'Aye, that's right, Jim,' cried one of the men, a big, powerful-looking fellow with a huge baulk of wood. 'Out o' the way, mister, or you'll be gettin' hurt . . . '

'If you're sensible you'll listen to what I have to say,' said Peter. 'Don't you understand that I'm only talking to you for your own good? If you don't behave yourselves, you'll all land in gaol and that won't do any good, will it? Go back to your homes. If this man Gourley has done anything wrong the law will punish him . . . '

'The law!' broke in Robson, and spat with contempt. 'The law's bin messin' about for nearly two years. The law ain't done nuthin', an' it won't *do* nuthin'. We're goin' ter stop his devil's games once an' for all . . . '

'Get out o' the way, mister,' roared the big man, and made a lunge at Peter with the heavy stake. He dodged the blow, but somebody else gripped his arm and dragged him aside. He was pushed and buffeted from one to the other until he found himself panting and dishevelled on the fringe of the crowd. The lust of destruction had them thoroughly in its grip, now, and they were blind and deaf to everything except the thing they had come there to do. Well, thought Peter, he had tried and failed. The only hope now was that the police would get there in time . . .

The door of the house was strong, but the axes prevailed and there was a shout from the throng as it finally gave way. They went streaming, elbowing and shoving, into the house, the flickering torches dancing weirdly, and Peter's heart sank. It was impossible, now, to save the property; he could only pray that Odds would turn up to prevent anything more serious. The din was tremendous. A bright glare flared up from inside the house and was greeted with a yell of delight. It died down, sprang up again, and was followed by an ominous cracking sound. A cloud of smoke billowed out through the broken front door, obscuring the people who surged round the porch. A crash of glass and the windows smashed as those inside began hurling out articles of furniture and, with the draught to fan them, the flames grew brighter. The old building was alight now in a dozen places, and the dull roar of the fire added to the pandemonium. Peter wondered what could have happened to Gourley. There was no sign of him. He concluded that by some lucky chance he must be out. The fire was gaining rapidly, lighting up the surrounding trees and throwing into vivid relief the figures that darted hither and thither. It was like a picture of hell; the moving figures rendered grotesque and unreal by the dancing flames; the billows of smoke and the changing, distorted shadows . . .

A car turned in through the gate and for a hopeful second Peter thought it was the police, but the car was an ancient and ramshackle coupé, and as it came into the red glare from the burning house, he caught sight of the driver's face and recognized Gourley. Now, he thought, there's going to be *real* trouble ... Some of the men had also seen the car. A shout went up.

'There's Gourley! There's Gourley 'isself!'

A party of fifteen or twenty broke away from the main crowd and surrounded the car ...

'String 'im up to one of 'is own trees,' shouted a voice.

'That's right, string 'im up!' cried a score of voices.

'What is the meaning of this outrage?' Ralph Gourley got out of the car and faced them angrily. 'What are ... ?'

'String 'im up. String 'im up!' shouted the crowd.

'Let me go, you damned rabble!' cried Gourley. 'How dare you ... ' But his words were drowned by the shouts of the mob.

Peter hurried over. He couldn't stand quietly by and see murder done.

'Let that man alone!' he said. 'Don't any of you realize that what you contemplate is murder? Isn't there a sane man among you? Do you want to hang, you fools?'

'We're goin' to 'ang Gourley,' cried a thick-set man, brandishing a hoe. 'You keep quiet, mister, an' get out o' the way . . .'

'If you hang Gourley it's murder, and you'll suffer for it,' shouted Peter. 'The police are already on their way here. You've done enough damage. For God's sake be sensible . . .'

One or two of the older and more sober among the crowd seemed inclined to listen to him, but the others, drunk with the power of destruction, were not going to be done out of their greatest thrill.

'They can't hang all of us,' cried Robson. 'Push 'im out o' the way . . .'

Peter was seized roughly and hauled away.

'If you had one ounce of brains among you, you'd listen to me,' he panted.

'Shut up!' snarled one of the men who held him. 'We're goin' ter finish what we came for, an' nobody ain't goin' ter stop us.'

Peter could see Gourley. He was

fighting desperately with a group of men, but the odds were against him. He went down heavily from a swinging blow which, more by luck than judgment, caught him on the jaw, and he was dragged over to where three other men had flung a long rope over the branch of a tree . . .

'You fools!' panted Peter, struggling to free himself. 'You'll pay heavily for this . . . '

'You shut up, or it'll be the worse for you,' said the man, threateningly.

The three men with the rope had made a noose, and Gourley was hauled to his feet and his head thrust through the loop. Peter fought desperately to free himself and go to the man's assistance before it was too late, but he was held too tightly . . . Two big labourers pulled on the slack end of the rope and Gourley swung off his feet. For a second he dangled like a giant pendulum and then . . . Two cars came tearing through the gate and pulled up with a squeal of brakes in front of the blazing house . . . Men in uniform and plain clothes tumbled out, and among them Peter saw Superintendent Odds and Detective-Inspector Donaldson.

Somebody shouted a warning and the swinging body of Gourley fell to the ground as the startled men on the rope let go.

It was soon over after that. The less hot-headed gave in at once, and the few who tried to put up a fight were quickly overpowered. Half an hour after the arrival of the police the mob was routed, but the house was doomed. The fire had gained too big a hold for the efforts of the local fire brigade to have any effect. When at last it burned itself out there was nothing left but hot bricks and charred beams. But the night had claimed its victim after all. Ralph Gourley collapsed and died on the way to the hospital. The shock had been too great. His heart had failed.

PART FOUR

ABSOLUTE EVIL

'The cunning livery of hell . . . '

WILLIAM SHAKESPEARE:
Measure for Measure.

1

The inhabitants of Fendyke St. Mary, with the exception of a few unregenerate spirits, went about their normal occupations, on the following morning, in a rather sheepish and shamefaced manner; much as a collection of small boys might have behaved after being detected robbing an orchard. Robson, and the men directly responsible for the attempted hanging of Ralph Gourley, had been arrested and, since Gourley had died as a result, looked like facing a serious charge. The general feeling about his death, however, was not one of sorrow. It may be summed up in a remark which Miss Tittleton was overheard to make to a customer: ' 'Tis a pity it should have happened as it did, but there'll be no more baby killings an' such-like, you mark my words.'

'The whole village is convinced that Gourley was responsible for everything unpleasant that has happened since his arrival,' said Peter at lunchtime. 'They have an unshakable belief that he practised witchcraft . . . '

'It's so like them,' said Miss Wymondham. 'They are really very childish and stupid . . . '

'There was nothing very childish about them last night,' interrupted Peter, grimly. 'Stupid, if you like, but certainly not childish . . . '

'Oh, but of course they were,' said his aunt. 'They behaved *just* like a parcel of children. Children are naturally very destructive and have no sense of moral values whatever. You were a *very* destructive child, my dear. I remember when you poured paraffin all over the gardener's new wheelbarrow and set it alight because he wouldn't let you eat any of the peaches, which weren't ripe, anyhow . . . '

'*Did* you do that, Peter?' asked Ann, laughing.

'I suppose so, if Aunt Helen *says* I did,' replied Peter. 'She has a remarkable memory for such things, and an even more remarkable aptitude for trotting them out at the most inopportune moment . . . '

'Well, really, Peter,' exclaimed Miss Wymondham, indignantly, 'I don't think you would call this an inopportune moment for mentioning what you did to the gardener's new wheelbarrow. It only proves that when I say these people behaved like children it was really a very good simile. I remember another thing too . . . '

'All right,' broke in Peter, hastily. 'I'll grant that you're right, Aunt Helen.'

'I'm sure that's very nice of you,' said Miss Wymondham, beaming at him. 'I always told you never to be ashamed of admitting when you were wrong. Of course, I don't want you to think that I *agree* with them taking the law into their own hands like that. It's very wrong and very dreadful, especially when you remember what happened to poor Mr. Gourley through it. Not that I can truthfully say that I ever liked the man, and I should imagine that it was really a merciful release — he always looked so *very* unhappy, poor soul . . . '

'Aunt Helen, you really are incorrigible,' said Peter.

'Why, my dear? What have I said now?' The old lady looked at him, her blue eyes wide with surprise. 'He always *did* look most unhappy and miserable . . . '

'Because a person looks unhappy is not a sufficient justification for bringing about his death,' remarked Peter.

'Of course it isn't. I never said such a thing,' declared Miss Wymondham, indignantly. 'Now did I, Ann . . . ?'

'Peter misunderstood you,' said Ann. If there was one thing that was quite impossible, it was to argue with Miss Wymondham. She had discovered that quite early in their acquaintance. It was purely a waste of time and breath and led nowhere.

'I should be the last person to uphold violence in any shape or form,' went on Aunt Helen. 'I think it's a disgusting and uncivilized thing. All I was trying to point out was that the people round here are very simple and have the wits of children. They don't realize the enormity and . . . and wickedness . . . '

'I dare say you're quite right,' interrupted Peter, hastily, and changed the subject. After lunch, when Miss Wymondham had gone to have her usual rest, Ann put a question which she had been unable to ask before.

'Do you think Gourley had anything to do with the Satanist cult?' she said.

Peter shrugged his shoulders.

'It's difficult to say whether he had or had not,' he replied. 'There might have been something in the house that would have told us, but if there was it's gone now for good. Everything that could burn is charred to a cinder . . .'

'What does Inspector Donaldson think?'

'He's instituting inquiries into Gourley's past history,' said Peter. 'He'd already started those before this happened . . .'

'Has he had any reply to his inquiry about the Reverend Gilbert Ray?' she asked.

'No, not yet.' He pulled out a packet of cigarettes, gave her one and took one himself. 'It's all going to be very difficult, you know, darling,' he went on, when both cigarettes were alight. 'These people belonging to the cult or the coven — whatever you like to call it — are going to keep very quiet, and so long as they do there's no means of finding out who they are or even if such a cult ever existed . . . '

'We still don't know that it ever did,' she said.

'No, that's true,' he agreed. 'We don't. But we have a fairly good reason for thinking that it did — in fact several good reasons. I think we are safe in assuming that such a cult *did* exist . . . '

'Even if it did, it doesn't account for the murder of Laura Courtland and the others,' said Ann, wrinkling her forehead. 'That's the snag, darling. And it doesn't help at all in suggesting who the fifth person was in the cottage that night . . . '

'Or how they worked the trick with the snow,' finished Peter. 'No, I'll admit we haven't got very far with that . . . '

'Actually we haven't got very far at all,' said Ann. 'We haven't got anything really *definite*, have we? It's all theory and conjecture . . . '

'And it's not going to be easy to get

anything definite,' said Peter. 'Although Donaldson agrees that we've probably hit on the right idea, he's not at all sanguine about being able to *prove* it. Something unexpected may turn up . . . '

'It *must*,' declared Ann. 'It's impossible that such sheer evil wickedness could be allowed to go unpunished.'

'I hope you're right,' answered Peter, but his tone was not very optimistic.

2

To say that Detective-Inspector Donald-son was not sanguine about the task that confronted him was a distinct understatement. He had reached that unenviable state of mind when he had not the least idea what to do next. Most of the crumbs which he had cautiously cast upon the waters had returned him nothing in the nature of a loaf of bread, and he was very doubtful if they ever would. It was all very well to evolve a plausible and fairly convincing theory, but quite another matter to prove that that theory was an actual fact. In his own mind he was quite certain that Peter Chard's suggestion that a band of Satanists were operating in the district was correct, but he could find nothing really tangible to support it. The people who *could* have supplied evidence of the existence of such a cult, and given the names of the members who belonged to it, were dead. There were, without doubt, a considerable number still alive, including the person responsible for the formation and running of the horrid sect, but how was he to know who they were? There was nothing about them, outwardly at any rate, that distinguished them from anybody else.

Chard had suggested that the Reverend Gilbert Ray might be the head of the coven, but he could produce nothing concrete to substantiate this idea — only a vague dislike of the man, and the fact that the hideous and ghastly rites of Satanism demanded the inclusion of a properly ordained clergyman — and you couldn't get very far on *that*.

Detective-Sergeant Porter was still searching the countryside for a likely place which these supposed Devil-worshippers could have used for a temple but, up to now, he hadn't been able to find it. And here again they were both handicapped by having to move with the utmost caution. There were several large houses within a few miles' radius and any one of these

341

could have contained a room adapted for the purpose. It was impossible to search them. The only method of finding out was the institution of discreet inquiries among the people who lived near by, and this not only took time but was a very unsatisfactory method. It was by no means thorough and rankled in Donaldson's precise and tidy mind. To add to all his troubles Colonel Shoredust was getting a little restive and impatient. Although the local police had not succeeded in doing anything at all over a period of nearly two years, he seemed to expect the London men to clear up everything in the space of a few weeks. The inspector thought this was a little unreasonable and, in consequence, felt aggrieved. He could not, in the circumstances, formulate the theory on which he was working. The Chief Constable would, without the slightest doubt, have pooh-poohed the whole idea as ridiculous and fantastic. He was forced, therefore, to answer all Colonel Shoredust's inquiries in the most vague and unsatisfactory manner. It was all very disturbing to a man of Donaldson's calibre and he heartily wished that he had never been put on the case in the beginning. However, he *had* been, and the next best thing was to get shot of it as quickly as possible. It was a thoroughly nasty, unpleasant business. He would be very glad, indeed, to get back to London and on to something more normal and prosaic.

Ruminating over a cup of coffee in the tiny police station which he had made his temporary headquarters, he was disturbed by the entrance of the nondescript Porter.

'Hello,' he said. 'You're back already? Any news?'

'Yes, sir,' replied Porter, unemotionally. 'I've got on to something that may be what you're looking for.'

'Sit down and tell me all about it,' said Donaldson quickly, with a gleam of hopeful interest in his eyes. 'What have you found?'

'Well, sir,' answered the sergeant, sitting down rather stiffly on a wooden chair.

'It's a barn. It's about a mile and a half outside the village and from what I can gather it don't seem to belong to anybody . . . '

'What do you mean? It must belong to someone,' said the inspector.

'Well, nobody seems to know who,' answered Porter, 'an' that's what made me think it might be the place we was after. It's quite a good-sized building an' it stands all by itself on a little patch of ground between two fields and it's been recently repaired and painted. The door's secured with an expensive-looking mortice lock — not the kind of lock you'd *expect* to find on a barn. They grow beets in the fields on either side of it . . . '

'Beets?' said Donaldson, momentarily puzzled.

'Beetroots, sir,' explained the sergeant. 'For sugar . . . '

'Oh, yes, of course. They grow a lot of them round here, don't they? Go on.'

'Well, sir, I saw the man who owns these fields,' said Porter, 'an' he says that the strip of ground on which the barn stands was the subject of a lawsuit about sixty or seventy years ago. The fields belonged to two different people then an' they each claimed the piece of land dividing them. After a lot of wrangling it was declared to belong to neither and was bought by a farmer who put up the barn. Until about two years ago the place wasn't used by anybody and had got into a pretty bad state of repair, and then some workmen arrived one day, repaired, painted it, re-glazed the windows, an' put on the new lock. They'd been instructed by a house agent in Hinton. I've been over to see this fellow, but he couldn't tell me very much. The barn and the land were bought by a person signing themselves B. L. Ackman, and the whole transaction was done over the telephone an' by letter. The money for the barn and the repairs was paid in cash an' sent by registered post from London. Who this B. L. Ackman is, nobody knows. The name's unknown in the district . . . '

'I believe you *have* struck something,' said Donaldson. 'It looks to me as if this is what we've been searching for. It's not quite accurate to say that it doesn't belong to anybody, though . . . '

'What I meant was that nobody's ever seen Ackman, sir, or knows anything about him,' interjected the sergeant.

'No, I don't suppose they have,' remarked Donaldson, thoughtfully. 'Queer name, when you come to think about it. Doesn't it strike you as queer?'

Detective-Sergeant Porter wrinkled his forehead.

'How do you mean — queer, sir?' he asked.

'B. L. Ackman,' said the inspector. 'Blackman or Black Man. Now do you see? Black Man was one of the old names for the Devil . . . '

'I never thought of that,' said Porter.

'It goes to show that this barn *is* the place we want,' said Donaldson, 'and it also goes to show that the idea we're working on is the right one. You've done a very useful piece of work, Porter. Somehow or other we've got to have a look at the inside of that barn . . . '

'Well, I don't know how you're going to do that, short of smashing the door, sir,' said Porter, dubiously. 'The lock's a pretty strong one an' the only window's high up in the front. Apart from which, breakin' in 'ud be against regulations . . . '

'I'm afraid we'll have to break regulations for once,' said Donaldson. 'I've got to see the inside of that barn . . . '

3

It was a cold night with a thin drizzle of rain and very dark. The barn made a black, smudged blot against the general blackness, that was barely distinguishable. Detective-Inspector Donaldson thought he had seldom seen a bleaker or more isolated spot and was glad because what he had come here to do could quite easily get him into considerable trouble if it should ever become known. The laws safeguarding property are very stringent and he was about to break most of them. If the result did not justify the risk he was taking he was liable to a severe reprimand if ever his superiors got to hear of it. He had brought with him Detective-Sergeant Porter and a locksmith from Hinton.

'I want the door opened, but I don't want there to be any sign that it's been tampered with,' he said. 'Do you think you can manage that?'

'I'll do my best,' said the locksmith,

and switching on an electric torch, examined the lock. 'It's a good lock,' he said, after a short inspection. 'One of the best makes . . .'

'If you don't think you can open it without damage,' said Donaldson, 'I'd rather you left it alone . . .'

'Oh, I can open it all right, sir,' answered the man, confidently. 'It may take a bit o' time, though . . .'

'You've got all night, if you want it,' retorted the inspector, shortly.

The man opened a small bag of tools which he had brought with him and went to work, while Porter held the light. He worked skilfully with the sure, unhurried touch of the expert, and it took him the better part of an hour. Donaldson, as he waited and watched, wondered what exactly would happen if anyone should pass that way. Not that there was much likelihood, for it was after midnight and the people in that district went to bed early, and the place was not near any main thorough-fare. But just supposing someone did — what would they imagine was happening? In that superstition-ridden place they might imagine anything. He would have been willing to bet a great deal that they would never come within several miles of the truth . . . He began to speculate on what they would find inside the barn. Would he find confirmation of what he suspected, or was he going to be disappointed? If this was the temple of the Satanists he might find a great deal more than he expected — perhaps even the list of membership of the cult, though that was almost too much to hope for . . . Chard would be interested to learn of his discovery. Probably he'd be a bit annoyed that he hadn't been asked to come along. He had thought of it, considering that it was Chard's idea in the first place, but he'd decided that the fewer people concerned in this preliminary scamper, so to speak, the better. It might turn out to be a pig in a poke after all . . .

'There you are, sir. She's open.' The locksmith's voice broke in triumphantly on his musings. 'Pretty tough nut to crack, too, but I managed it . . . '

'Good,' said Donaldson. 'Now you just wait here until I come out. I shall want you to relock the door. You can do that, I suppose?'

'Oh, yes, I can do that,' affirmed the man.

'You stay with him, Porter,' Donaldson continued. 'I'll be as quick as I can.'

He had brought a large pocket electric lantern with him and, switching this on, he entered the barn. The first thing he noticed was a queer smell — a pungent smell like incense and yet subtly different. The second was the intense blackness that surrounded him. The light from his lamp seemed to become eaten up and absorbed. He discovered that the cause of this was the fact that the interior of the barn was draped from floor to roof in a dull, soft, black material that was like heavy *crêpe*. A very thick carpet of the same funereal hue covered the floor. He advanced farther into the place and swept his light about. At the end facing the door was a raised dais and on this a long, low, altar-like table covered with a pall of thick black velvet. Flanking the dais on either side were tall black wooden candlesticks, each containing a partly consumed black candle. Smaller candlesticks of the same pattern and hue stood on each side of the altar, which was backed by a high screen of velvet stretched, apparently, on a wooden frame.

Donaldson stood in the centre of this weird chapel and felt suddenly cold. It was not the same cold as he had felt outside, but an unpleasant, *inner* chill which crept slowly up his spine to the back of his neck. The atmosphere of the place was full of a horrid, almost tangible, evil that seemed to reach out and clutch at him. There were forces here all around him, invisible but potent — a latent power that made him feel *afraid* . . .

He shook off this feeling and began to make a closer inspection. All round the walls were small, low settees covered with black velvet, there must have been nearly thirty of them all told, and they constituted the only furniture. From the centre of the draped roof hung a large sort of chandelier made of some black wood and holding twelve lamps which, he concluded, must be fed with oil since it was unlikely that either gas or electricity would be laid on. To the right of the altar was a curtained recess, containing a cupboard which was locked, two oil-burning radiators, and a row of hooks on which hung two scarlet cassocks, two white surplices of fine linen and lace, and a richly embroidered robe. Donaldson would have liked to inspect the interior of the cupboard, but it was stoutly built, and the lock looked a strong one. He could have called in the locksmith, but he thought it would be wiser not to. There would be an opportunity, later, to find out what that cupboard contained, and some of its contents he could guess. He went over and examined the altar. In several places the thick pile of the velvet was matted and hard . . . The light of the lamp showed that the irregular stains were reddish — like rust . . .

Donaldson turned away abruptly. He was not normally an imaginative man, but he felt suddenly rather sick . . . The full and ghastly ritual of the Black Mass had been celebrated here in all its hideous detail . . . He was glad to get out into the clean cold air of the night.

'Did you find anything?' asked Porter, curiously.

'Yes,' answered Donaldson, shortly. 'Relock this door, will you?'

The locksmith began his task. When he had finished Donaldson said: 'I want you to make a key for me that will open that door. Can you do that?'

'Yes, sir,' said the locksmith. 'I'll have to take an impression o' the wards . . . '

'Can you do that now? I shall want the key first thing in the morning?'

'I think I can manage that, sir,' said the man.

'Good,' said Donaldson. 'And remember. There's to be no talk about this, you understand? If anything leaks out I shall hold you responsible, since only you, I, and Detective-Sergeant Porter, here, know anything about it.'

'You can trust me, sir,' said the locksmith.

'I hope so — for your sake,' said Donaldson, curtly.

4

'Damn and blast it!' spluttered Colonel Shoredust. 'Are you asking me to believe in fairy tales?'

'No, sir,' said Inspector Donaldson.

'But you *are*, man!' exclaimed the Chief Constable. 'That's just what you are doing. What else do you call it?'

'There's nothing,' said Donaldson, quietly, 'at all like a fairy tale about it, sir.'

'But . . . ' Colonel Shoredust almost choked and the colour of his red face deepened. 'You don't expect me to blasted-well take all this rubbish seriously, do you . . . ?'

'It's very far from being rubbish, sir,' said Donaldson. 'Mr. Chard will bear me out on that.' He looked across at Peter. They were seated in the room in Hinton police station where the first conference had taken place and, as before, it was uncomfortably crowded. There were present, as there had been on that first occasion, Colonel Shoredust, Detective-Inspector Donaldson, Detective-Sergeant Porter, Superintendent Odds, Sergeant Quilt, and Peter. The only difference was the absence of Doctor Culpepper and Doctor Mipplin. It was the afternoon following Donaldson's visit to the barn, and the inspector had just finished explaining the theory which Peter had presented to him, and what his investigations had led to.

'So far from being rubbish,' remarked Peter, in reply to Donaldson's appeal, 'the cult of Satanism is a very hideous and horrible fact. I should recommend you to read this book' — he tapped the volume by Montague Summers which he had brought with him — 'if you are in any doubt on that point.'

'What is it?' The Chief Constable leaned forward. '*The History of Witchcraft?* Good God! You don't believe in all that nonsense, do you? Witches' Sabbaths and pacts with the Devil? Lot of blasted nonsense.'

'You can't just dismiss it as a lot of — er — nonsense,' said Peter, quietly, 'because it's anything *but* nonsense. I'm afraid the trouble is that very few people know anything about it, but it exists for all that. The cult of Satanism with its foul, wicked, obscene, and blasphemous ritual still has its devotees today as it did in the time of Louis XIV's court when the Abbé Guibourg, during the celebration of the Black Mass, sacrificed a child on the naked body of Madame de Montespan, the King's favourite. I am not suggesting that all the people who belong to the cult *believe* in the Devil or that their principal object is to worship. The majority are out for a thrill — for something *different* in the way of vice and sexual indulgence. The orgies which are part and parcel of this filthy, beastly, and hideous cult offer an opportunity for really unbridled lust, and the ritual forms a setting which stirs the blood and acts like an aphrodisiac to these perverted and morally corrupt creatures who participate in the abominable practice . . . '

'But . . . but . . . ' stuttered Colonel Shoredust incredulously. 'That's all very well in the Middle Ages . . . I mean to say, Louis XIV and all that . . . Everybody knows *they* were a depraved lot . . . But *today* . . . '

'There were outbreaks of Satanism in Europe in 1925,' said Peter. 'Several in America between 1929 and 1933. Inspector Donaldson, himself, was recently engaged on a case in London . . . '

'That's right, sir,' said Donaldson, nodding. 'That's really why I was ready to listen to Mr. Chard when he suggested that Satanism was at the bottom of *this* business. I'd had some experience, you see, sir . . . '

The Chief Constable sagged back in his chair and blew out his cheeks. He rubbed his forehead and passed his hand over his hair. 'You really believe — *seriously* believe — that . . . that these children were — *sacrificed* in some diabolical ritual?' he said.

'Yes, I do, sir,' answered Donaldson, looking at him steadily. 'The altar cloth of black velvet, which I described to you, was stained in several places. The stains were quite obviously blood . . . '

'They might not have been human

blood, though,' remarked Superintendent Odds, speaking for the first time.

'Perhaps all of them are not,' said the Inspector. 'I believe this business started with *lambs*, didn't it? However, it will be easy to tell, when the stains are analysed.'

'Look here!' exploded Colonel Shoredust suddenly. 'Let's get the thing clear. You're suggesting to me that the reason why these children were kidnapped and killed was to provide sacrifices for a bunch of Satanists. You say that these blasted people have been carrying on their Devil-worship, or whatever they call it, in a barn, a mile and a half outside Fendyke St. Mary. But what you don't say is what all this has blasted-well got to do with those four people who were poisoned in the old cottage. Or are you going to ask me to believe that they were poisoned by the Devil and that's why he was able to get away without leaving any marks in the snow . . . ?'

'No, sir,' said Donaldson, with a slight smile. 'I'm not going to ask you to believe anything so absurd.'

'I'm glad of that,' grunted the Chief Constable.

'To be perfectly candid, sir,' went on the inspector imperturbably, 'I don't know what connection there is between the poisoning of those four people and this other business — except that they were undoubtedly members of the cult. I believe there *is* a very close connection — the two things are bound up together, so to speak — but *how* I don't know — yet.'

Colonel Shoredust uttered a queer little sound. It was partly a clearing of the throat and partly a grunt. It was altogether disparaging. 'What about this man Gourley?' he inquired. 'Was he mixed up in it?'

'No, sir, I don't think so,' answered Donaldson. 'Of course I'm not sure, but I don't think so. I've had a report about him from the Yard. It seems that some years ago he got himself into trouble for performing an abortion for a friend. The facts leaked out and he was struck off the register. Prior to that he was, apparently, considered a brilliant man with a great future, particularly in research. The loss of his reputation appears to have embittered him. He came here with his books and settled down to a life that was practically a hermit's, going out very little, and spending most of his time continuing his researches . . . '

'H'm,' interrupted the Chief Constable. 'Well, if *he* wasn't in this business, who blasted-well is?'

'The four people who were poisoned, sir,' said Donaldson. '*That's* certain . . . '

'I know that,' snapped the colonel, irritably. 'At least you've already told me that. What I want to know is who else? I suppose there must be *somebody* running this Devil-worship mumbo-jumbo . . . ?'

'Oh, yes, sir,' said the inspector, and looked at Peter.

'Well, who is it?' demanded the colonel impatiently. 'Or don't you know?'

'I've no proof, sir,' said Donaldson, cautiously, 'and so I'd rather not say who I think it *might* be. There's a locked cupboard in this barn I told you about, and I'm rather hoping that it contains information concerning the identity of these Satanists . . . '

'Then why the blasted hell don't you open it and see?' exclaimed the Chief Constable irritably.

'I was about to suggest that we *all* went there, sir,' said the inspector. 'I have had a key made to the barn and I've no doubt you would like to see for yourself . . . '

'Huh? Oh, yes . . . yes, of course,' said Colonel Shoredust, without any great show of enthusiasm. 'When do you suggest . . . ?'

'Now, sir,' broke in Donaldson, firmly. 'We could drive there in a quarter of an hour . . . '

Colonel Shoredust shifted in his chair. Quite clearly he had no particular wish to make the journey. But, since there was no really plausible excuse that he could think of for *not* making it, he reluctantly capitulated. They went out into the damp, misty air of the afternoon. Peter had come over to Hinton in his own car and he offered to take Donaldson, Porter, and Odds, if Colonel Shoredust would take Sergeant Quilt. With Donaldson sitting beside him to show him the way, and

Porter and Odds in the back, they started off, Colonel Shoredust following, with Quilt, in his two-seater sports coupé.

'He doesn't,' remarked Peter, 'believe a word of it. He thinks we're all crazy as coots . . . '

'I was afraid he would,' answered Donaldson. 'That's partly the reason why I suggested he should come and see this place for himself.'

'The other being that you don't want to take *all* the responsibility for breaking open that cupboard on yourself,' said Peter, and Donaldson smiled faintly.

'That's very smart of you, Mr. Chard,' he answered.

'I take it,' Peter went on, 'that you expect to find a record of the members of the cult there?'

'That's what I'm hoping, sir,' said the inspector.

'Well, at least there can be no doubt, now, that we were right,' said Peter. 'What you found in the barn proves *that* without question . . . '

'Yes,' agreed Donaldson. 'You take the second turning on the left here, sir . . .

Yes, but it doesn't help us very much over the death of those four people in Witch's House. We still aren't any nearer knowing why, how, and who, are we?'

Peter had to agree that he was right. And that was the major problem. They had got no further in finding a motive for the poisoning of Laura Courtland, Mallory, Fay Bennett, and Severac, nor to the identity of the murderer or how he had succeeded in making his escape from the snow-bound cottage. Colonel Shoredust had pounced on that. That the rendezvous at the cottage on the Eve of All-Hallows was intimately connected with the Satanist cult seemed pretty certain, but its object was less clear. It seemed likely that some kind of abominable and unholy rite had prompted it. Probably the reputation of the cottage and its ancient associations with witchcraft had rendered it a suitable setting for whatever had been planned to take place there. Certainly what had *actually* taken place had been completely unexpected by at least four of the people concerned. They could have had no pre-knowledge that they were going to their deaths. Only the unknown fifth person — the person who had administered the poison — had known that. But why, if he was also a member of the coven, had he decided to kill them? And if he was *not* a member of the coven how had he known anything about the meeting, or managed to take part in it without arousing suspicion? The foul and hideous secret life which bound all those people together had, of necessity, to be a rigid and closely guarded secret. Only those they knew and could thoroughly trust, which meant only those who were involved in the same black and evil practices as themselves, would have been admitted to such a gathering . . . 'You're not going to ask me to believe that they are poisoned by the Devil,' Colonel Shoredust had said. Well, no . . . and yet, if one let their imagination run away with reason, it wasn't difficult to conjure up a picture of that dirty, sordid room with the table laid for a meal and lit by the flickering light of the candles and those four people sitting staring with dumb horror at the awful occupant of that fifth chair . . . The expression on their faces had been just such an expression as might have come to people who had steeped their souls in Absolute Evil, and suddenly been confronted with the source of *all* evil . . .

'Round to the right here, and then keep straight ahead,' Donaldson's voice, calm and prosaic, put to flight Peter's fantastic imaginings, like a gunshot that disturbs a flock of birds. 'The barn is on the left.'

In another ten minutes Peter saw it and brought the car to a stop. It was, he thought, in as lonely and dreary a setting as anyone could wish — ideal for the ghastly purpose to which it had been put. On every side stretched flat, unbroken fields, without a sign of life or human habitation. At some periods during the day men might work in the fields, but at night, from sunset to cockcrow, the place would be completely deserted.

Colonel Shoredust and Quilt joined them as they left the car, and Donaldson took the key from his pocket.

'The whole place is draped with black stuff,' he said, as he put the key in the lock, 'which makes it pitch dark inside.

You'd better wait until I switch on my lamp . . . '

The key fitted stiffly and he had some difficulty in turning it, but he managed it eventually and opened the door. They crowded behind him as he entered, sniffing at the stuffy, incense-laden air.

'Ugh,' grunted Colonel Shoredust, disgustedly. 'Blasted filthy smell . . . '

Donaldson produced his lamp from his pocket and the light dispersed the blackness.

'The altar's on a platform at the other end, sir,' he said, moving forward. 'And . . . ' He stopped abruptly. There was something there that hadn't been there on the previous night — something that lay sprawling half on and half off the dais . . .

With a muttered exclamation Donaldson stumbled quickly forward and turned his light downwards. The something was a man. He lay on his face on the soft black carpet, his arm flung forward . . .

'My God . . . ' cried Peter, in sudden and startled recognition of the clothes the man was wearing. 'I know him! It's Sherwood — Anthony Sherwood . . . '

5

'Is he dead?' asked Colonel Shoredust, in a voice that was more throaty than usual.

'I'm afraid he is, sir,' said Donaldson, giving Odds the lamp to hold and stooping over the body. 'There's a wound in the side of his neck. It looks as if he'd been stabbed.' He looked up at Peter. 'How did you identify him so quickly, Mr. Chard?'

'By his clothes,' said Peter. 'He was wearing that suit when I last saw him . . . '

'Somebody ought to go for Mipplin,' broke in the Chief Constable, suddenly and surprisingly practical.

'You go, Quilt,' said Superintendent Odds. 'Perhaps Mr. Chard will let you take his car . . . '

'Yes, yes, of course,' said Peter, quickly.

'Better arrange for an ambulance, too,' said Donaldson. Sergeant Quilt nodded briefly and hurried away. 'We'd better not move him until after the doctor's seen him,' Donaldson went on. 'He'll be able to tell us approximately when he was killed. It must have been after two this morning. Sergeant Porter and I were here until then.'

'Is Sherwood the man you said you suspected?' asked Colonel Shoredust.

'No, sir,' replied the inspector. 'I don't know how he comes to be mixed up in it . . .'

'Wasn't he dining with you on the same night as Miss Courtland, Mr. Chard?' asked Superintendent Odds.

'Yes,' said Peter, absently. He was thinking of April Sherwood and the effect the news of her husband's death would have on her. Telling her was going to be an unpleasant job, but he thought that he ought to volunteer for it. It might be better coming from somebody she knew than from strangers. Perhaps Ann would go with him . . .

'Well, it looks as if the same person who killed those other four killed him too,' remarked the Chief Constable. 'What do you think?'

'I don't know what to think, sir,' admitted Donaldson candidly. 'I was utterly unprepared for anything like this . . . '

'That goes for all of us, if it comes to that,' grunted Colonel Shoredust. 'The question is who killed him and why . . . '

'And what was he doing here,' put in Odds. 'It seems that he must have belonged to these Devil-worshipping people to be here at all . . . '

'I don't think that's at all likely,' interrupted Peter. 'He wasn't the type . . . '

'What was he doing here, then?' asked Odds. 'He must have known about this place and what it was used for . . . '

'He may have been *brought* here,' said Peter.

'Why?' demanded Colonel Shoredust. 'Why should he have been brought here if he had nothing to do with this blasted cult?'

'The answer to that, sir, lies in the answer to the question, who killed him and why,' remarked Donaldson, 'and that can be answered when we find out why those four people were poisoned in the cottage . . . '

'That's exactly what I said before,' growled the Chief Constable, irritably. 'Look here, all this blasted arguing and conjecturing isn't getting us anywhere. We did enough of that over the other affair. The point is that somebody's going about killing people *ad lib.*, and whoever it is has got to be found . . . '

'I appreciate that, sir,' said Inspector Donaldson, patiently, 'but I can't see that we can do any more than we are doing. We have at least established the fact that a circle of Satanists exists in the neighbourhood, and that the motive for *all* these crimes can in some way be attributed to them . . . '

'That's all very well so far as it goes,' said Colonel Shoredust. 'The trouble is, it doesn't blasted-well go far enough. Who are these Satanists? Who's at the head of 'em . . . ?'

'That's what we've still to find out, sir,' said Donaldson.

'You said earlier that you suspected somebody,' said the Chief Constable. 'Who is it?'

'I'd rather keep that to myself, sir, for a

371

little longer, if you don't mind,' answered Donaldson. 'I'm not trying to be mysterious or anything like that, but it's really only a rather wild guess at present. There's nothing whatever to justify it . . . '

'Oh, well, have it your own way,' grunted Colonel Shoredust rather crossly. 'What about this cupboard you were talking about? Didn't you suggest that it might contain evidence of the identity of these blasted people?'

'Yes, sir, I thought it was possible,' said the inspector. 'It's in this alcove . . . ' He led the way and they followed.

Colonel Shoredust stared about him and his prominent eyes bulged even more than usual.

'It looks like a church vestry,' he exclaimed.

'Yes, sir,' agreed Donaldson. 'In a way that's what it is . . . '

'What d'you mean?' demanded the Chief Constable.

'It has been used for the same purpose,' explained Donaldson.

'The first part of the Black Mass

follows the orthodox Communion service in almost every particular,' said Peter. 'It is only *afterwards*, when the bread and wine have been consecrated, that the foul, blasphemous, and ghastly ritual takes place . . . '

'But how can the orthodox Communion service be celebrated without a properly ordained priest?' said Colonel Shoredust with a puzzled frown.

'That's just it, sir, it can't,' replied Donaldson, briefly.

'But . . . Good God . . . You don't mean to tell me that . . . a *priest* . . . ' The Chief Constable gaped at them.

'Yes, sir,' said the inspector, 'I mean just that . . . ' He went over to the cupboard and tried the door. It was locked as he had expected. From the breast-pocket of his overcoat he produced a strong-looking chisel which he had borrowed for the purpose from Police Constable Cropps's tool-box. Inserting it in the crack of the door, just above the lock, he pressed his weight upon the handle. The wood cracked protestingly but the lock held. He tried again, and at the second attempt the door flew open.

'Show your light here, will you?' he said to Odds, and the superintendent flooded the interior. The cupboard was divided two-thirds of the way up by a shelf. Below this, on hooks, hung an alb of the finest linen and, beside it, a chasuble. On the shelf was a silver chalice and a paten, also of silver. And that was all. Donaldson made no immediate comment, but his face was expressive of his disappointment.

'This removes any remaining doubt there might be,' said Peter gravely, 'as to whether the full, horrible ritual of the Devil's Mass was celebrated here . . . '

The inspector nodded.

'There wasn't much doubt, anyway,' he said. 'But these things supply evidence that can't be refuted. Unfortunately the books of the cult aren't here . . . '

'I was afraid they wouldn't be,' said Peter. 'You can depend that they are in the personal possession of the man who founded it, and very carefully guarded. They represent his personal safety, don't forget — the hold he has over all the other members of the coven.'

Again Donaldson nodded.

'There was a chance they might have been here,' he said. He sighed and his shoulders hitched in a barely perceptible shrug. 'We'd better concentrate for the moment on this new development, I suppose . . . '

'Look here,' broke in Colonel Shore-dust. 'It looks to me as though you're right about this Devil-worship stuff, although I admit I don't blasted-well understand it. How any *sane* people can bring themselves . . . However, that's not the point. I've seen enough to convince me that there's something in it. Now what I want to know is — whom do you suspect?'

Inspector Donaldson looked at Peter and hesitated.

'I've nothing whatever to go on, sir,' he began reluctantly.

'You've already told me that,' said the Chief Constable, impatiently. 'Good God, man, I'm not blasted-well *binding* you to anything. I just want to know whom you *believe* is at the bottom of this Devil's cult, or whatever you call it.'

'Well, sir' — Donaldson drew a long breath — 'I think it *might* be the Reverend Gilbert Ray.'

Superintendent Odds uttered a queer little gasp.

'The curate at Fendyke St. Mary?' he exclaimed incredulously. 'That's a bit far-fetched, isn't it?'

'Why?' asked Donaldson, who, now that he had burnt his boats, was prepared to make a swim for it.

'Well . . . ' Odds pursed his lips and shook his head.

'I'm prepared to believe anything after *this*,' grunted Colonel Shoredust, waving a hand round the black-hung barn. 'Why do you think it's Ray, eh?'

'I've already said, sir, that I've no evidence . . . ' said Donaldson.

'But you must have *some* reason,' said the Chief Constable.

'Well, sir,' said the inspector, 'for the *full* ritual of Satanism there has *got* to be a properly ordained priest, and if the *full* ritual has *not* been carried out in this instance then our entire theory falls to the ground. Ray is the right *type* . . . '

'He's suave and charming,' put in Peter, in an endeavour to help Donaldson out, 'but there's an atmosphere about him that's unpleasant and unwholesome . . . '

'It seems hardly sufficient to warrant such a terrible accusation,' said Colonel Shoredust. 'I'm not saying that you may not be right. But you'll have to go damned carefully. We dare not make a move until we've got absolute, irrefutable *proof* . . . '

'Nobody realizes that more than I do, sir,' agreed Donaldson. 'And that's just the difficulty. How are we going to *get* the proof? *This* isn't going to be any too helpful, you know. We can't keep the existence of this place dark any longer — which means that we've got to admit that we know about the cult. If these people were careful before they'll be doubly careful now. They'll realize that their filthy practices are finished for good — at any rate in this district — and they'll just quietly disband . . . '

'Which means that it will be next to impossible to bring a case against 'em,' growled the Chief Constable.

'Unless the records of the cult can be found,' said Peter.

'They've probably been destroyed by now . . . ' began Colonel Shoredust.

'No, sir,' interrupted Donaldson. 'They are the only safeguard that the head of this diabolical sect possesses, and he'll take care to see that nothing happens to them. While they exist nobody *dare* give him away — they'd only involve themselves. If what we believe is correct *all* the members of the coven are accessories to murder, don't forget . . . '

Colonel Shoredust shuddered.

'The whole thing's blasted-well horrible,' he said. 'It's almost impossible to believe that people could be so disgustingly foul . . . '

'In that, I believe, you are in company with the majority,' said Peter. 'Most people wouldn't believe it, because they've never come in contact with it. If they've ever heard of Satanism at all, they regard it as something belonging to the far-off past — certainly not contemporaneous. It seldom raises its ugly head in the placid, ordinary, normal stream of

378

life. The persons connected with it take good care of that. If it once became generally known and accepted that such practices existed there would be a greater chance of stamping it out for good and all. As it is it flourishes in secret, nourished by that minority of depraved and morally corrupt portion of the community who pursue evil — real, absolute evil — for its own sake and because it stimulates their jaded appetites. Satanism caters for, and panders to, the bestial lusts of the flesh. That is its chief attraction and always has been throughout history. The celebration of the Black Mass upon the naked body of a woman prepares the way for a wild orgy of drunkenness and unlicensed sexual debauch — carried to extremes that are beyond the imagination of most people. *You* find it difficult to believe? *I* should say that this circle is only one of many, both in this country and abroad. While human nature remains as it is there will always be devotees to the hideous and ghastly rites of Satanism . . . '

'I can realize something of what you

mean,' said Colonel Shoredust, seriously. 'But it's going to be very difficult to convince a jury . . . '

'Yes, sir, I agree with you,' said Inspector Donaldson.

6

Doctor Mipplin came, listened to what they had to tell him with a face that expressed neither surprise nor any other emotion, and made his examination of the body. Sherwood had died, he said, from the result of a stab in the side of the neck which had missed the jugular vein but had penetrated the trachea. Death would not have been instantaneous, but would have followed very shortly. In his opinion death had occurred between the hours of three and four in the morning — certainly not before three and not later than four. He made his report in a dry, rasping, toneless voice as though somewhere inside his bony frame a rather worn gramophone record was grinding out a set speech. When he had finished he came to an abrupt stop and said nothing more. Peter fancied he could hear the needle grating in the grooves. Inspector Donaldson and Superintendent Odds made a search of the dead man's clothing, but found nothing at all to suggest why he had come to the barn or why, and by whom, he had been killed. That was one of the two things which had been puzzling Peter for the past several minutes. The other was: why, if Sherwood had died between three and four that morning, April had not missed him or, if she had missed him, why she had taken no steps to find out what had happened to him. He waited until the body had been placed in the ambulance and it had driven off, taking Doctor Mipplin as well, and then he mentioned the matter to Donaldson.

'I've been wondering about that too, Mr. Chard,' said the inspector. 'It seems rather queer to me, though most likely there's a simple explanation. Perhaps Mrs. Sherwood has been worrying but hasn't made up her mind to do anything about it. The main thing that puzzles me is how Sherwood is mixed up in this business. What brought him to this place at such a time? Did he come in company with his murderer or did he come alone? If he came alone he must have known of the existence of the place before and that looks as though he must have also known what it was used for . . . '

'Perhaps he came here to keep an appointment with somebody,' said Peter.

'H'm, queer time to keep an appointment,' remarked Donaldson. 'Unless . . . ' He stopped, stroking his nose thoughtfully.

'Well?' inquired Peter, after a pause. 'Unless what?'

'Unless he knew something,' said the inspector, 'and that's why he was got here and killed . . . '

'Couldn't he have been a member of this blasted cult?' suggested Colonel Shoredust.

'He *could*,' said Peter, 'but I should think it was very unlikely. I should think the very thought of such a thing would have filled him with horror. Sherwood was a very well-balanced, sane, and normal type, and so is his wife. The only reaction they would have to Satanism would be loathing and disgust . . . '

'Maybe he found out something about this thing,' said Odds. 'Sort of stumbled on the fact that it existed and who was running it and tackled 'em with it . . . '

'That's a great deal more likely,' agreed Peter, nodding.

'Well,' said Donaldson, 'perhaps Mrs. Sherwood will be able to tell us. There isn't much we can do here, so we may as well lock the place up and go along and see her . . . '

'Look here,' said Peter. 'It's going to be a terrible shock for her. Don't you think it would be kinder if I and my wife were the first to break the news? Mrs. Sherwood knows us. It would be better coming from us than from a stranger . . . '

'Blasted good idea,' grunted Colonel Shoredust approvingly, but Donaldson did not seem too pleased with the suggestion.

'I suppose it wouldn't do any harm,' he said reluctantly, 'but I'm anxious to see her as soon as possible. She may be in possession of important information . . . '

'An hour can scarcely make any difference,' urged Peter, 'but it will give her an opportunity of recovering from the first shock.'

Rather grudgingly Donaldson agreed. At Superintendent Odds's suggestion,

Sergeant Quilt was left on guard until such time as he could be relieved by a man from Hinton — Colonel Shoredust was going back there and promised to attend to it — and Peter drove the others to Fendyke St. Mary. Dropping them at the police station he went on to Wymondham Lodge. He was not looking forward to the job of breaking the news of her husband's death to April, but for humanity's sake he didn't see what else he could have suggested. The bald, official statement, however kindly put, coming from Inspector Donaldson, and followed up with a string of questions, would have been unnecessarily harrowing.

Ann and Miss Wymondham were in the drawing room when he burst in upon them with his news. As he had expected they were both very upset. Anthony and April Sherwood had an especial place in Miss Wymondham's affections and, although Ann had only known them for a short while, she, too, had taken a very great liking to them both.

'My dear, of course you could do nothing else,' declared Miss Wymondham, when

Peter told them what he had arranged. 'Poor child! It will be a terrible shock for her. Do tell her how very, very sorry I am . . . not that other people's sympathy is ever very helpful on these occasions, I'm afraid, but it's all one can offer, isn't it? Really, I don't know what this place is becoming . . . nothing but murders and sudden deaths. It's really dreadful . . . ' She was still repeating how dreadful it was when they left her.

On the way to the Sherwoods' house, Peter gave Ann a more detailed account of what had happened since he had last seen her. In front of Miss Wymondham he had thought it wiser not to say anything about the contents of the barn or the use to which it had been put. His wife listened in silence and when he had finished gave a little shiver.

'It's horrible, Peter,' she said, almost in a whisper. 'Horrible and beastly and ghastly. There can be no doubt *now* that we were right . . . '

'That *you* were right,' corrected Peter. 'I've taken the credit for it, but it was your idea originally . . . '

'Why was Anthony Sherwood killed?' she broke in. 'What had *he* got to do with it?'

'Why were those other four killed?' said Peter.

'That's different,' she answered. 'They belonged to the cult. But he ... I'm afraid April's going to take this very badly, Peter ... '

'I'm afraid she is, darling,' agreed Peter. 'What I can't understand is why she hasn't missed him and done something about it.'

They both discovered the reason for this when they reached the house, and Peter's ring was answered by the maid.

'Mrs. Sherwood's away, sir,' said the girl in reply to Peter's inquiry. 'She went to London the day before yesterday. She won't be back until tonight, I don't think.'

'Do you know what time?' he asked.

'No, sir. Mr. Sherwood would be able to tell you, only he's out, too. He was going over to Hinton to meet Mrs. Sherwood with the car.'

Peter looked at his wife, a little undecided what to do. Inspector Donaldson would be arriving in under an hour . . .

'Thank you,' Ann smiled at the maidservant. 'Will you tell your mistress that we called? Come along, darling.' She took Peter by the arm and pulled him away.

'What . . . ?' he began, but she interrupted him.

'There's only one thing to do,' she said calmly. 'We must find Inspector Donaldson, tell him that April is not expected back until late this evening, and then go over to Hinton and meet that train . . . '

7

The London train, due to arrive at Hinton at 8.32, was six minutes late. To Peter and Ann, waiting in the gloomy and rather depressing station, that six minutes seemed like six hours. They both dreaded the arrival of April and yet at the same time were anxious for her to come so that they could get their unpleasant task over.

The train came at last, steaming along the platform with a great deal of hissing, and stopped to the accompaniment of a deafening, screeching roar from the engine that drowned every other sound. Doors opened along the long line of carriages and people began to tumble out. There were not many, and April was among the last. They saw her, at the end of the long platform, struggling with a mass of parcels, and as she came towards them, Peter mentally braced himself for the coming ordeal.

'Hello,' she said in surprise, which

changed almost at once to a welcoming smile, 'what are you doing here? Where's Anthony?'

'He couldn't come,' said Ann, 'so we thought we'd meet you . . . '

'Well, that was nice of you,' said April, managing after some difficulty to extract her ticket from her glove and give it up to the collector. 'But why couldn't Anthony come?'

'Let me help you with those parcels,' said Peter hastily.

'Thank you. There *are* rather a lot of them,' she said. 'Every so often I go up to Town and indulge in an orgy of shopping. It's one of the best tonics I know — spending money on things that aren't really necessary just for the sheer fun of spending it. Why couldn't Anthony come to meet me?'

'I'm afraid he's not very well,' said Peter.

'Don't tell me he's caught a cold,' cried April, as they made their way to the car. 'He's been boasting so triumphantly that he *never* gets a cold . . . '

'No, it's not that,' said Ann. 'We'll get in the back, Peter, and you can put April's parcels on the seat beside you . . . '

They seated themselves with a rug over their knees, the parcels were stowed on the front seat, and Peter got in and drove out of the station approach. It was a long time before he forgot that drive back to Fendyke St. Mary. Even years afterwards, at odd moments, the memory of it would escape from some hinterland of his brain and conjure up a vivid picture . . . The dark, twisting road, somehow eerily unreal in the light from the car's lamps . . . the sudden ghostly glimpses of gates and trees . . . the rhythmic, soporific hum of the engine . . . and the low murmur of Ann's voice . . .

Ann told April during that short journey from the railway station at Hinton to Fendyke St. Mary and she listened, tearless, and without any outward sign of grief or emotion. But Peter realized just what the news of Anthony Sherwood's death had done to her when they reached the house. It had been a smiling, happy, *living* girl who had got into the car at Hinton. It was a dead woman who got out.

8

April retained that stony, blank-faced, unnatural calm throughout the interview with Inspector Donaldson which took place soon after they arrived. She listened politely to what he had to say, but it was only the shell of a woman who sat rather listlessly in the big armchair. 'She herself, the real woman, is not there,' thought Peter, watching her. 'This is only an automaton. The essential spark, the *something* that made her an individual personality, is somewhere else . . . ' It was more poignant than any wild display of grief could have been. If she had broken down; if the hot, blank, dry eyes, that looked like shuttered windows, could have found relief in tears; if the strained mask of her face would relax, even for a moment, and release the pent-up emotions within, so that they could be dissipated and exhausted, they would all have felt easier and less constrained. As it was the atmosphere was full of tension which affected even the official stolidity of Inspector Donaldson. He was ill at ease and embarrassed; acutely conscious that he was intruding into a grief that was so deep that it lacked the power of all normal expression.

'Would you mind leaving now?' said April, tonelessly, before he could begin the questions which he had come to ask her. 'All of you, please. I'll tell you anything I can tomorrow morning, but I should like to be left alone now. I'm very tired . . . '

'Are you sure you'll be all right?' asked Ann, and realized after she had spoken how futile it sounded.

'Yes, thank you,' answered April, with that frozen politeness which had characterized her attitude all along. 'You've both been very kind, but I would rather be alone . . . '

'Come along, darling,' murmured Peter, taking his wife's arm.

'I should like to see you as early as possible in the morning, Mrs. Sherwood,' said Donaldson hesitantly. 'The sooner I am in possession of any information you can give me the better . . . '

'Come at half-past nine,' she answered. 'Will that be early enough? I'm sorry that I don't feel equal to answering questions tonight . . . '

She had forgotten their existence before they reached the door.

Peter looked back as they went out. She was sitting, without expression of any sort, staring at the fire . . .

★ ★ ★

'The shock has stunned her,' said Peter. 'Like a severe wound. The pain will come when the numbness wears off and she begins to *feel* again . . . '

'Poor girl,' said Ann. 'I'm not at all happy leaving her there all alone . . . '

'There's nothing we can do, darling,' said Peter. 'Nobody can do anything . . . '

'If only she'd cry,' said Ann, 'or show any sign of — of animation. It's that deadly, horrible calm that worries me . . . '

Inspector Donaldson cleared his throat.

'It's a pity she wasn't able to talk to us tonight,' he said. 'but it was quite obvious she wasn't up to it. Queer kind of dazed look about her, as you say, Mrs. Chard. I wonder if she'll be able to help us? Of course, being away at the time . . . '

'I rather doubt it,' said Peter. 'How do you expect her to be helpful?'

'Well,' replied Donaldson slowly, 'if her husband got to know something about this business he may have talked to her about it . . . '

'How *could* he have got to know anything about it?' asked Ann. 'The only people who *would* know anything about it would be the actual members of the coven, and I'm quite sure Anthony Sherwood wasn't *that* . . . '

'All the same he must have got mixed up in it somehow,' said the inspector, 'otherwise he wouldn't have been killed. You can take it from me, ma'am, that he found out something that was a source of danger to those people, or at any rate to *one* of 'em . . . '

'It's quite likely,' said Peter, a little impatiently, 'but it's too cold standing about here conjecturing. Can I drop you and Sergeant Porter at the police station?'

'Well, I won't say no,' said Donaldson. 'We walked here and it's a goodish stretch . . . '

'All right, hop in then.' Peter opened the door of the car. 'You get in the front beside me, darling.'

It began to rain as they started, and by the time they reached Wymondham Lodge it was coming down in sheets. Peter pulled up at the porch for Ann to get out and then drove round to the garage to put the car away. The rain was so heavy that even the short walk back to the house made him wet and he had to go straight upstairs and change. Miss Wymondham was in the drawing room talking to Ann when he came down.

'Oh, here you are, Peter,' she said, breaking off in the middle of a sentence. 'What a shocking night it is to be sure. Did you get wet? Really, it's the most extraordinary weather . . . I'm so dreadfully sorry to hear about poor April. Ann tells me that she's taken it very badly, poor child, but then, of course, she would. They were a most devoted couple. Quite a lesson to a good many people, I always thought. He was always so willing to do anything for anybody and nothing was too much trouble. Why *anyone* should want to murder Anthony Sherwood I cannot imagine . . . '

'Perhaps April will be able to suggest a reason when she's well enough to talk?' said Ann, during the pause that Aunt Helen took for breath.

'If she'd been aware of any reason I think she would have told you at *once*,' declared Miss Wymondham. 'If I know anything of April her one thought will be to get the person responsible punished as soon as possible, and if she knew anything that would do that she wouldn't wait a second. And, after all, you can't blame her for feeling like that. She's suffered a dreadful loss, and it's only natural that she should be vindictive. Anthony was very popular in the village, too, and I'm sure everybody will be terribly grieved. He always used to play in the cricket eleven against Marshton St. Paul, and at the vicarage fête, in aid of the church fund, he used to do wonderful tricks on horseback and tightrope walking and lassooing. He was born in a circus, you know — and he was really very good indeed . . . My dears, just hark at the rain. I do believe it's getting worse.'

'It can't go on very long as heavy as this, surely?' said Ann. 'The roads will be flooded . . . '

'It's not the roads that are important, my dears,' said Miss Wymondham, a tiny worried little pucker appearing on her smooth forehead. 'It's the dykes. The sluice gates of the Great Dyke haven't been too sound for a long time. The Conservancy Board have promised and promised to have them seen to over and over again, but nothing is ever *done* about it. It would really be very awkward if they gave way, and with all the snow and now this rain there must be an abnormal strain on them . . . '

'You mean if they gave way the place would be flooded?' asked Ann.

'Yes, all the *lower* parts,' answered Miss Wymondham. 'It wouldn't affect us because we are on higher ground, but all round Witch's House would be flooded. The Great Dyke runs close by there, you know, and even normally the land is very marshy. Although we shouldn't actually be flooded, the village would probably be cut off completely — like an island entirely surrounded by water . . . '

'Has that ever happened?' asked Peter.

'Not for nearly sixty years,' said Miss Wymondham, 'and *that* was the last time that the sluice gates were renewed, so it's no wonder that they are getting a little worn out by now. Of course, they've been repaired any number of times, but what they really want is renewing . . . '

'Well,' remarked Peter, yawning. 'Let's hope we don't wake up in the morning and find ourselves marooned. From my short experience of Fendyke St. Mary *anything* could happen . . . '

9

Ann turned over restlessly and opened her eyes. A cold, grey blur marked the position of the window and she could hear the heavy patter and rustle of the rain. The place where Peter should have been beside her was empty but still warm. There was a movement in the room and raising her head she saw him, dimly in the half light, moving about.

'What is it, darling? What's the matter?' she asked, drowsily.

'It's all right,' he answered. 'I'm getting up. Go to sleep again . . . '

'Getting up?' she said, in surprise. 'What are you getting up for? What's the time?'

'Nearly half-past seven,' he said.

She sat up in bed and blinked the sleep from her eyes.

'What on earth are you getting up for?' she demanded. 'What's happened?'

'Nothing's happened,' he answered,

reassuringly. 'I've got an idea, that's all, and I'm going to test it . . . '

'Where are you going?' she asked, pulling the bed covers round her, for it was very cold.

'Out,' he said, vaguely.

'Out — at this hour?' She stared at him through the gloom. 'But it's scarcely light and pouring with rain . . . '

'I know,' he said. 'Now just you snuggle down and wait until Roberts brings the tea . . . '

'But where are you going?' she insisted.

'I'll tell you when I get back,' he replied. 'I shan't be long.'

He opened the door and slipped out before she could question him further. The servants were moving about downstairs and as he reached the hall Hewson, sketchily clad in a dressing-gown, came out of the dining room.

'Good morning, Hewson,' said Peter. 'I'm just going out for a while. I shall be back to breakfast.'

'Yes, sir,' said the old man. 'It's a very wet morning, Mr. Peter . . . '

'I know,' said Peter. 'But I shall be all

right. I'm taking the car.'

He pulled on a raincoat, wound a muffler round his throat, and picked up his hat. Hewson watched him with frankly astonished eyes as he opened the front door and went out into the cold, wet greyness. The gravel of the path round to the garage was a morass of yellow puddles. The rain had abated very little in violence during the night and there was no sign that it was likely to. The sky was a leaden tent. Peter began to wish that he had not been so impatient to find out if the idea which had come to him during the night was feasible. The morning might have been less depressing after breakfast.

He unlocked the garage and got into the car. It was only after several attempts that the cold engine consented to function and he backed slowly out . . .

The light had strengthened when he reached Witch's House, and getting out of the car, he picked his way towards the desolate old building, avoiding with difficulty the numerous puddles which were the size of small ponds. His objective was the porch. Here, if there was anything in his idea at all, he might expect to find confirmation. And he found it. What his imagination had suggested might be there *was* there. He felt a glow of satisfaction that his reasoning had proved to be correct. This, then, was how the trick had been worked. This was how the murderer had come and gone without leaving any marks on the snow. As simple as that . . .

10

A reply from the *Sûreté* arrived for Detective-
Inspector Donaldson that morning, and
he read it while he waited for Peter, who
had promised to take him to April Sherwood's house. He read it with deepening
interest, to the neglect of his coffee which
grew cold at his elbow. One paragraph in
particular he read several times. The report
had been forwarded from Scotland Yard
after being translated from the original
French, and several relevant notes appended.
It contained a fairly comprehensive account
of the Reverend Gilbert Ray's career, but,
with the exception of that one paragraph,
there was nothing that had any bearing on
the present case. He had come to England
at the age of seventeen and had been
ordained at the age of twenty-five. He had
held several curacies in various parts of
the country but, apparently, had never
been very popular. There had been vague
rumours, nothing substantiated, linking his

name with a number of women, and in no instance had he held an appointment for very long. But there had been no open scandal. Donaldson's eyes came back to the paragraph which had held his attention before, and dwelt there thoughtfully.

'*The name of Ray is an Anglicized version of de Rais. The family is a very old one in France, tracing its origin back to Gilles de Rais of notorious memory . . .*'

Of notorious memory . . . ? Donaldson reached out a hand and picked up the volume by Montague Summers, which had come by registered post addressed to André Severac. Turning the pages until he found the place he was seeking, he read slowly and carefully. He was still reading when Peter arrived.

'Good morning, Mr. Chard,' he said, resting a hand heavily on the open book before him. 'Have you ever heard of a man called Gilles de Rais?'

'Yes,' answered Peter. 'He was a French nobleman who went in for hideous and horrible practices, witchcraft, Devil-worship, and murder. He was tried and convicted with several others for the abduction, torture, and murder of a number of children in 1441, I believe . . . '

'I've just been reading about him here, sir,' said Donaldson, patting the book.

'Not very pleasant reading,' remarked Peter. 'He gave a detailed description at his trial of the sensations he experienced when he cut his victims' throats . . . '

'Gilles de Rais,' said Donaldson, slowly, 'was an ancestor of Gilbert Ray.'

'*What!*' Peter's ejaculation was full of startled surprise.

'Ray is an Anglicized version of de Rais,' explained the inspector carefully. 'Gilbert Ray comes from the same family as this Gilles de Rais we've been talking about . . . '

'How did you discover that?' demanded Peter.

'The report from Paris has just been forwarded to me from the Yard, sir,' said Donaldson. 'There's very little in it apart from that. Here, you can read it for yourself.'

Peter picked up the report which he tossed over, and glanced through it.

'There seem to be certain rumours . . .' he began, and Donaldson interrupted him with a grunt.

'They're not much good to us, Mr. Chard,' he said. 'They may help to confirm our own opinion, but that's all. It's evidence we want. Real, concrete, four-square evidence that can be put before a jury. Even the fact that Ray is a descendant of this de Rais is only interesting from a psychological point of view. It wouldn't cut any ice in a court of law . . .'

'I should say that it was a clear case of heredity,' said Peter. 'A throw-back . . .'

'And I agree with you, sir,' said the inspector, instantly. 'But it wouldn't hold water with a jury — not without something more substantial to back it up. I daren't take any action without more proof. There'd be a colossal row and probably a case for damages . . . We'd better be getting along to see Mrs. Sherwood, hadn't we, sir . . . ?'

Peter agreed and Donaldson got up and put on his hat and coat. It was still pouring with rain — a steady, determined downpour that seemed to have decided to go on for ever. Everything was wet and grey and cold and unutterably depressing. Even the discovery which he had made that morning, and which he had decided for the present to keep to himself, failed to bring Peter any sense of elation. He should, he thought, as he sent the car splashing through the streaming morning, be feeling very pleased with himself, but he wasn't. He had found the solution to the puzzle of Witch's House, but it brought him no sense of pleasure . . . The gloomy greyness of the morning not only surrounded him, but seemed to have seeped through flesh and bone to his innermost being . . .

The maidservant who had admitted them on the previous evening came to the door in answer to Donaldson's knock.

'Oh,' she said, when she recognized them. 'I'm sorry, but Mrs. Sherwood is not at home . . . '

'But we had an appointment with her for half-past nine,' broke in the inspector, sharply. 'Where has she gone?'

'I don't know, sir,' answered the servant. 'She went out just before nine . . . '

'Did she say how long she would be?' asked Peter.

The girl shook her head.

'No, sir,' she replied.

Donaldson's forehead puckered with annoyance and he looked reproachfully at Peter as though he were to blame.

'I'm sure Mrs. Sherwood cannot intend to be long,' said Peter. 'She was definitely expecting us this morning . . . '

'She didn't say nothing about it, sir,' said the girl. 'Maybe she forgot. She looked dreadfully ill — terrible — an' she didn't go to bed all night . . . '

'I think we'd better come in and wait,' suggested Peter. 'I'm quite sure Mrs. Sherwood will not be long . . . '

The girl looked doubtful. She was obviously worried about her mistress and didn't want to do anything that was likcly to cause her any more distress. Rather reluctantly, however, she admitted them and ushered them into the room where they had left April Sherwood on the previous night.

'I don't like this, I don't like it at all, Mr. Chard,' grunted Inspector Donaldson, when they were left alone. 'I oughtn't to have agreed last night to leave things until this morning . . .'

'I don't see what else you could do,' remarked Peter. 'She obviously wasn't in a fit state to answer questions . . .'

'It looks to me as though she was trying to dodge answering questions altogether,' said Donaldson, who seemed to be still a little ruffled at the turn events had taken. 'It looks to me as though she's cleared off . . .'

'Oh, nonsense,' interrupted Peter, though he was feeling more than a little uneasy about this disappearance of April's. 'Why should she?'

'Well, I don't know, sir,' admitted Donaldson. 'But she isn't here, is she?'

'She's probably gone out for a breath of air, or to see someone,' said Peter, not very convincingly.

'I hope you're right, sir,' said Donaldson, dubiously. 'I hope that's *all* it is . . .'

'What else could it be?' demanded Peter. 'What's at the back of your mind . . . ?'

'I don't know, but I wish I'd insisted on carrying on last night,' answered the inspector, staring gloomily out of the window. 'This is all wasting time, Mr. Chard. Mrs. Sherwood may be in possession of vital information about her husband's murderers. She may know *why* he was killed, or at least be able to offer a suggestion . . . '

'I think you're right about that,' interrupted Peter. 'Look here, Donaldson, I wasn't going to say anything until we'd seen Mrs. Sherwood this morning, but now I think I ought to. I believe I *know* who killed those four people at Witch's House and how the snow trick was worked . . . '

Donaldson swung round from the window. His face was full of startled surprise.

'You do, sir?' he said, sharply. 'You do . . . ?'

'I think Mrs. Sherwood knows too,' went on Peter, rapidly. 'That's why her husband was killed. If you come with me to that old cottage I'll show you what I found this morning and what I think it means. It won't take long and by the time we get back Mrs. Sherwood will probably have returned . . . '

'Can't you tell me, Mr. Chard,' said Donaldson, doubtfully. 'I don't want to . . . '

'I want you to see with your own eyes,' broke in Peter. 'You'll understand better that way. We're not doing any good hanging about here, are we? We can do the whole thing in under half an hour and be back . . . '

'All right,' agreed Donaldson, suddenly. 'Who do you believe poisoned those four people?'

'You'll know that when I show you how the trick was worked with the snow,' said Peter, 'because only *one* person could have possibly done it.'

★   ★   ★

They left word with the worried and distressed maidservant that they would be returning in half an hour, and asked her to inform her mistress, if she should come back in the interim, and set out for

412

Witch's House through the steadily falling rain. Donaldson was curious and a little excited; Peter doubtful as to whether he had, perhaps, been a trifle premature after all in divulging what he had discovered, and unable to shake off the depression that still gripped him. As they passed through the village he saw several groups of people chattering excitedly and apparently heedless of the rain. It was unusual, and he wondered in a lukewarm, detached way what the excitement was about. His mind was too occupied with his immediate errand to give it more than a passing thought, however. On the road leading to the old cottage, a man on a bicycle came splashing towards them, pedalling furiously, and as he went by he shouted something, but the noise of the rain on the roof and the hiss of tyres drowned whatever it was he said.

'What did he say?' grunted Donaldson, but Peter shook his head.

'Probably something rude because we splashed him with mud,' he answered. 'The people who haven't got cars always resent those who have. The pedestrian dislikes the cyclist and the cyclist dislikes the motorist, and the motorist dislikes the man who has a bigger car than his own. It's the same with most other things, too. The vast majority of people hate anybody to have anything better than they have themselves . . . Hello, here's another cyclist. This road seems to be unusually full of traffic this morning . . . '

The second cyclist seemed to be in as great a hurry as the first. With his head bent down over the handle-bars, he drove his machine forward with powerful thrusts on the pedals, skidding and splashing over the muddy, rutted road. But unlike the first, he slowed down as he saw the car approaching him.

'Get back!' he shouted. 'Get back . . . '

Peter pulled up and lowered the window.

'What's the matter?' he called.

'The sluice gate's goin' . . . ' panted the man. 'On the Great Dyke . . . You'd best turn back, mister. They're doin' their best, but they say it can't hold much longer . . . When it does go this bloody road'll be ten foot deep'n water in a matter of seconds . . . '

Peter glanced quickly through the curtain of rain to where Witch's House was mistily visible in the dip. If the sluice went the old cottage would be almost submerged.

'You'd best get a move on, mister,' warned the man on the bicycle urgently. 'There won't be no time when once she goes . . . '

'Look!' exclaimed Donaldson, suddenly. 'There's somebody there — in the porch of the house . . . I saw them move . . . '

'Well, I'm on me way,' broke in the cyclist, impatiently. 'You can do what you like, but you'll be a bloody fool if you don't turn back an' quick.' He thrust off with his foot and began pedalling for all he was worth.

'I can't see anybody,' said Peter. 'What do you think we ought to do, Donaldson. Go back?'

'If there's danger of the sluice gate going, I suppose we ought, sir,' said the inspector. 'There wouldn't be much chance if we were caught down in the hollow. I'm sure I did see something move in the porch of the cottage . . . '

'Imagination,' said Peter. 'This is a damn nuisance. I wanted to show you . . . '

There was a sudden muted boom, followed by a rending sound, like the falling of a heavy tree in a thick forest, and then a dull roar that grew momentarily louder.

'That's it!' cried Peter. 'That's the sluice gate . . . ' He pressed on the clutch pedal and slid the gear lever from neutral into first . . .

'Look!' shouted Donaldson, in alarm. 'Here comes the water . . . '

The edge of the Great Dyke running behind Witch's House was no longer a straight and unbroken line. It seemed to bulge and move and heave like something that was alive. A great boiling mass of water reared up in a solid wall, broke, and thundered down the bank. It came flooding forward; a huge wave that spread with a rapidity that was uncanny, engulfing everything in its path, swirling and hissing and booming; a released torrent that nothing could check. Even as Peter sent the car forward preparatory to turning round, the mass of water reached Witch's House and broke around it in a deluge of spume and spray. A man burst suddenly from the dark mouth of the porch, was caught by the rushing waters and hurled forward like a piece of driftwood, spinning and bobbing and wildly struggling in the seething whirl-pool . . .

'My God!' cried Donaldson. 'Did you see that? There *was* someone there . . .'

Peter, hurrying frantically to turn the car in the narrow road, said nothing. They were powerless anyway. Whoever it was, was beyond help. The strongest swimmer would be helpless in a fight against that maelstrom. The old cottage was already half submerged and the flood was rushing relentlessly forward; a tumbling, frothing cataract that in a few seconds would reach the car . . . Peter backed it, wrenched the wheel round, and sent it jerking forward. The tyres slithered and slipped in the semi-liquid mud and the right wing scraped the hedge. There was a bump and a jolt that nearly shot them out of their seats and then the car was round and facing the way they had come. Peter's foot came down hard on the accelerator and the car gave a quivering leap forward, its back wheels sending up a fountain of water and mud as the first wave of the flood came bubbling round them.

'Just in time, I think,' said Peter, through his teeth.

Donaldson nodded. As they sped away from the onrushing waters to safety, he looked back. Only the roof and chimney of Witch's House were visible above the water — the roof and chimney and the thin, tapering branches of the pollard willows . . .

11

April Sherwood had not returned when they got back to the house, neither had there been any message from her. They waited for nearly an hour with growing impatience and uneasiness, but she did not put in an appearance.

'Where on earth *can* she have got to?' muttered Peter, and Donaldson, who was pacing up and down the room, stopped and shrugged his shoulders.

'Heaven knows, sir,' he grunted, irritably, 'but there's going to be a hell of a lot of trouble if she doesn't turn up, and the brunt of it'll fall on me. I should never have given her this opportunity, Mr. Chard, and that's all there is to it. But I never imagined for one moment that she wouldn't keep her appointment . . . '

'I can't understand why she hasn't,' said Peter, frowning. 'Unless,' he added, quickly, as a thought occurred to him, 'the flood has anything to do with it.

Perhaps she has got cut off . . . '

'That *might* be possible,' said the inspector, but without any very great enthusiasm at the suggestion. 'But where would she be likely to go to? Had she any particular friend whom she would be likely to turn to in her trouble?'

'Not that I know,' said Peter, shaking his head. 'But then, of course, I've only known her for a very short while. Probably Lily could help there . . . '

Lily, the maidservant, could offer no help whatever. Mrs. Sherwood, she said, knew most of the people in the village and was on friendly terms with nearly all of them, but she couldn't think of any particular person she might have gone to.

'Well, I can't hang about here all day,' said Donaldson, gruffly. 'Will you tell your mistress to ring me up at the police station *immediately* she comes in.' He scribbled the number on a card and gave it to the girl. 'And please tell her that it is urgently important that I see her as soon as possible.'

Lily promised. She was obviously both mystified and worried at her mistress's continued absence.

'She might at least have left a note,' said the inspector, as they left the house, 'saying where she was going and how long she'd be. It looks to me as though she were trying to avoid answering any questions about her husband's murder.'

Peter made no reply to this. He was wondering if, perhaps, Donaldson wasn't somewhere near the truth in his surmise.

'Now what about this discovery of yours, sir?' went on the inspector, when they were on their way to the police station. 'You say you know how and who killed those people in the cottage. Suppose you . . .'

'Wait till we get to the police station,' interrupted Peter hastily. 'I'll tell you all about it then.'

They found Fendyke St. Mary in a state of seething excitement. Refugees who had been lucky enough to get away from the flooded area before the rising of the waters stood about in uncertain groups with such belongings as they had been able to get together and bring with them, in forlorn little bundles. Rescue-parties were being hastily organized to go to the help of the less fortunate who had been marooned. Timber for the construction of improvised rafts was being requisitioned and boats of all sizes and types were arriving on trucks and carts. The usually placid village was now a place of feverish activity. Near the church of St. Mary, Peter caught sight of the Reverend Amos Benskill talking to a man and a woman, obviously two victims of the flood, and pulled up. The vicar recognized him and came over to the car, his fat face worried and anxious.

'This is a terrible catastrophe, Mr. Chard,' he said. 'Terrible. The low-lying portions of the district are already completely under water and it is still rising . . .'

'We nearly got caught in it,' said Peter. 'We were close to Witch's House when the sluice gate went . . .'

'It is monstrous,' said Mr. Benskill, his face reddening with righteous indignation, 'that the Conservancy Board should have neglected to attend to the sluice. Absolutely criminal! Hundreds of people have been completely cut off and are in considerable danger. We are doing our best. Mrs. Dilly is providing hot coffee and sandwiches at the vicarage, and the schoolroom and the church are being prepared for those poor souls who have been rendered temporarily homeless. We need volunteers for the rescue work, Mr. Chard. As many as we can gather, for this is a case of working against time. I should be glad if we could count on your help? Your car would be invaluable . . . '

Peter looked at Donaldson.

'I s'pose we ought to do what we can, sir,' muttered the inspector. 'There's no doubt about the urgency of it . . . '

'You can count on us,' said Peter, and the vicar beamed.

'Splendid, splendid,' he cried, rubbing his hands together. 'Your aunt and your wife are already preparing to look after some of the stranded. Perhaps you would go and see Tom Acheson, who is organizing transport? I'm afraid I must go and see what has happened to the mattresses and blankets . . . All these poor people will have to be provided with somewhere to sleep tonight and until their houses have been rendered habitable again . . . I wish I could find my curate. His help would be invaluable at this crisis, but I haven't seen him since this morning when he left the vicarage with Mrs. Sherwood . . . '

'What's that?' said Peter curtly.

'I said I hadn't seen the Reverend Gilbert Ray since this morning,' repeated the vicar, looking rather astonished at Peter's tone. 'Mrs. Sherwood called to see him and they went out together . . . All right, I'm coming, I'm coming.' Somebody called to him from across the street and he went trotting away to see what they wanted.

'So *that's* where she went?' said Peter. He should, he thought, have guessed that, all things considered.

'The question is, sir,' remarked Donaldson, 'where did she go to *afterwards* — when she left with Ray? And where are they both now? You know, Mr. Chard, it's a very queer thing that she should have gone to Ray at all. It almost looks as though *she* had the same idea about him as we have . . . '

'It wouldn't surprise me to know that she did,' answered Peter, sending the car moving slowly forward. 'Look here, Donaldson, suppose we shelve the whole thing until we're through with helping to rescue these people from the flood?'

Donaldson gave a sidelong glance and his lips curved into a slight smile.

'Twice you've put off telling me your idea about the murders in Witch's House, sir,' he said. 'And now you're putting it off again . . . '

'I know,' said Peter, 'but a few hours won't make much difference, will it . . . ?'

'I don't know about that, sir,' disagreed the inspector. 'It might make . . . '

'I can assure you it won't,' broke in Peter. 'You can take my word for *that*.'

'I've got an idea that we're thinking very much along the same lines, sir,' remarked Donaldson, shrewdly.

'*That* wouldn't surprise me,' said Peter.

* * *

They worked till it was dark, fetching people and their goods and chattels from the rafts and boats that brought them across the wide expanse of the flood-waters. Mattresses, beds and blankets had been collected and brought to the schoolroom and the church; articles of clothing and food. Miss Wymondham, voluble as ever and full of abuse against the Conservancy Board, whose negligence had been the direct cause of the disaster, took charge of the schoolroom and, assisted by Ann and half a dozen helpers, received the wet, frozen, and exhausted victims of the flood and administered to their creature comforts with dry clothing, tea, and hot soup. When the schoolroom could take no more, they were diverted to the church, where the Reverend Amos Benskill and another band of helpers administered a similar treatment. The devastated area was enormous. Fendyke St. Mary was surrounded on three sides, and the water lapped sluggishly at the foot of the High Street within a few yards of the *Red Lion*. Hinton was completely cut off and the railway line submerged for nearly a mile. Peter found time for a brief word with

Ann while he hastily swallowed a cup of tea and a sandwich.

'Enjoying your holiday?' he asked. 'From battle, murder, and sudden death, good Lord, deliver us!'

'Did you see April?' she said. 'How is she . . . ?'

'I haven't seen her,' he answered, quickly. 'She was out when we got there this morning . . . ' He told her briefly what he had learned from the vicar.

'But, Peter, why did she go to Ray?' said Ann.

'I think I know,' said Peter, a little grimly. 'I think I know nearly everything, or I can guess. I can't stop now, though, darling. See you later . . . '

It was late that evening when the last raft-load was brought safely in, and when the shivering old man and his wife and their few belongings had been got ashore, one of the weary rescuers touched Peter on the arm.

'We've got sump'n else 'ere, sir,' he said hoarsely. 'Bumped agin the raft as we was bringin' 'er in an' my mate caught 'old on it an' towed it arter us. It's a dead 'un,

I'm afeared, sir . . . '

He jerked his head towards his companion, who was crouching over the side of the raft, dimly visible in the faint light of the hurricane lamp, holding on to something that was invisible in the water.

'We didn't say nuthin' to old Copley an' 'is missus, sir,' went on the man. 'All right, George, I'll give you a 'and now . . . '

'What is it?' asked Donaldson, coming up and joining Peter.

'A body,' answered Peter. 'I think it must be the man we saw come out of Witch's House . . . '

The sodden, limp thing, shinily black in the light of the lantern, was hauled on to the raft and turned face upwards . . .

'My God,' whispered Peter. 'It's Ray . . . '

12

Peter and Donaldson sat facing each other across the shabby desk in Fendyke St. Mary's inadequate police station. They both looked tired and a little haggard. In front of the inspector were two large books with thick board covers and furnished with brass locks. Police Constable Cropps, also looking tired and haggard and in his shirt-sleeves, came in with two large mugs of steaming coffee, set them down on the desk and withdrew.

'Well, these clinch the matter, Mr. Chard,' remarked Donaldson, after a gulp from his mug. 'This book' — he laid his hand on one of the volumes — 'is a *Grand Grimoire* . . . '

'The ritual for the Black Mass?' interpreted Peter, and he nodded.

'The *full* ritual,' said the inspector. 'Complete in every horrible and ghastly detail. There's no doubt that they went the whole hog, sir. And this' — he touched the second book — 'is a list of the people comprising the coven. And it doesn't end with being just a bare record of names and addresses, either. One section of it is like a kind of minute book. What took place when the cult met is set out in detail and *signed by every member*. There's enough evidence here to hang the whole blasted lot of 'em, and it makes you sick to read it . . . '

'Pretty clever to have got *everybody* to sign it,' said Peter. 'It acted as a complete safeguard against anybody giving anybody else away . . . '

'Yes,' said Donaldson. '*And* as a pretty good basis for blackmail. There's going to be a whole lot of people charged with accessory to murder because of this . . . Ray was the head of the whole filthy business, and Mallory, Severac, Bennett, and Laura Courtland formed a kind of committee. Bennett and Courtland seem to have taken a leaf out of Madame de Montespan's book and acted on several occasions as a *living* altar . . . There's a description here of the blood running over Courtland's naked body as she lay

430

on the altar . . . '

Peter shuddered and felt his forehead go cold and damp.

'It's difficult to believe that anyone could be so vilely corrupt,' he said huskily. 'When you think of those poor children . . . '

'It doesn't bear thinking about for long, sir,' snapped Donaldson, his face stern and set in a hard line. 'The principal people concerned have paid the penalty and the others have got it coming to 'em. That's the only comfort we can cling to . . . ' He took another gulp of coffee, pulled a packet of Players from his pocket, helped himself to a cigarette and held out the packet to Peter. He had found the books in a locked bureau in Gilbert Ray's room at the vicarage. The man's death had given him the opportunity, and the keys, both to the books and to the bureau, he had found on the body.

'It's a strange trick of heredity,' remarked Peter, after a pause. 'He must have inherited all the characteristics of Gilles de Rais . . . It makes you wonder if there may not be something in reincarnation after all . . . '

'There was a cash end to it as well,' said Donaldson. 'The subscriptions for membership to the cult were enormous. He must have made a lot of money . . .' He smoked for a moment in silence. 'Now suppose you come across, Mr. Chard,' he said suddenly. 'Who poisoned those people in Witch's House and how did they do the snow trick?'

'You know, don't you?' said Peter quietly.

'I may have guessed *who*,' answered Donaldson, 'but I haven't guessed *how*. I'm waiting for you to tell me, sir.'

Peter drank some of his coffee, drew deeply at his cigarette and slowly exhaled the smoke.

'Anthony Sherwood,' he said.

'I thought that was what you were working up to, sir,' said Donaldson, nodding. 'Now tell me how he did it and why?'

'Let's reverse the order of that, shall we?' said Peter, 'and take the 'why' first . . .'

'Do you know the 'why' . . . ?'

'I don't know it as a *provable* fact. I don't suppose we shall ever be able to prove it. If this was a story, Donaldson, Sherwood would have left a full and detailed confession somewhere to be found at the appropriate moment, but it isn't a story. It's real life, which doesn't as a rule make a habit of dotting all the i's and crossing all the t's neatly, so I shouldn't think there was anything of the kind. However, I believe you'll agree that the motive I suggest is a completely plausible one and, personally, *I* believe it's the true one. Anthony Sherwood was very concerned over the murders of those children. The first time I met him, when Doctor Culpepper broke the news about little Joan Coxen, both he and his wife were in a white-hot rage against the person responsible. Now he was, as you know, a student of witchcraft. He knew all about Satanism and Devil-worship and all the hideous details connected with the celebration of the Black Mass. I think he had put two and two together and come to the same conclusion which we eventually came to, that a coven of Satanists was operating in the district and that the child murders were directly attributable to it. I don't think he had any proof, but I should say that it was possible he suspected that, if such a cult existed, Laura Courtland, Fay Bennett, Mallory, and Severac were probably mixed up in it. It would be natural to suspect them. They were the right type.'

Donaldson nodded slowly but refrained from comment.

'If you had known Sherwood, even as little as I did,' Peter continued, 'you would agree that once he had become *certain* that these people were what he suspected they were, he would, in his rage and loathing, have gone to any lengths to put a stop to their horrid activities. He would regard them as worse than vermin. In my opinion he *did* become certain. He discovered, how I can only conjecture, about the rendezvous at Witch's House on the Eve of All-Hallows. You know we came to the conclusion that this meeting was a sort of subsidiary one before the full meeting of the coven at the barn, arranged between Courtland, Bennett, Mallory, and Severac? I believe they planned it as an additional thrill before the serious debauch of the night and that their object was an attempt to conjure up the Devil, or something of a similar nature. I don't suppose any one of them expected for an instant that they would be successful, but the idea, on such a traditional night and in such surroundings, offered possibilities for new sensations . . . '

'What about the fifth person, sir, who was supposed to occupy that empty chair . . . ?'

'There wasn't any fifth person in the original scheme. The chair, in my opinion, was to accommodate the Devil, should he materialize. The fifth person who *did* appear was totally unexpected.'

'Sherwood?'

'Exactly,' said Peter. 'In the middle of that weird meal, perhaps while they were reeling off some gibberish incantation, the door opens and not the *Devil* but *Sherwood* arrives. Can you imagine the scene? I can. The dark, dirty, dilapidated old room, dimly lit by the candles flickering in the draught, and full of dancing shadows . . . Those four startled people sitting round the table and, probably, in the first instantaneous shock of his appearance believing that they *had* evoked the Devil . . . And then Sherwood making them admit, at the point of a pistol most likely, all the foul, hideous, and ghastly things of which they had been guilty, and, later, in a cold fury at this revelation of moral corruption and absolute evil, forcing them to drink that poison . . . No wonder their faces were such twisted masks of horror and terror when they were found, for they must have died in a paroxism of fear, facing their executioner . . . That's what I believe happened in that old cottage that night, or something so near it as makes no difference. As I said in the beginning, none of it is provable, now . . . '

'Yes,' said Inspector Donaldson. 'Yes, Mr. Chard. But why are you so sure it was *Sherwood* . . . ?'

'Because,' replied Peter, 'he was the *only* person who *could* have worked the snow trick . . . '

'I'm waiting to hear how he did that, sir,' said Donaldson.

'It's very simple,' said Peter, and he could not keep a faint trace of triumphant complacency out of his voice. '*He walked along the top of the wire fence which runs close to the back of the old cottage.*'

13

'Sherwood was born in a circus,' said Peter. 'He told me that himself and I ought to have guessed then, but I didn't. It was only when my aunt, Miss Wymondham, was telling us the other night how he used to do tricks with lassoos and tightrope walking at the annual vicarage fête, that the idea occurred to me. Look, you'll be able to understand better if I show you on paper . . . ' He found an odd scrap of paper on the desk and took out his pen. For a moment he sketched rapidly, pushed the result towards Donaldson and, getting up, came round to the back of the inspector's chair and leaned over his shoulder. Donaldson frowned at the rough sketch before him.

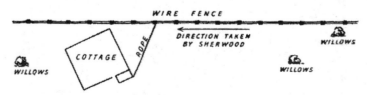

'He ran a rope from the nearest support of the wire fence to a hook in the post supporting the porch. From here to here,' explained Peter, his finger moving over the sketch, 'I found the hook this morning when I went to look for it. It was a double rope, looped over the hook and both ends taken back and fastened to the support holding up the wire fence — they are placed all along at equal distances. All he had to do when he left the cottage, after locking the door on those four dead people, was to walk along the rope to the fence — that, by the way, must have been when Belton saw him — slip down on to the *lower* wire, give a smart, *undulating* flip and tug to the rope, which jerked it off the hook and back into his hands — remember that he was a expert with the lassoo — and make his way back along the wire fence to the willows. Result — no marks of any kind on the snow near the cottage.'

Donaldson drew a deep breath and looked up.

'That certainly explains it, sir,' he said.

'When did he fix this rope in the first place, though . . . ?'

'Well, it must have been *after* the snow had started and *before* it stopped,' said Peter. 'After, because there would have been no need for it at all if it hadn't snowed, and before it stopped, so that any marks he made would be obliterated by fresh snow. I should say it was during the previous night . . . '

'You seem to have worked it out very well, Mr. Chard,' remarked the inspector, approvingly. 'Though there are a lot of loose ends . . . '

'There's bound to be,' said Peter. 'There's nobody who can tell us positively what happened . . . '

'Except Mrs. Sherwood, sir,' broke in Donaldson. 'She must have known . . . '

Peter nodded. His face was suddenly grave and concerned.

'Yes, I am sure she did,' he replied. 'But I don't think she'll ever be able to tell us. I think Ray took care of that.'

'You mean . . . ?'

'I believe she either knew, or guessed, that it was Ray who killed her husband. It must have been Ray, you know, Donaldson. Sherwood had found out too much and was a danger. I think Ray decoyed him to that barn on some pretext or other. Perhaps he demanded proof of the existence of the coven and Ray agreed to hand over the membership record. He could have got him to go to the barn for that purpose . . . '

'It's logical so far as it goes, sir,' said Donaldson, 'but what I don't understand is, if Sherwood discovered all this why he didn't go to the police . . . ?'

'Neither he nor his wife had any very great opinion of the police,' answered Peter. 'You must realize that for nearly two years the police here had done nothing. And he hadn't any proof. He was probably afraid that any accusation he might make would merely be laughed at as fantastic — as it probably would. He preferred to take the matter into his own hands. I doubt if he regarded the killing of those people as murder — more in the sense of extermination, I should say.'

'I can understand that,' said Donaldson. 'I'd like to know how he found out that the meeting in the cottage was going to take place on All-Hallows' Eve. He must have known it long enough in advance to make his preparations . . . '

'I've puzzled over that,' said Peter. 'There are several ways in which he might have found out, but I think this is the most likely. If he had suspected the existence of a cult of Satanists in the district it's reasonable to suppose that he would have looked round for a likely place in which they held their orgies. Why shouldn't Witch's House have suggested itself, and why shouldn't he have been exploring the old cottage at the precise time that two or more of those four people elected to go there to make preparations for the Hallowe'en tryst? The glass and china, etc., had to be taken there well in advance and almost certainly by night. I suggest that Sherwood was lurking in the vicinity of the place when this happened and *overheard* sufficient to tell him what was contemplated . . . '

'Yes, that's reasonable, sir,' agreed Donaldson. 'But of course it's all conjecture. There's no real evidence . . . '

'Does it matter?' interrupted Peter, impatiently. 'There's no question of preparing a case for a jury, is there? Sherwood's dead and Ray is dead and so, in my opinion, is Mrs. Sherwood. If Sherwood were still alive, I tell you quite candidly, Donaldson, I should have kept my mouth shut. My sympathies are all with Sherwood. I'm not at all sure that I shouldn't have acted in exactly the same way as he did. If anybody ever deserved to die it was those four people, and the rest of the foul bunch, too . . .'

'So far as they go, sir,' said Donaldson, grimly, 'there's enough evidence here' — he tapped the record book — 'to convict all of 'em. The majority of them live in London and I'm having them all rounded up first thing in the morning.'

'So that actual proof of what Sherwood did doesn't matter,' said Peter. 'All we want to do is to satisfy *ourselves* as to what happened, and so far as I'm concerned, I've done that . . .'

'You've satisfied me too, sir,' said Inspector Donaldson. 'I'll admit that. There's only one thing I'd like to know.

How did Sherwood get hold of the poison?'

Peter shook his head.

'I can't tell you,' he answered. 'Perhaps we shall find out and perhaps we shan't. The thing is that he *did* get hold of it.' He got up stiffly and stretched himself. 'I think I'm going to call it a day,' he said, with a yawn. 'And *what* a day . . . '

14

Inspector Donaldson discovered how Anthony Sherwood had 'got hold of the poison' when he made a search of the dead man's house on the following day. Part of the cellar was fitted up as a 'dark room' and among the bottles of photographic chemicals on the shelf beside the sink was one labelled *Pot. Cyanide* bearing the name of a London chemist. The bottle was quite empty. It was here, too, that he found a long length of fairly thin but very strong rope, loosely coiled, and hung on a hook behind the door. Its discovery was not, in the circumstances, of very great import, but it tended to confirm Peter Chard's theoretical reconstruction of how Sherwood had entered and left Witch's House without leaving any footprints in the snow. That was all he did find. There was nothing else in the house that had even the remotest connection with the case. An inquiry at the chemist's, whose name appeared on the bottle of poison, elicited the information that it had been sold to Anthony Sherwood six months previously. He had said that he was experimenting with a style of photography known as a 'Cyanotype' and, since he was an old and valued customer at the shop, the chemist had let him have it without scruple. He had signed the poison book and the transaction had been quite open and above-board.

Colonel Shoredust received Donaldson's full report with a mixture of astonishment and incredulity. But the last lingering doubt in his mind regarding the actuality of Satanism was blown to the four winds of heaven when he was shown the two books which the inspector had found in Gilbert Ray's room at the vicarage.

'I should never have blasted-well believed that such things could happen,' he declared. 'Still beyond my comprehension, though you've got it there in black and white. You think that this woman, Mrs. Sherwood, is dead?'

Donaldson said he did.

'Best thing that could have happened for her sake,' grunted the Chief Constable. 'Good thing for her husband, too. If they'd still been alive we'd have had to blasted-well charge 'em with murder. Those wretched people damned-well deserved what they got, but it was murder all the same. Pity Sherwood took the law into his own hands. If he'd come to us and told us what he suspected he'd be alive now. It's your idea that his wife guessed who killed him and went and tackled Ray on her own? Stupid thing to do. If *she'd* said what she knew, *she* would be alive too.'

Donaldson pointed out that she could hardly have done that without confessing herself to be an accessory to murder.

'Suppose not,' agreed Colonel Shoredust. 'Wonder how he persuaded her to go with him to Witch's House? Ray, I mean. Oh, well, it doesn't matter, does it? The whole thing is practically finished, bar the blasted shouting. Horrible business altogether . . . '

A horrible business indeed, thought Donaldson, as he made his circuitous journey back to Fendyke St. Mary, which involved a wide detour to avoid the flooded area that lay between the village and Hinton. He was very glad that the end of it was in sight. The eighteen people whose names appeared in the register of membership, together with their signatures, should all be under arrest by nightfall if the Yard had acted on the information he had telephoned. Of course there was still a lot to be done. The case for the prosecution had to be prepared, but it wasn't likely to prove difficult, thanks to those books, and he could attend to it from his own home . . . It would be nice to see his family again — the missus and young Alice . . . There was nothing like being able to go home after a hard day's work . . . He'd be very thankful to see the last of Fendyke St. Mary . . . A nasty and unpleasant business . . .

★ ★ ★

It was nearly three weeks before the flood waters subsided, leaving behind a waste of mud and wreckage. Amidst the ruins of Witch's House, which had partially collapsed, Superintendent Odds found the body of April Sherwood. She had not died by drowning. In the side of her neck was a knife wound similar to the one which had killed her husband.

★ ★ ★

The morning was warm and sunny, one of those almost perfect mornings that sometimes come in early spring. Through the open window of his study, Peter Chard could see the big lilac tree in the middle of the lawn just beginning to show signs of the buds that would in a week or so become trusses of delicate, sweet-scented bloom. He was feeling particularly pleased and contented that morning. The new book which, after many false starts and initial labour, he had begun just before Christmas, was finished and he thought it was far the best thing he had yet done — more mature, more truly imaginative, than anything he had previously attempted. He was looking at the pile of manuscript waiting to be packed up and sent to his typist with an inward glow of self-satisfaction, when the door opened and his wife came in.

'I've just had a letter from Aunt Helen, darling,' she said, perching herself on the edge of the desk and displaying a large portion of very shapely leg in the process. 'She writes just the same as she talks and she never bothers to punctuate at all. It's very difficult to decipher what she means sometimes . . . '

Miss Wymondham's letter was crammed with news: Hewson had fallen downstairs and hurt his knee; Tom Twist had caught a severe chill through sitting all night on a tombstone in the churchyard and had nearly died as a result; the repairs to the houses in the flood-devastated area were still going on; the Reverend Amos Benskill had got a new curate, 'a very nice young man, my dear, with glasses and a wart on the side of his nose, but, of course, he can't help that and he really seems most enthusiastic and conscientious . . . ' Wedged in amongst all this small fry was an item of news that brought back vividly to Peter's mind the events of that November month. Robson and the ringleaders of the riot, during which Gourley had died, had been tried and received varying sentences for manslaughter . . .

'That's one of the things I've always been wondering,' said Ann. 'Why was Gourley so friendly with Fay Bennett? I know you can't tell me, but I *would* like to know.'

'Can't you guess?' asked Peter, looking at the curve of her swinging leg with approval.

She shook her head.

'Well, I may be wrong, but I should have thought it was obvious,' he went on. 'Gourley was a doctor. He was also very hard up. And he had previously got into trouble for performing an abortion. The rites of the cult to which the Bennett woman belonged include a great deal of sexual debauch . . . Add it all up and you should come to the same conclusion that I did . . . '

'Oh, I see,' she said. 'Yes. I never thought of *that* . . . .' She stood up and smoothed down her dress. 'You know, darling, I think sometimes that it was all a horrible kind of nightmare . . . That it never really happened . . . '

'It was real enough,' said Peter, grimly. 'Horribly and hideously real, though there were quite a number of people who refused to believe that such things could happen. Look at all the letters that were written to the newspapers during the trial of the rest of the coven. It was a good thing that Donaldson was able to produce those books. *Nobody* would have believed it if he hadn't, and those wretched people would never have been sent to the gallows. Sherwood knew that. He knew that nobody would have believed him. That's why he acted as his own judge, jury and executioner. I'm ready to bet that the greater part of the population are *still* sceptical — even after all the facts that came out at the trial . . . '

He got up and put his arm round his wife's shoulders.

'Let's go out in the garden and see what's coming up,' he suggested. 'I'm not going to do any work today. I think after that' — he jerked his head at the heap of manuscript — 'I deserve a rest.'

THE END

We do hope that you have enjoyed reading this large print book.

Did you know that all of our titles are available for purchase?

We publish a wide range of high quality large print books including:
Romances, Mysteries, Classics
General Fiction
Non Fiction and Westerns

Special interest titles available in large print are:
The Little Oxford Dictionary
Music Book, Song Book
Hymn Book, Service Book

Also available from us courtesy of Oxford University Press:
Young Readers' Dictionary
(large print edition)
Young Readers' Thesaurus
(large print edition)

For further information or a free brochure, please contact us at:
Ulverscroft Large Print Books Ltd.,
The Green, Bradgate Road, Anstey,
Leicester, LE7 7FU, England.
Tel: (00 44) 0116 236 4325
Fax: (00 44) 0116 234 0205

Other titles in the
Linford Mystery Library:

THE CLEVERNESS OF MR. BUDD

Gerald Verner

Responding to an urgent telephone request, solicitor Larry Graham drives to the Yorkshire Moors home of a client, Benjamin Starl, who is gravely ill. However, when Starl's secretary, Margaret Lane, shows Larry to his bedroom, his client has been brutally murdered — a knife embedded in his blood-drenched body! And soon, even more shockingly, Superintendent Budd from Scotland Yard arrives and asks if they can explain why the dead body of a strangled man is lying on the steps outside . . .

TH.... ...HING DEATH

Niel Vane

Thieves, breaking into a mortuary to steal the body of a woman, are disturbed by a police constable, and they escape, dropping their burden in the street. Then, days later, a lorry grazes a speeding car, dislodging a hamper attached to its roof. Neither vehicle stops. Inside the hamper, the police find the body of a recently murdered man whose corpse had been stolen whilst awaiting police examination. Who's behind the would-be body-snatcher — and what is their sinister purpose . . . ?